Alba, the L

David Stephen

C

CENTURY PUBLISHING
LONDON

Alba, the Last Wolf

For my wife and her wolves
Marquis and Magda
and in memory of Lisa
who fostered them

Prologue

When was the last Scottish wolf killed? The usual answer is that it was killed by one Macqueen in 1743 on the Slochd near the River Findhorn. But that is no answer. Macqueen may have been the last man known to have killed a wolf in Scotland; it doesn't follow that he had killed the last one. The last one, for all anybody knows, could have died of disease, accident, or old age.

The only certainty is that the Scottish wolf survived long enough to become British. By the incorporating Act of Union of 1707 Scotland the nation ceased to exist; the wolf did not. It existed into the eighteenth century, until 1743 at least. But why not 1746? Or 1750? Or even later?

In 1756 the president of the Royal Society, Lord Morton, told the great naturalist Buffon that wolves still existed in Scotland. He said he had this on the authority of 'a Scotsman worthy of the greatest credit and respect, and proprietor of large territories in that country'. Buffon's editor disputed this, insisting that 'it is universally known to the inhabitants of Scotland that not a single wolf has been seen in any part of that country for more than a century past.'

Nothing of the kind was universally known in Scotland, and Buffon's editor obviously hadn't heard about the wolf killed by Sir Ewen Cameron of Lochiel at Killiecrankie in 1680. He didn't even know about the one killed by Macqueen only thirteen years before. Nobody knows whether or not Lord Morton's worthy Scotsman was right, but everybody knows that Buffon's editor was wrong. There was more excuse for the English naturalist Pennant who understood, or misunderstood, that the last wolf killed in Lochaber was the last in Scotland.

1

Lochiel's wolf was around for a long time after death, and was on offer at the London museum sale in 1818 as Lot 832: 'Wolf – a noble animal in a large glass case. The last wolf killed in Scotland by Sir E. Cameron.'

There is no scarcity of 'last' wolves in Scotland, but each was claimed as the last in a district, not in the country. Tradition has it that the last one in Banffshire was killed in 1644. The last wolves in Sutherland were killed between 1690 and 1700. But where or when the last one in Scotland made its exit bow is anyone's guess. It is beyond reason to believe that any man could walk in one day with a corpse and announce that he had just killed the last wolf in Scotland, at a time when the Highlands were trackless wilderness and ordinary communications non-existent.

More important than the time or place of the last wolf's death is the kind of beast it was. Folklore has given it the same kind of reputation that history foisted on John Graham of Claverhouse, and you can still sell horror tales about either more easily than you can make a gift of the truth. Acts of the Scottish parliament – and there were many – were concerned entirely with the wolf's predation on domestic livestock, and it became mandatory for landowners to hunt wolves at least three times a year. Great tracts of forest were burned down to smoke them out, and bounties of one kind or another were paid to the killers. On one day in 1563, in the presence of Mary, Queen of Scots, five wolves were killed on Athole during a deer drive, the queen herself ordering a long-dog to be slipped at one of them.

The wolf had been hunted in Scotland throughout recorded history, and there are many surviving accounts of such hunts, including single-handed killings by named hunters. Right down to the time of Macqueen it is clear that the beasts were hunted because of their predation on domestic livestock.

The legendary King Dorvilla, who reigned two centuries before Christ, ordained (according to Boece): 'The slayer of ane wolf to have ane ox to his reward. Oure elders persewit this beast with gret hatreut, for the *gret murdir of beistis* done be the samin.'

Eidir, a contemporary of Julius Caesar, 'delitit in no thing more than in chais of wild beistis, with hounds and rachis, and especially of wolffis, for they are *noisum to tame bestiall*.'

2

In 1527 Boece wrote: 'The wolffis are *richt noisum to the tame bestiall* in all parts of Scotland except ane part theirof namit Glenmores ...'

Yet folklore has the wolf a ravening, bloodthirsty hunter of men, a view still shared by a great many people to this day. Evidence for this is scant, but when attacks on man did take place they were probably made by rabid wolves. This could be inferred from the death of Ferquhard II in the year 668. He was such a bad king that the Bishop of Lindisfarne declared the vengeance of God would overtake him. Holinshed wrote of this: 'And sure his words proved true; for within a month after, as the same Ferquhard followed in chase of a Wolfe, the beast being enraged by pursuite of the houndes, flew back upon the king, and snatching at him, did wounde and bite him righte sore in one of his sides, immediately whereupon, whether through anguishe of his hurt, or by some other occasion, he fell into a *most filthie disease.*' Rabies?

True or not, that account could be accepted by any modern wolf researcher. Bishop Leslie of Ross, writing towards the end of the sixteenth century, is less convincing with his mixture of fact and fancy. 'Our nychbour Inglande has nocht ane wolf ... but we now nocht few, ye contraire, verie monie and maist cruel, cheiflie in our North contrey, quhair nocht only invade they scheip, oxne, ye and horse, but evin men, specialie women with barne, outrageouslie and fierclie they ovirthrows.'

What of the single-handed hunters? Despite the almost inevitable temptation to gloss or dramatize their encounters, their accounts are mostly straightforwardly exciting. The Macqueen story is a model in this respect.

Macqueen was a big man – six feet seven inches tall – noted for his strength, for the quality of his hounds, and for his skill as a deer-stalker. One day he received a summons from the Laird of Mackintosh to attend a *tainchel* (gathering) and lead the hunt for a black beast, supposed to be a wolf, that had killed two children the day before. Instead of joining the *tainchel*, in the morning Macqueen went straight to the hill with his long-dog, and it was late in the day when he turned up to meet an angry crowd and a fuming Mackintosh.

'*Ciod e a chabhag?*' ('What's all the fuss about?') Macqueen asked.

After the Mackintosh had exploded, Macqueen lifted his plaid and displayed the wolf's bloody head. *'Sin e dhuibh!'* ('There it is for you!') he said, and threw the head on the ground.

Sir Thomas Dick Lauder tells a fuller story, in which Macqueen described his exploit in Scots, an unlikely tongue for a Highlander of that day, but a jewel of brevity:

'As I came through the *slochk* by east the hill there, I foregathered wi the beast. My long-dog there turned him. I buckled wi him, and dirkit him, and syne whuttled his craig, and brought awa his countenance for fear he might come alive again, for they are very precarious creatures.'

Brief, brilliant, honed to the bone. Personal danger? The Macqueen didn't say. Personal prowess? He made no claim. He merely grappled with the beast and dirked it. And the wolf let him. The surprising thing about the story is that it is no surprise. It would find favour today because it fits the facts about the wolf as now known.

There were hunters long before Macqueen's day who carried out similar exploits, singly or in pairs, including those who killed wolf pups in the den with little or no interference from the parents. A touch of near comedy, and credible, is provided by the story of the old woman of Cre-lebhan on the north side of Strath Glass who killed a wolf with a griddle. She had borrowed the griddle, and was resting on the way home, when a wolf poked its head from a hole by her side. Instead of running away in terror she clouted the wolf on the skull and killed it.

Modern research makes such stories acceptable. D.H. Pimlott of Ontario is on record thus: 'In spite of one of the highest wolf populations in the world in that area, thousands of children canoe and camp in the wilderness section of Algonquin Park each year, and there are no accounts of any one of them having been attacked or threatened by wolves.'

Lois Crisler's husband took a whole litter of pups from a den while the adult wolves 'bounded around crying'. Robert Hodge, a conservation officer-pilot in Minnesota, who has shot hundreds of wolves from the air, tells how he once landed to finish off a wolf whose forelegs he had broken. He says he was met by a meek, docile animal wagging its tail like a frightened dog. Dr David Mech tells how he and his associates freed a snared wolf who allowed herself to be held by the scruff of the neck while he ear-tagged her, fastened a radio collar round her neck, and examined her teeth. She remained as docile as though she had been anaesthetized.

D. F. Parmalee of Kansas State Teachers' College, and a co-worker chased a dog wolf and four pups on Ellesmere Island, North Canada, caught two of the pups and carried them off. On their way back to camp they shot several ptarmigan which they slung from their shouldered gun barrels. In the dark they heard something behind them, and found it was the bitch wolf following so close that she was nosing the dead ptarmigan. Several times they had to drive her off with snowballs, and she skulked about their tents all night.

Adolph Murie, a pioneer in modern research on the wolf, tells how he crawled into a den in Alaska and took a wolf pup just after the bitch had bolted. Dog and bitch did nothing more than howl and bark in the distance until he left. Murie's strongest impression of Alaskan wolves was their 'friendliness', and Mech says they have a personality that in humans would be called 'agreeable'.

The Russians are in broad agreement with the Americans on the subject of wolves attacking people. Their view is that 'such stories probably are based on attacks by rabid wolves, with the usual exaggeration as they are passed on, eventually becoming established in folklore.' One Soviet biologist, who tried to document reported attacks by wolves on human beings, found that 'it was impossible to do so, and it was concluded that, with the exception of possible killing of small children wandering alone into remote areas, reports of such attacks had no basis in fact. People like to believe that wolves are dangerous.'

Indeed they do, and despite all the evidence to the contrary they hang on to their misconceptions, preconceptions and prejudices. What the evidence indicates is that attacks on humans were made by rabid wolves, which makes them no different from rabid dogs. But there is the Russian suggestion that small children wandering alone into remote areas might be at risk. It seems strange that the Soviet researcher could give no actual cases. Alongside this there is the belief, still widely held in Russia and Europe, that wolves will sometimes rear human children, the archetypes being Romulus and Remus. This belief is held mostly by people who think the wolf is dangerous, and is rejected by those who are sure it is not: an odd dichotomy.

In the 1970s the Soviet news agency Tass released a story about a Russian child who had been lost and told her rescuers that she had been kept warm by a big, shaggy dog. The only tracks the rescuers could find in the neighbourhood were wolf tracks. Yet it is on record that the Russians killed 42,000 wolves in 1946 and 8,800 in 1963 (Plotnikov), the policy being to exterminate the beast in European Russia. Taken together, these two official reports suggest that the wolf in Russia is being killed for the same reason that it was in Scotland – as a threat to domestic livestock – and because of the threat from rabies.

Professor Ritchie, whose classic work *The Influence of Man on Animal Life in Scotland* is a gold mine on the subject, says that wolves were so numerous in the sixteenth-century Highlands that a man was taking his life in his hands to travel through the wilds of Lochaber or Rannoch: such places were almost impassable because of their savage tenants. As a result, hospices or spittals were built wherein travellers could seek refuge after dark. The Spittal of Glenshee is a present-day reminder of them. What happened to travellers who failed to reach the shelter of a spittal? Were they killed and eaten? Tradition is silent on this.

Ritchie is less than objective about the wolf, falling too readily into the traditionalist camp with his use of terms like 'plague', 'pestilence', 'scourge', 'savage marauders', and 'wolfish breed'. No writer of sensational animal fiction in the past hundred years could have outdone this, except perhaps by using the word 'evil'. He maligns an already much maligned animal by making it a confirmed hunter of people, which is contrary to all modern experience.

The poets also have had their say about the Scottish wolf. Mrs Ogilvie gave us the 'pitiless eyes that scare the dark with their green and threatening light', ending with: 'And he digs the dead from out the sod/ And gnaws them under the stars.'

In the *Orkneyinga Saga* the skald wrote about the battle between the Vikings and the Skyemen: 'There I saw the grey wolf gaping/ O'er wounded corpse of many a man.'

So wolves were battlefield scavengers and grave robbers, but at least the people they scavenged or dug up were already dead. Tradition has it that the people of Ederachillis had to bury their dead on the island of Handa to prevent the graves being robbed by wolves, or as Ritchie has it, 'there to lay the poor bodies in peace far from the reach of the prowlers of the night'. Bram Stoker couldn't have done better than that.

The wolf is a prodigious digger, the equal of the badger, and excavating a grave would have presented it with no problems. The tradition about grave robbing is a strong one. It is believed on Loch Awe side that Green Island was used as a burial place to secure the graves against wolves. One island on Loch Maree was used for the same reason. The isle of St Mungo, off the Argyll coast, was another burial place. In Athole it used to be the custom to bury the dead in flagstone coffins to secure the bodies against the wolves.

So the Scottish wolf was a sometime grave robber and a sometime scavenger of battlefield casualties, and probably only a threat to man when it was rabid, as is the case today. The difficulty is in discovering where and how often such things happened. Tradition can be a pitfall as well as a guide. Aside from the kernel of truth which there has to be in folklore, the wolf of Scottish tradition bears more resemblance to the beast of discredited fiction than to the animal that emerges from modern research.

As to when the last Scottish wolf died – the year or the day isn't important. Lord Morton was convinced the beast was still around in 1756, and he could have been right. Nobody knows. Nobody was there monitoring the decline and demise of a doomed race. So nobody can say whether or not there was a pack of four wolves alive on a March morning in the year 1745. For the purposes of this story there was ...

1

Iolair the eagle was lazing on the wing above Beinn a Ghlo, soaring and gliding at ease in the high familiar cold – a dark shape against the vaporous blue of the sky, wide-winged, with pinions spread-fingered and upcurved: a young male but mature, in the morning of his life, with crown of gold – the True Bird in the ancient language of the Gael.

Below him the white crown of Beinn a Ghlo sparkled in the sun. On the lower slopes the last of the snow lay shrunken in the shadow of boulders and heathery hillocks, or in dark ravines where it had drifted deep on north-facing steeps. Down in the glen the Tilt was a riot of water, fed from hill streams gorged by thaw and avalanche. The riverside trees were awash, and the eagle could see goosanders preening along the floodline. Nine stags were grazing on the flat close to the river, unaware of the eagle gliding more than three thousand feet above them. At that height he was beyond their knowing or their interest, and Iolair had no interest in them because they were outside his prey range.

A raven flapped from the dark side of Beinn a Ghlo, where his mate was sitting on eggs, and beat up on the currents of air towards the eagle. Iolair had no fear of ravens, but their threat flights unnerved him because they could always outfly him, so he banked away eastward, round the massif of Airgiod Bheinn, and into the corrie where he had his roost on a rock above the eyrie.

The sun brightened through the haze like a lens cleared of breath, and its light fell on the eyrie, which was on a ledge above a burn that brulzied into a narrow gorge, its leaping waters brandishing dirks of sunlight. The pool below was a simmer of foam. Birch, rowan and aspen held precarious foothold in the gorge, and above and round the eyrie. It was a hidden, enclosed place, with no view of the glen or the mountains stretching to the Cairngorms and the forest of Mar. Even Iolair, on his high roost, could see nothing beyond his immediate surroundings.

So Fior-eun, his mate, flying up from the gorge with a tuft of heather in her talons, was almost at the nest before he knew she was coming. She pitched on the edge of the eyrie, folded her wings, and released her hold on the heather. She glared right and left, with the sun highlighting the facing hazel eye. She shook a drip of water from her crown, then, with ponderous, flat-footed steps, she stalked round the eyrie – a cartload of sticks and heather packed and flattened by the weather – picking up a branch here and a tuft there, loosening the entire top layer, rearranging it, and uncovering many stained bones and shreds of skin and sinew. It seemed random rummaging, but all the while, close to the bottom of the rock overhang, she was fashioning a shallow, closely knit base where, presently, she would lay her eggs and sit. Her work over, she hopped to the edge of the eyrie and stared down the gorge, not distracted even when Iolair lifted from his perch and disappeared over the top of the crag.

Motionless, almost unwinking, she stood there, harking to the deeving waters; but her ears could still hear lesser sounds, and the nuance of a hoof-tap, coming from overhead, alerted her at once. Craning her neck she looked up with one eye, through the scrawny screen of birches and aspens, to where five goats were mincing along a crumbling terrace, led by a patriarchal billy, bearded to the knees.

Fior-eun, although hungry, let them go – perhaps because the confined place, steep and scroggy, was not suitable for a strike – and it was some time afterwards before she opened her wings and thrust herself from the eyrie, up and over and into the corrie. Nine stags, cudding there, jumped to their feet, threw up their heads, and stood still with nostrils flared and ears twitching. But when she flew over them, low and fast, they broke away, one of them shedding an antler as he plunged behind a sheltering rock. After a sweep round the corrie Fior-eun tilted away, levelled off, then swooshed over their heads,

10

turning her head to glare at them before swinging out towards Glen Loch.

She was hunting now, and side-slipped into the slope of Carn nan Gabhar to fly its length. She drifted low, almost breasting the heather, lifting and dipping to hold steady height above the contours, with hardly a wing flap – ettling to flush, by her awesome proximity, any hare, grouse, goat or goat kid below her flight line. A low ridge ahead forced her up, at increased speed, and she overshot the hollow on the other side, where a goat was sheltering among scrub birch with a newly born kid at her flank. Fior-eun swung from the slope, threw up with a mighty buffet of wings, then came round withershins, positioning herself for her power swoop back to the hollow and her strike at the goat. The goat, fearing her return, had coaxed her kid against a low rock face and was holding him there with her flank, fronting for him against assault, bleating and stamping with a foot.

But there was to be no assault from the eagle. Fior-eun was on the down turn, muscling for her power swoop, when she checked suddenly, flapping like a hovering kestrel, and changed direction. Drifting out sideways from the slope she poised on the deeper air, wing tips quivering, to view with more critical eye the strange apparitions on the long snowbank below. Now, with plenty of room to manoeuvre, she swung right and left, patrolling their line at eye level, while the outlandish beasts padded along the snowbank, following a trail already well trodden and darkened by the hooves of deer and goats.

Their like Fior-eun had never seen, although her forebears had known them since the retreat of the glaciers, before the coming of man. Dogs they looked like; but dogs they were not. She knew dogs, for she had seen them often enough near human dwellings, or on the hill in the company of men. Small dogs of terrier type she had seen, and dogs of other shapes and sizes. And she knew well the giant *rachis* – the savage hunting hounds – descendants of the beasts that Eidir had followed at the time of Julius Caesar, wolf-killers and deer-killers whose ancestry dated back to the days of Romulus and Remus. But the dogs she was seeing now were not *rachis*. They were wolves. And wolves were outside her experience.

Yet the great wilderness of Athole had known the wolf in the not far distant past. Here Mary Queen of Scots had ordered slipped the fiercest *rachis* at a Royal Hunt, when two thousand Athole kerns, bare-legged and many barefoot, had driven the vast forests of Athole and Mar, Moray and Badenoch, and the day's end had seen five wolves killed, besides eighteen score red deer and some roe. The wolf was still howling, more rarely and from afar, when the Great Montrose was camped at Blair. But not since Cameron of Lochiel killed his wolf at Killiecrankie, nine years before John Graham of Claverhouse died there in the moment of victory over the army of William III, had the wolf call been heard in Athole. And neither Iolair nor Fior-eun had ever seen one.

The wolf pack being shadowed by Fior-eun was the last in Scotland: a remnant pack of a doomed race, now British by accident of political timing. They trotted on at steady pace, heedful of the eagle patrolling their flank, because they knew about eagles even if Fior-eun knew nothing about wolves. When she eddied closer to them on the updraught, swivelling her head, with beak half open, the leader stopped, and the others with him, to stare at her with expressionless amber eyes. And Fior-eun turned away.

There were four wolves in the pack, all with earned wisdom behind them – grey beasts in thick winter fur, long limbed and deep of chest, with tongues flacking, treading almost in the slots of the one in front. Their short ears were pricked, and they were carrying their tails at the relaxed slope, lightly brushing their hocks. Under their thick fur their flanks were lean and hard, for they had made no kill for five days and the hunger gripe was in their bellies. But long hunger had sapped neither their fitness nor their strength: the wolf is built for fasting and gorging, and muscled for marathons.

The pack leader Saighdear was a giant wolf, five years old, wide-skulled, with dark mane and ruff, a pale throat patch, and fine-furred legs of silvery grey. Padding in his tracks came Alba, his mate, lesser in stature than he, more lightly built, with mask and body fur the colour of oak bark. Although close to whelping she was showing little sign of it; but she was wearying for a refuge where she could give birth to her puppies in peace.

Behind Alba came the bitch wolf Dileas the faithful, her sister, who had been running with her since puppyhood. They were four years old. Dileas had never had a family of her own, nor was she likely to have one so long as the pack stayed together and Alba remained the ranking bitch. Bringing up the rear came the dog wolf Sgian, a powerful and strong-willed three year old, who had been accepted into Saighdear's band after Alba's last year's puppies, her first, had been dirked to death by Mackenzie shepherds and herdsmen in Kintail.

The pack had taken a year to get together, because a wolf could have howled over a thousand square miles and heard only dog barks in reply. Alba and Dileas had fled from Wester Ross as wolflings after the family had been scattered by hounds, and for a year they were wanderers, travelling and hunting by night and lying up by day, hiding wherever the forest still stood, comelings never again to be homelings because the first sight of men or dogs sent them stealing furtively away. After a year they had met Saighdear, who had spent most of his life in the Rannoch wilderness of fearful repute, leaving it only at the tailend of winter to wander hundreds of miles seeking a mate. In Kintail the trio had met Sgian, who had to play camp follower for a month before he was accepted.

Saighdear had led the pack from Lochaber, and the previous day they had travelled thirty miles, making detours and climbing high to keep away from even the smallest and loneliest settlements. A few days before they had been in Cameron country, where they had spent the winter unsuspected and unmolested. Lasting snow, with frequent blizzards, had been their ally, and in the pathless back country they had survived on deer, deer carrion, goats and hares, with sometimes a blackcock, red grouse or ptarmigan. Wisely they had resisted the temptation to raid the sheep folds, or molest the inbye cattle.

It is the wolf's behavioural misfortune that he has to sing, singly or in company, even within earshot of his arch enemy Man. The pack chorus is a social affair, an ululant, cadenced pibroch not confined to season or time of day, and the wolf can no more control or unlearn it than the nightingale his song or the red stag his roaring. And in the end their ritual chorus was heard by Cameron ears.

With the snow in retreat before the spring thaws men became more active, and one day the wolf howl was heard by a party of raiding Camerons, homing with cattle lifted from the Grant lands to the north. The plaided kerns, red-shanked with the cold, were gentling the beasts on the final drive across Cameron land when they heard the quavering pack cry on the high ground to the west.

Although the pack chorus could hardly be mistaken for anything else they were puzzled, then incredulous, for no wolf had been heard or seen in Lochaber in their lifetime. Yet there they were thinking the unthinkable, for they had the clan memory of folklore, and had heard the sayings of old men, long dead, who had been with Claverhouse at Killiecrankie. And, of course, they knew about their great chief Lochiel, who had himself killed a wolf there sixty-five years before. So, while they mixed their drammach of oatmeal, they conjectured about what they were hearing.

'It will be some wandering hound,' said one.

'To be sure there's more than one,' said another, 'and I am thinking they are wolves we are hearing.'

'But there is not a wolf in Lochaber or anywhere else in the country,' the first one insisted. 'Or so it is said. And is it not for sure that the last one was killed at Killiecrankie by our own Lochiel of the time?'

A third man said: 'They are wolves out there I am sure. I knew a man from Moidart who was out in '15, and he was telling me that he had seen a true wolf on Ben Alder that very year. I believed him at the time, for he was an experienced man who would be knowing a wolf from a wolfhound.'

At home they were first greeted with laughter and scorn; but later, at a hastily summoned *tainchel* (gathering) of shepherds, herdsmen and tackmen, their story was talked over, doubted and refuted, and in the end believed to be worth looking into. A wolf pack howling is a wolf pack howling, in Gaeldom as anywhere else, and these were mountain men who knew every nuance of sound in their wild fastness of Lochaber. If the cattle raiders thought they had heard wolves, they were as likely to be right as wrong. And there were many who believed they were right.

So two youths were sent at once on ponies to Acharacle to fetch the *rachis* – deerhounds and wolfhounds: the dogs that Fingal bred. Others left hurriedly to warn the clansmen over a wide area, while the men left at home held council to plan the wolf hunt on the morrow.

14

But Saighdear and his band did not wait for the morrow and *rachis*, for they knew what was coming. Wisest of their kind, they had learned long ago how to stay alive in country where the hand of every man was dedicated to the destruction of their race. To their natural fear of man was added their experience of him. Before the Cameron raiders had reached home to tell their story, Saighdear was already travelling east, leading his band in single file, with Sgian at the tail.

All that day, and well into the night, facing a freezing east wind that put the iron back in the ground, they covered the miles at a tireless trot, using forest cover to the tree-line, then running the ridges, well below the crests, when they left the glens. Halfway to first light they stopped to rest on the slopes of Ben Alder, sheltering from the wind behind a crag, where they bellied down, with tongues a-loll and dripping, facing their back trail. Saighdear, tireless and wakeful, with muzzle on outstretched forepaws, stared into the dark with slitted eyes. Alba gathered herself and slept muzzle to flank.

Long before daylight Saighdear had them on foot again, running the west shore of Loch Erricht northwards. A travelling wolf pack will usually turn aside to kill if they surprise or scent a prey animal close to their line; but Saighdear and his band ignored deer and goats, even hares rising almost at their feet, because they knew what lay behind them. On a bare crest they put on foot a big wildcat, which would have been an easy prey, but no wolf broke line to hunt it.

Daylight found them at the head of Loch Erricht, but the pack turned east again without resting, and padded on until mid morning, while Cameron hunters were seeking them in Lochaber, having no way of knowing they were now in Badenoch. It was Alba who called a halt by lying down to rest among rocks in a south-facing corrie. Saighdear approached her, with tail level, sniffed her muzzle, and threw himself down close by her. Dileas joined Alba, and Sgian moved up through the rocks to find a place for himself.

Two hours before sunset the restless Saighdear had them travelling again. On a high ridge they were spied by an armed Macpherson who slipped a long-dog after them, but they lost him in a wild tract of burnt-over forest and reached Gordon country at darkening. They were soon across the narrow strip of

Gordon land, and running south-east through Glen Feshie into Athole. And now they were following a deer path leading to the corrie of the eagles on Beinn a Ghlo, with Fior-eun escorting them and a hollow with a goat and her kid just ahead.

They were tiring, and Alba wanted to rest, but when they winded the goat they became excited and crowded together, wagging their tails. Alba nuzzled Saighdear's muzzle, and when he lifted a lip she licked his teeth. Then, as though they had come to a decision, they rushed towards the hollow, with Saighdear leading and the three following abreast. The goat, seeing them on the rim of the hollow and considering them to be dogs, pressed closer against her kid and stamped a foot; but she broke when Alba, thrusting ahead and flanked by Saighdear and Sgian, bounded into the hollow and stopped, with tail high, within a few wolf strides of her.

A fleeing prey is the end of pondering for wolves warming to the kill, and the pack rushed at her. They caught her on the rim of the hollow and pulled her back, Sgian taking her by the neck and Saighdear biting deep into her rump. She died with a gurgling bleat as Alba and Dileas killed her kid, severing the head from the body with their rending teeth.

Alba carried the kid behind a rock and lay down with it between her forepaws to tear the warm flesh. Saighdear hefted the nanny from the slope to the flat. There Sgian and Dileas also took hold, and the three pulled against each other, growling and grimacing but not fighting. Soon they had the body almost dismembered, and were chopping entrails and gobs of flesh, discarding only the long coarse hair and eating the leg bones down to the trotters.

The Beinn a Ghlo raven, whose sharp eyes missed little that happened on his range, flew down to a knuckle of lichened rock on the lip of the hollow, with a grumble in his throat and his head full of crow nonsense. He croaked challengingly at the wolves, bowing and tap dancing, with beard bristling and the feathers of his crown raised like a porcupine's quills. Many a time he had played the taunt, mooch and pilfer game with foxes; now he had a mind to try the same with wolves, although the sight of four together was a little daunting even to his braggadocio. Alba, in the act of crushing the kid's skull, raised

16

her head to look at him, then went on eating. The others ignored him.

The raven knew what the wolves were feeding on: he could hear the crunching of bones and recognized goatskin when he saw it. A scavenger of long experience, he was looking for leavings. What he didn't, and perhaps couldn't, realize was that while a fox or an eagle left much of a dead deer, four wolves were unlikely to leave anything of a goat and a kid. Still, he was hoping, and was not likely to be distracted. Even when Fior-eun flew over low, with a mighty swoosh of wings, he danced in a rage and stabbed up at her, croaking harsh raven contumely; but he resisted the urge to fly after her. He was more interested in the wolves.

Although he could play the buffoon when it amused him to do so, he was no buffoon: he was an alert, cunning and resourceful bird. But patience and he were ever restless bedfellows, and his natural boldness was fast overcoming his inborn wariness, a dangerous lapse for a raven confronting wolves, as many of his kind had discovered to their cost in the past. He danced and croaked himself into such a rage that at last he flew down and ground-skipped, with wings half-open, to within a hop and a wing flick of Alba's rump.

First he snatched a tuft of goat hair, danced away with it, and tossed it over his shoulder. Then he sidled towards her flank, keeping a guardian eye on the other three, hop-skipped round her rump, and tweaked her bushy tail hard with his powerful beak. The nip brought her instantly to her feet, with her tail high and the long hair of her mane bristling, and he skimmed out of reach. She made a short, threatening rush at him, but there was more of irritation than savagery in it, and she returned to her prey without trying to drive him from the hollow.

So far the wolf was playing the game by fox rules, and maybe the raven was thinking, if he was thinking at all, that she was just another fox – a big one to be sure, but a fox of a kind whatever. So he came back again and hopped close to her flank, taunting her. This time Alba stayed down, doing no more than turn her head with a growl muted in her throat. Instead of harassing her further, the raven turned his attention to the other three bellied down round the remains of the nanny goat. Alba changed position to face out from the rock so that she could keep her eyes on him. She had plenty of experience with ravens and knew he was likely to come back.

Twice, croaking and *kronking*, the bird snatched goat hair from behind Sgian's back before the three took any notice of him. Then they rose, turned about, and squatted down to watch him with their pale say-nothing eyes, each with fur at ease, ears erect, and teeth locked away. It almost seemed as though there were some sort of tolerant understanding between wolves and bird. The raven danced close to Dileas, making mock snatches at her whiskers, then back and sideways to *pruk* at Sgian and Saighdear with his crown feathers quilled. Dileas made a half-hearted pounce at him, but the movement was more annoyance than threat display. Sgian, too, made a short dash towards him, with hackles raised but teeth unbared, then lost interest in him when he skipped aside.

In the end the trio turned their backs on the raven and stalked across to join Alba, leaving him to strut and crow-swagger about, chortling and pecking, and swallowing the morsels they had left. He made a great show of ignoring them, but for all his swagger and mock indifference he was keeping them well in view. Tolerance, truce or whatever, he was not going to be caught off guard.

Saighdear threw himself down beside Alba and curled up muzzle to flank, with eyes slitted; he wanted to sleep and digest his meal. Dileas and Sgian lay down nearby, fox like, with tails over muzzles and guard hairs screening their eyes. Alba whimpered and touched noses with Saighdear. There was a growing restlessness in her – the commanding warnings from the life kicking inside her. She knew what she was looking for, and it was not in the hollow of the goat. Without any visible signal to the others she trotted from the hollow and turned north along her back trail on the shoulder of Carn nan Gabhar. Dileas was the first to rise and follow her; but the pair had not gone far before Saighdear and Sgian leaped up and loped after them. Saighdear ran on to head the line, while Sgian stayed back to keep the old order of march.

Saighdear kept below the snowline, round the north shoulder of Beinn a Ghlo, and led them on a long slant down towards the Tilt. A parcel of red deer hinds stampeded from a corrie when they saw the wolf pack padding over a knoll below them and bounded uphill in a frightened bourach, not stopping until they were on the skyline. Perhaps they thought the wolves were *rachis*, for they had several times been hunted by deerhounds. Saighdear slowed to a walk when they broke, then stopped to look after them, with tongue out and cat whiskers of misted breath curling from his teeth. Iolair and Fior-eun came circling down to view and follow but turned away when the pack splashed across the first of the many mountain streams spilling down to Loch Loch.

From time to time Saighdear halted, always at places where rocks or remnant woods provided cover for wolves to hide in, and there was an urge in him to lie up in daylight and travel the unknown country by night, but always Alba fronted him and her urgency kept him on foot. Rounding the high ground on Meall a Mhuirich, where they were slowed by the drag of hock-deep snow, he led them steeply down to tree cover above the Tilt, where they stopped beside a waterfall to rest and drink.

The trees were pine and birch, with oak and alder lower down, a vast hanging wood that was yet a mere remnant of the old Caledonian Forest, the great Wood of Caledon that the Romans knew, which once stretched from Glen Lyon and Rannoch to Strathspey and Strathglass, and from Glencoe to Mar. Now the great Wood, wherein once dwelt elk and bear, wild boar and beaver and wolf, was mostly gone, although much still remained. Centuries before, the Vikings had begun the destruction, setting the forest alight to smoke out the natives – a practice continued in later centuries by people like the notorious Wolf of Badenoch, Robert the Bruce and Oliver Cromwell. While Cromwell was devastating Lochaber to smoke out the natives, the natives were firing tracts around Loch Treig to smoke out wolves. The firestick was a weapon frequently used to drive wolves from the forest, on Athole as elsewhere, and the signs were there – sheened, lichened stumps and skeletal roots – on the ground over which Saighdear and his band had just travelled.

But the forest was resilient, and a thousand years of firing had not destroyed it because the ground, bared of herbage and enriched by its ash, provided an ideal bed for seeds that became seedlings then trees to replace the dead charred obelisks that

19

were their parents. Over centuries and millennia lightning had lit the fires that created the ground tilth for seedlings to thrive in, and old trees felled by storms opened clearings to give them light; but destruction by man far exceeded the ravages of lightning, without the rewards, and the great Wood was disappearing. Fellings yet to come would all but complete its disappearance from the map. Caledonia stern and wild was being born.

The pine beneath which Alba was resting, close to the waterfall, was a wide-armed, muscular tree, with the short bottle-green needles, ruddy bark and domed crown typical of its race. It was a seedling when King James IV of Scotland was paying rewards for the slaughter of wolves in the kingdom more than two centuries before. Wolves had roamed in Athole for half its lifetime, but Saighdear and his band were the first to pass that way for more than seventy years.

Alba rose, stretched herself and yawned; she was restive to be on her way. Saighdear headed the pack downhill to Allt Fheannach, a tributary of the Tilt, and padded along its near bank to the river. They ran the river bank, close to the water, startling a heron from a side pool where it had been fishing. The sudden spring of the bird, with its eagle spread of wings and kranking call of alarm, startled the wolves in their turn, but they checked only momentarily before leaping the narrow channel that fed the pool.

On the level now, they kept steady, tireless pace, splashing through a channering freshet and crossing two more hill streams cloudy with clots of melting snow. A mile later they reached another waterfall and turned downstream to the Tilt, but the river was wild with snow melt, a riot of broken water and foam-crested waves, thundering its way to join the brawling Garry. Alders on the face of the bank were awash and some, their roots undercut by the torrent, were leaning over, trailing their purple catkins in the water. The wolves stared across the river, with water lapping round their feet. They wanted to cross; but not here. Strong swimmers they were, but they had no stomach to attempt a crossing of the raging Tilt.

Instead they turned along their back trail to the waterfall and crossed the stream below it. All the hill streams were running full, gushing, spouting, cascading, breaking against boulders in bursts of white spray, but they were no obstacle to the wolves, who forded them at stepping stones or plunged in and splashed across, sometimes up to the neck in water. Oyster-catchers leaped from their path and circled overhead in jerky flight, piping in alarm. A buzzard lifted from the crown of an alder and mounted, mewing, then drifted down-river to pitch in another tree, where he ruffled his feathers and rubbed his head against a wing elbow before drawing up one leg and falling asleep. Three blackcocks, pecking at alder catkins, craned their necks to view the wolves passing below, then went back to their feeding.

Here Alba fronted the line, with Saighdear running second. On the other side of the river was where she wanted to be, but no wolf could have faced its tide-race of snow-fed water and lived. And she knew it. So she loped on, spring-footed, with the others running her tracks, through straggles of oak and birch and pine, holding close to the river, keeping her eyes on it and looking for a crossing place. Presently, after they had crossed another stream below an empty shieling roofed with heather and sods, their ears alerted to the faraway muted thunder of falling water, which became a deafening roar when they reached the junction of the two rivers where the Tarf's white cataract crashed into the boiling Tilt. The junction pool was a cauldron, a volcanic eruption of mushrooming water necklaced with foam. Its scattering sparks of spray drenched the wolves on the rim, and they turned away. There was no crossing for them here.

With Alba still leading they continued upstream, stampeding small parcels of red deer on the way. Less than two miles from the falls, where the channel narrowed, they splashed across, barely out of their depth, and shook the water from their fur. Alba turned west, then south below the eastern crags of Coire na Creige, where she called a halt. She was wearying again, and wanted to rest. On a knoll near the base of a crag she lay down in the heather, turned muzzle to flank and fell asleep with the sun just coming round on her. Saighdear and Dileas stayed near her, but the restless Sgian wandered off to explore, perhaps to hunt on his own.

Alba slept the daylight away, and well into the dark, now and again whimpering and twitching in sleep. Clouds had rolled across the sky while she was asleep, but shortly before midnight an eye opened revealing a pupil of sky with a cat's claw of moon

21

as highlight. The pupil opened wider, the clouds drifted apart and the stars came out, presaging frost by morning. A light wind stirred from the east, lightly ruffling the fur of Alba's back. She rose, yawned and stretched, then trotted over to Saighdear, who met her with wagging tail. After she had touched noses with him he sat down, pointed his nose to the sky and howled.

The howl, mournful and far carrying, excited Dileas and Alba, and they ran to him, wagging their tails like dogs. Within seconds Dileas joined in, then Alba, and Saighdear raised the pitch and power of his voice, ending his first long note in a crescendo that could have been heard two miles away. After three short *ow-ow-ows*, with head lowered, he pointed his muzzle skyward again and howled on another long rising note. Their display was a true chorus, three voices in wolf harmony, not the babel it might have seemed to a human ear, had there been human ear to hear. There was none. The pack chorus was also a rallying cry. Sgian, more than a mile away on the north bank of the Tarf, heard it and howled in reply. In under two minutes the session was over, and Alba was ready to go.

2

Alba was still leading the line when the trio came on Sgian in a juniper brake on the face of a ridge sloping down to the storming white waters of the Tarf. But he was not coming to the rallying cry.

He was scraping at a hole in an undercut, gravelly bank where a mountain hare, in coat of winter white, had sought refuge after he had coursed her on a short uphill burst. Waywise, she knew it was there, as she knew her own well-trodden trail leading to it. Perhaps she had even excavated it, for the hare of the mountains, unlike its brown kin in the low glens and straths, will go readily to ground, and sometimes dig burrows for itself. Sgian knew where she had gone, and he knew she was still there because his nose was full of the tantalizing smell of her, just as the hare's was saturated with his warm breath every time he stuck his face in the hole to snort and sniff. He looked up momentarily when the rest of the pack arrived, then returned to his digging. Saighdear sat down to watch him, and stayed down when Alba padded away with Dileas at her flank.

The bitch pair kept to the low ridges, following the course of the river, but three times in as many miles they had to go down to glens and up again to cross streams in their path. At the fourth they turned upstream, through scattered alders and birches, rowans and juniper, into a wild glen between snow-clad mountains with forested lower slopes – another remnant of the once vast Wood of Caledon.

The glen had no north exit; at its head stood the snow-clad massif of An Sgarsoch. The stream the wolves were following had its source on the east side of the mountain, high above the

23

snowline. Two miles below the source they waded, plunged and swam across, with the current pulling at their legs, then trotted uphill through alders and birches into the shrub layer of the ancient forest. They climbed through to the tree-line, turned right along the open face of the mountain and down again into the forest, coming to a halt in a clearing of rock outcrops and scree.

Alba became excited and cast about, whimpering, with her tail held high; she squatted and soaked a dry, rasping tussock with urine. But she did no more prospecting. Instead she lay down to rest in the shelter of the pines below the clearing. The long marathon from Lochaber was telling on her now. Dileas went to the tussock where Alba had squatted and added her urine to it, then she stood up, pointed her muzzle to the sky, and howled. She howled for only half a minute, and was answered by Saighdear and Sgian from afar.

Her howl was almost certainly more than a simple call for vocal contact with the absent pack members. Howling is a complex ritual, more than social choristing or the expression of emotion, and more than likely each wolf in a pack can recognize the voices of the others. So perhaps Dileas was signalling that Alba's quest was over and that the pack now had a base. She might even, instinctively, have been warning any intruding wolf, or wolves, that there was a pack in possession of the ground, for she had no way of knowing there was none to answer her.

Saighdear and Sgian arrived after daylight and the bitches ran to them and greeted them with tails wagging. Alba went down on a shoulder, grappled Saighdear's neck with her forepaws, and showered him with affectionate play-bites. She rose and rubbed against his flank. He pawed her playfully and took her muzzle gently in his powerful jaws, not pressing with his teeth as he would have done in a gesture of warning. After a few minutes they parted. Alba, followed by Dileas, began to search among the rocks and above: she wanted cover – a dark, secret place where she could give birth to her puppies. Sgian skulked into the downhill timber and squatted to lick his paws before falling asleep. Saighdear also slept, full-bellied with Sgian's hare inside him, for he had stepped in to kill her when she was at last

24

unearthed, and growled the protesting digger off with hoisted tail and eyes closed to slits.

While the dog wolves slept Alba began to explore the clearing, questing under huge rocks, along tortuous alleyways and deep tunnels, disappearing and reappearing with tongue quivering over teeth, with her shadow Dileas standing by and not interfering. At the end of one tunnel she came face to face with a big sow badger lying up with small cubs in a massive nest of withered grass and leaves. She had seen badgers before, but not face to face and never underground, so she was perplexed and angry, and showed her anger with growls and a display of teeth that would have daunted any beast of badger size – except a badger. Growling and snapping the sow pushed forward, and Alba retreated before the dart-dart-dart of the black and white striped arrowhead with its crushing jaws and crippling teeth.

The badger came out after her, blinking and grumbling, and she wisely withdrew to search elsewhere. Soon afterwards she · found what she was looking for, at the end of a long walkway under a pile of rocks lodged and ankylosed by weight, plant debris and weather – a massive roof that would seal her nursery against the worst of snow, sleet or rain. Satisfied that this would be her nursery, she came out, ran to Saighdear and licked his muzzle. Then she went back in and stayed. Dileas, her shadow, followed her and lay down at the entrance.

Alba spent most of the day digging six feet into the hard-packed pebbly bank from the walkway under the scree, rounding out the end of the burrow into a chamber spacious enough for herself and her family. Between spells of digging she slept a half-waking sleep, and once she came out to lap water from a sap below the clearing. Like the fox, but unlike the badger a little distance away, she carried no bedding into the den. The dry, padded earth was all the nest her puppies would need. No wolf howled all that day, but Saighdear and Sgian, exploring uphill and down in the timber, left their scats in prominent places, as foxes do, perhaps as territory markers.

Crested tits, working through the trees, hopped down to low branches to view the newcomers to the forest; crossbills, flickering red and green in the pine tops, were feeding on cones; a red squirrel dropped the pine cone he had been shredding and

25

watched the wolves, bright-eyed, from behind a trunk. A cock wheatear, newly arrived, flittered from rock to rock in the clearing, ignoring them. When he paused, he became invisible against the lichen on the scree.

Frost, with Arctic cold, came when the night was far gone, and in the morning there was taloned wind with threat of snow. The sun came up, plaided in cramassie, like a monstrous flower rayed with flame, suffusing with rose and amethyst the snow-crowned peaks and gilding the crescent of moon now at its setting. Rime mildewed the heather and blaeberries; the hoar lichened the pine cones and tipped with silver the manes of the wolves. Saighdear and Sgian were lying above the scree, clear of the grizzled pines, with a commanding view over the lower forest to the opposite side of the glen, where deer were moving in the open. Dileas, still keeping tryst with Alba, was curled half-asleep at the entrance to the walkway – chin on hocks, eyes closed to slits, and breath vapouring in the frore.

The wind rose to a rant that made a tide race of the grass on the lower slopes. It clawed at the crouching alders, and bent the birches on the banks of the stream, still running clear with a flotsam of old alder cones, birch twigs and catkins. And suddenly there was a hurricane of snow, hard and fine as granite dust, that sealed the rock clefts of An Sgarsoch and wrapped in ermine the eagle on her eyrie above the headwaters of the stream, where she was guarding her first egg. This Fior-eun's territory was north of the Tarf, which was her frontier with the eagles of Beinn a Ghlo.

When the snowstorm passed on and the sky cleared, the ground was white from the high tops to the Tilt. But the wind's barbed fury and skelloch were slow to die. While the sun glimmered wan through the spindrift over An Sgarsoch, it scourged the high ridges to the bone, exposing the shapes of white hares running downhill, and sculpting the drifts into long, corniced ridges from the high ground to the riverside flats. Already the first white hares were down, seeking heather tips blown clear of snow, scraping away snow to uncover them, or gnawing rushes and twigs of willow and rowan near the water's edge. Red deer were scraping through the snow on the flats across the Tilt, or browsing the riverside trees; beyond them

Iolair the eagle, hare hunting, was scouting the mid slopes of Beinn a Ghlo.

The wind backed at darkening, and in the white starlit silence Sgian left the rock clearing and padded down through the forest to the glen, leaving a plain trail of outsize dog tracks to mark his going, and now and again the drag furrow of his tail tip where it touched the snow. Two great birds, one with the seeming bulk of an eagle, startled him when they crashed from a low pine branch ahead of him and clattered from the forest in headlong flight. The birds were capercaillies, cock and hen, the biggest grouse in the world, now rare in the forests of Athole and like the wolves a dying race.

Saighdear left the clearing soon after Sgian and trotted up through the pines into the white open to explore in the opposite direction. This being unknown ground to him he was not waywise, so he had to reconnoitre, and he chose to go high and into the hinterland rather than down to the glens. Prey might be scarcer in the great mountain wilderness, but his wolf sense told him that men might be so also.

Dileas, whimpering, watched the dog wolves go, and resisted the urge to join one or other of them. Instead, she stalked along the walkway to Alba's den and touched noses with her. There was a great bond between them, but Dileas knew her place in the pack order of dominance, and when Alba grumbled irritably at her she back-tracked a few paces and crouched down, in scent contact. When Alba continued to grumble she rose and left the walkway, and lay down in the snow at the entrance to keep vigil.

By then Sgian was out of the timber and running the flat top of a ridge above the stream, where the wind had blown the snow to a scowder barely deep enough to cover his feet in their slots. Behind him he left a neat line of tracks – the trail of a walking wolf which, like a walking fox, prints hindfoot on forefoot. But the two could never be confused, because the wolf's tread is huge compared with the cat-footed fox's, although a man might easily have mistaken it for the footprint of a big dog.

The stream was running no higher than on the day before because the savage night frost had sealed off its tributaries of melting snow. Sgian, high stepping, splashed across where it was shallow and running over pebbles, with the wind combing and parting the long hair of his mane, and the rippling water sleeking the fur of his flanks. The current, surging under him, tried to lift him, but he kept his feet and swam the last few yards in a swirl of deeper water to a spit where he shook the loose wet from his fur.

The snow on this bank was hock deep, and slowed him down; but he had an eye for ground, and from there to the head of the stream he followed the lee side of the long drifts, rarely floundering and never trapped. Two lesser streams, from their sources below the eyrie of the An Sgarsoch eagles, joined the main one at its head, forming a fork, and a group of seven red deer stags had crossed below the junction that morning. Sgian crossed their trail, but his nose told him nothing because their foot scent was smothered under the new blanket of drifted snow. Like other hunters, he tracked by scent, not by visible footprints holding none.

He followed the left fork of the stream until he was below the great fissured crag where the An Sgarsoch eagles had their eyrie. Below the crag he halted to pant in a cloud of steamy breath, knowing nothing of the eagle above him, well down on her nest and mantled in snow, waiting for the morrow when she would lay her second egg. She had her first one on the outside of her breast feathers, protecting it but not warming it, as she would after she had laid her second. When she saw the wolf below her, a dark shape against the white, she rose to a crouch to look at him, at the same time shaking off her mantle of snow. But she settled again at once, having no notion about leaving her precious egg, even for a moment, to chivvy a prowling wolf which she probably thought was a dog.

Sgian plodded along below the eagles' crag, in snow up to his hocks, and turned the head of the left fork into the open ground between it and the right. The sources of the two prongs of the fork were less than a mile apart; from their junction with the main stream they were like the antlers of a switch stag. Sgian ploughed his way to a ridge between the prongs, unaware that he was being watched by the eagle, or that Saighdear had come round the shoulder of An Sgarsoch and was on the other side of the right fork. From the ridge he could see seven stags below him, black against the snow; but they could not see him because he was not in silhouette, and could not smell him because he was

28

down wind of them. Sgian bellied down to watch them, while they spread out to scratch through the snow with hoof and antler in search of a bite.

The wind was still gathering clouds of snow and swirling it into drifts, and before long the stags started uphill to seek the bield of the eagles' crag. Sgian crouched low, realizing that they were going to come right on top of him. The stags high-stepped towards him, five with full heads and two with one antler. They were within twenty-five yards of the waiting wolf when the An Sgarsoch raven, for reasons known only to himself, made a sweep flight in the snowy half-dark, playing tricks with the wind, and swooped low below the ridge. If he had not seen the wolf before, he was seeing him now, and said so, and his *kronk-kronk* of discovery was not lost on the deer.

They stopped at once and looked right, left and over their shoulders, with ears harking back, forward and sideways, and flared nostrils asking questions of the wind. But the wind told them nothing. Yet they heeded the raven, as they would have heeded an alarmed grouse bursting from the heather, or a yarring crow, or a hare in panic flight. They did not always have to see, hear or smell for themselves. So they turned away across the face of the slope in a tight group and broke down wind, with noses watching their back trail and eyes questing ahead. But they were not running in panic: they were running because the raven was a bird they listened to.

With alerted deer well away on a strong run, and difficult terrain between, hunting wolves may not give chase at all; when they do, they will break off, more often than not, if they cannot close up within a short distance. The long run, mile after mile, in pursuit of a strong quarry, is not their usual way.

But this wolf was Sgian, with his own thrawn personality. All wolves are individuals, with their own personalities clearly expressed within the discipline of the pack. Saighdear was an individual, as were Dileas and Alba. But there was a stubborn streak in Sgian. He would have run on where Saighdear broke off; attacked where Saighdear withdrew. He was wilful, rash even; and sometimes bold to the point of recklessness. Now the pack discipline, however often it might have irked him, saved him from himself.

The fleeing deer were two hundred and fifty yards away,

pounding the snow into spindrift, when he leaped from his ambush to give chase. With his shrewd eye for ground, he closed to within fifty yards of them before they had gone three quarters of a mile, heading for the narrow of the fork at the head of the stream. He kept directly uphill of them. If they changed direction to avoid the ridge drifts across their front he wanted them on a downhill run.

The stag leading the run was a big switch, with long rapier antlers unforked above the brow tines. He had come late to the rut in the autumn, and lost little weight, so he was well fleshed and strong, despite the hard winter, and was only a little below peak condition. The tail stag was a royal, with six points on each antler: brow, bay and tray tines with three-point top. Coming late from the rut, and caught by early snow when he was in low condition, he had not recovered his full strength. Every stag in the group now knew the wolf was there and crowded closer on the switch, leaving the royal still farther behind. The switch veered left but, faced by a wide drift ridge, he turned downhill again, ploughing through knee-deep snow until he reached a windswept knoll where it was barely over his fetlocks. And there he stopped, and wheeled to face the oncoming wolf. His followers rushed past him, stumbling and floundering, and slashing deep gashes in the snow. Then, realizing he had halted, they faced about, stamping and milling, and crowded behind him, with mouths open and nostrils spouting vapour.

Sgian slithered to a stop a few bounds from the stag now set to face him, with head down, brandishing his rapiers, and showing the whites of his eyes. No sane wolf would attempt a frontal attack on a big stag standing firm and prepared to defend himself. Sgian recognized the signs and his innate wolf wisdom took control of his ardour. Instead of rushing recklessly to the attack he bellied down, with his tail sweeping the snow, to ponder.

Yet he was reluctant to break off altogether: that was the dourness in him. Rather than break off at once, as Saighdear would have done, he had a mind at least to test the switch's mettle: that was the wilfulness in him. Rising warily he stalked to the right, threatening to turn the switch's flank, but the stag stamped round to face him. He tried a threat stalk to the left, bellying over the snow and showing his teeth, but the switch kept facing him. And Sgian backed away: that was the wolf wisdom in him.

But for Sgian breaking off from the switch was not the end of the hunt; his mind was now on the other stags crowding behind. They might break in disarray if directly threatened from behind. He made a wider detour round the posturing switch, found unerringly ground over which he could run at speed, and bore down on them in tremendous bounds, leaving great slashed slots like bear tracks behind him. The stags broke and stampeded downhill, with the royal lumbering in the rear. Sgian rushed to head him, spurning up gouts of snow with his hindfeet – a dark menace of hard muscle and flowing hair, never faltering, knowing exactly what he was going to do. From the far side of the right fork Saighdear howled. He heard it clearly but made no reply. He kept silence and ran on, and before the leading stag reached the head of the stream he had turned the royal into a long ridge drift. When the beast was rearing and plunging there, with mouth open and snow on his tongue, he ploughed through to the attack. With the stag trapped in the drift, unable to use antlers or hind hooves, he could do so safely, in classic wolf style, from behind.

Although he now knew that Saighdear was less than half a mile away he kept silence and attacked alone; what he did not know was that his pack mate had winded the deer, and seen them against the snow, and was already across the fork on the way to join him. Clambering on to the royal's haunch and grappling with his forepaws, he sank his enormous canine teeth into the lean rump. The bite was deep and opened a gaping wound from which blood began to spill. The stag struggled, trying to rear from the drift, but he could not extricate himself and Sgian pressed the attack, tearing away hide and muscle and laying bare the bone. Now he was joined by Saighdear, who attacked the stag's flank, low behind the rib cage. Blood gouted from the wounds, running warm on the muzzles of the wolves and staining and spattering the snow. And the stag's struggles weakened with the loss.

Sgian tore more flesh from the rump, then moved round to the other flank, opposite Saighdear, and began to slash there, forward of the groin, opening a terrible wound that exposed the entrails. The stag gasped, rolling his eyes, while the wolves ripped and tore, and the snow was churned and trampled to bloody slush. Death was near for the royal, and when Sgian tore out his entrails he died. The warmth from his gralloched body clouded on the cold night air, misting the heads of the wolves as they gobbled entrails and gorged on gobs of flesh.

The other deer were now across the main stream, facing back, unmoving silhouettes standing in a cloud of their own breath, with mouths open and flanks heaving. They guessed, or knew, as deer do, that the wolves would not be hunting them again that night. Presently they turned away and headed down to the Tarf at an unhurried, spring-footed trot.

Though lean, with little fat on him, the stag was still a lot of wolf meat, and the pack would not go hungry for several days. By the time the wolves had eaten their fill, bolting the meat in choking gulps, each had devoured more than the weight of a big mountain fox. With their own hunger sated for the moment, they could now carry for Alba, so they tore off two more heavy strips from the haunch of the royal and scrambled out of the drift with them in their jaws. Nothing was moving in the white silence; the raven, after his night sortie, had gone back to roost. Saighdear took the direct route to the den, across the left fork near its junction with the main stream, and Sgian followed in his tracks. By that route the distance from the kill to the den was no more than a mile.

Under the pines, below the rock clearing, they dropped their meat and scraped snow lightly over it, watched from a low branch by a tawny owl *wee-wicking* in query and clicking his beak. Both wolves urinated near the caches before padding into the clearing. Dileas was still lying at the entrance to the walkway. When she saw Saighdear she became excited, and ran to him to sniff his muzzle and lick his face, wagging her tail and whimpering. She could read the sign and smell the blood, and became even more excited. After the greeting she stalked back trail and found his cache, which she uncovered with her forepaws. The owl blinked at her, clicked his beak, gulped, bowed on his perch, and wafted silently away.

Dileas could have eaten all the meat in the cache; she could have eaten what was buried in both. Instead she bolted down the meat from Saighdear's cache where she stood and carried Sgian's back to Alba, who was bellied down at the entrance to the walkway, facing out. Alba took the meat and backed away with it to her den, rumbling in her chest. Dileas whined, with tail wagging, but did not stay; she turned back along the walkway. At the entrance she met Sgian, looking in, and lifted her lips at him, warning him off. He padded away without show of anger or resentment, and when he threw himself down among the rocks she stretched out beside him. Saighdear was out of sight, bedded behind a boulder, dozing in an agony of comfort.

After an hour's rest Saighdear rose, stretched himself, and loped away along his back trail to the left fork, followed by Dileas running in his slots, and Sgian some distance behind. They returned to the body of the stag, where Dileas gorged herself before tearing off about six pounds of meat to carry away. And again the dog pair ripped and bolted down flesh, each swallowing the equivalent of a white buck hare; and again they tore off meat to carry away. Sgian sheered off a shoulder with his powerful cutting teeth, hefted his load, and loped after Dileas along their back trail. Saighdear tailed them, carrying another bloody chunk of torn rump, now chilled, from which no drips fell to stain the snow.

The trio crossed the left fork together in line ahead, but were running abreast when they approached the clearing, with their heads high and their tails down-curved at ease. Dileas headed the dog pair before they left the cover of the pines and ran with her mouthful to the entrance to the walkway, where she put it down for Alba. Saighdear cached his lightly in the same place as before, but Sgian trotted through the clearing into the forest above until he found an ancient tree, half-uprooted by storms. Below the undercut roots he hid the shoulder of meat, pushing it out of sight with his nose before scraping snow and pine needles over with his feet.

Long before daylight the dog pair made another journey to the carcass of the stag. This time Saighdear tore and scraped off most of what remained of the haunch, while Sgian cut out the saddle, crunching through bone to free it and exposing the spine, on which the remaining morsels of flesh quickly dried and darkened. They were greeted by Dileas when they returned to the clearing, and the three jostled and scrummaged in great excitement, pawing and play-biting, with tails wagging. They chased each other through the rocks, rearing shoulder to shoulder in pair, and using their teeth on ruff and mane in mock threat. This over, they grouped, raised their muzzles and howled. Alba came out to fuss, but she neither frolicked nor howled, and stayed for only a few moments before skulking back to her den. She was near her time.

Although the chorus came muted to Alba in her deep den, she could recognize the three voices of it. It lasted for no more than a minute, and was heard by deer and goats, hares, foxes and ravens, and by the An Sgarsoch eagle on her nest; but it was unheard by human ears, for Blair was twenty miles away, with peak after peak between, and the deep corrie trapped the sound. A wolf on Tarf bank could have heard it, but not a human ear between Blair and the forest of Mar.

Just before dawn Saighdear and Sgian left the clearing again to make another visit to the kill, leaving Alba in the den and Dileas on her vigil at the entrance to the walkway. This time the kill had other visitors, as the wolves could easily see while they were yet some distance away. A big mountain fox, red of leg, in prime coat, with white-tipped brush, was eating at the carcass, with the An Sgarsoch raven skirmishing at his heels, snapping up morsels, fanning his wings, and croaking with his neck feathers on end. Two hoodie crows, grey-bodied with black head and wings, were standing by thigh-deep in snow, waiting on, endlessly patient, alert and wary, realizing there would be more than enough left for them when the others went away. Although they too could chivvy a fox when they had a mind to, they had no mind to with a raven present as well. Uphill, on a rock, the An Sgarsoch eagle was perched, standing on one leg, waiting his moment, when he would eat before carrying part of the kill to his mate on the nest.

All of them saw the approaching wolves, but the fox and the raven made no move to draw off until Saighdear was breasting the drift with Sgian at his heels. Even then, at the last moment, the raven took time to nip the fox's left hind pad while he had his bloodied face half into the rib cage of the carcass. Saighdear was almost on them, slowed by the depth of the snow, before they surrendered possession – the raven lifting off wideways and the fox scrambling, hock-deep, towards the waiting crows.

The wolves stood over the carcass and began to tear at it. Despite the depth of snow they managed to haul the body over, exposing the untouched shoulder, flank and lower rump of the other side. Saighdear worked on the lower rump, rending and stripping, while Sgian tugged at the spine, with its long side cushions of lean meat. This time neither of them stopped to eat more than a mouthful of cold entrails. The light was coming up when they cantered away, one with a fillet like a short fat eel and the other with a blue-sheened wedge of lower rump.

They were hardly clear of the drift before the raven was back, and when the fox joined him the bird displayed at him, but moved aside at the last moment to elude the snapping jaws. The hoodie crows moved in closer, still patient, still pondering, but not taking risks. The eagle remained on his rock: he would be in before the crows, but it would be after the raven and the fox had gone.

3

The An Sgarsoch eagle had laid her second egg, and was beginning her forty day sit, when Alba whelped five puppies in three hours and nosed them against her warm belly, where they soon found her nipples and mouthed them to suck. Thrice the weight of fox cubs, blind and deaf but not mute, they mewed and squeaked as they sucked in the dark, engulfing warmth of her body, treading with their small fish-hook nails against her swollen breasts while she licked their gummed eyes, their napes and under their tails. Relaxed now, with the milk flowing, she was breathing deeply, and now and again she sighed. The stress and strain of the long run from Lochaber were in the past. Her den was her world and the puppies her life. And there was Dileas close at hand, bellied down at the entrance to the walkway, head in and rump out, with the rump and tail of her mantled in snow.

Outside, beyond Alba's knowing or caring, the wind had ranted to new fury, and the glens and tops were a chaos of swirling, drifting white in which nothing was moving. Below the clearing the tawny owl was standing tall and shrivelled against the trunk of his pine roost, with eyes closed and breast feathers ruffled, unable to hunt. Saighdear and Sgian were crouched on an exposed rock flat above the walkway, like carvings ruffed and mantled in snow, facing the blast with slitted eyes, with no thought of seeking shelter although there was more than enough in the clearing for a score or more of their kind. Their thick fur gave them high resistance to cold, and under their skins they were as warm as Alba in her den, where she had her puppies

36

gathered between thigh and belly – milk-happy, quiet and asleep.

The wolves knew all about the vagaries of mountain weather, with its moods of shriving winds and Arctic cold, and white storms blanketing the hills, so were not troubled by a spring blizzard like the harbinger of a new Ice Age. They had remembered experience of it – winters of white hurricanes and crags of ice, and sprindrift of mare's tail waterfalls blown skywards again like geysers; spring days becoming winter in an hour, silencing lark-song, the keening of peewits, and the plaintive whistles of golder plovers; freak storms of May and June, bringing the deer back into the forest from their summer heights and roofing with ephemeral snow the ptarmigan on their nests. The eagle, too, had known her halo of flies replaced by a crown of snow on the threshold of summer, when she had pied, puling eaglets under her wings, and cuckoos were calling in the riverside trees along Tarf. All this the wolves knew, so they were content to lie up until the storm had passed.

But it lasted for two days and into the third, now in fierce blasts of snow, driving and swirling to the gale's banshee pibroch, now backing to a gentler wind and a slow dance of eddying flakes, with sometimes the clouds opening into a blue vault of sky. The wolves fed on cached meat, most of it taken by Alba and carried into the walkway, at the entrance to which Dileas still kept vigil. No member of the pack was yet irked by hunger, and none questioned, by posture or threat, Alba's right to take what she wanted.

In the gentle spells between snowstorms Saighdear and Sgian prowled in the forest, uphill and down. The wide-spreading, flat-domed crowns of the pines were mushroomed with snow. Under their white canopies red squirrels were running on the branches or sitting up shredding cones. They were curious, but not alarmed, when they saw the wolves passing below, padding along alleyways in the ground herbage, from which they brushed ostrich plumes of snow with their shoulders. Ahead of them the wolves could hear the purring of crested tits, true birds of the pine forest, like the giant capercaillies and, like them, doomed to dwine with its shrinking. Of deer sign there was none: the beasts were all down in the lower forests, trampling the snow and browsing on the shrub layer under the trees.

On the third day Alba came out, shook herself, touched noses with Dileas, and padded down through the timber below the clearing to lap water from a sap, with her pack mate and shadow following in her tracks. She lapped thirstily and noisily, then found the last cache of meat which she uncovered with a forepaw and bolted down where she stood. Then she hastened back to her puppies, who squirmed over her belly, mewing and yelping, and seeking her nipples. Until then they had known only darkness, the warm comfort of her, and her abundant milk; now they could smell, and her body scent added another dimension to their world. She turned them over, pummelled them and licked them, and when they emptied their bowels she swallowed the contents and washed under their tails with her tongue. Dileas did not resume her watch at the entrance to the walkway; she trotted past it and up into the timber to seek Saighdear and Sgian. She was ready to hunt again.

When she met them high above the clearing the three sat down, raised their muzzles and howled – three voices orchestrated and distinguishable. Two buzzards, soaring and gliding overhead, mewing like cats, fell silent and circled down to harken to the medley, with its *ow-ow-ow-ow*, its *ow-oo . . . ow-oo . . . ow-oo*, its quavering, rising cadences, and the gruff half-barks of Saighdear. The chorus lasted less than ninety seconds. At the end of it the trio fussed each other, with tails wagging, then set off downhill with Saighdear leading. They turned the south shoulder of An Sgarsoch and down to the lower ridges above the Tarf, along which the snow was lying in razor-edged escarpments and cornices. Hares and ptarmigan were already down in the glen, refugees from the heights to which they would return with the retreat of the snowline. Saighdear held the pack to the low ridges, running west at a steady lope, not waywise, not knowing what lay ahead, seeking sight or scent of prey, or chance encounter.

Wolves are tireless runners, muscled for marathons, and soon the pack had left eight miles of tracks behind them. They crossed many streams, and on the bank of one surprised a hare facing out from a burrow in a snowdrift. Saighdear snatched it and killed it before it could get into its run. When the others rushed in to share the worry he growled them off, and they left him behind to dismember and gulp down the warm prey. He caught up with them where another stream joined the Tarf, and here Sgian broke away to chase an otter on a snowbank by the river's edge. The otter, carrying a fish, dived into a pool and surfaced later under the bank upstream, out of his sight and out of his nose. Sgian bounded back to rejoin the others, spurting a wake of snow from his hind pads, and took his place again behind Saighdear, with tail hanging slack, his moment of indiscipline over. Wolves like a prey animal to run before they attack: Sgian still had the puppy habit of chasing anything that moved.

Two hours from the den they reached another forested glen, and Saighdear turned uphill through the first outlying trees, with the wind at his back. At the tree-line he swung left into the timber, then downhill: now he had it on his face. Overhead the cock eagle from An Sgarsoch was wheeling eastward with a white hare dangling from his talons: the glen was the boundary of his range to the west. Deer sign was plain all through the timber – old tracks without scent in them, newer tracks with a trace, and fresh tracks that any wolf could have followed with its nose in the air.

The pack found a fresh trail of hinds with yearling calves at foot and became excited, nuzzling each other, rubbing shoulders and wagging their tails. But they had no need to track deer by their foot-scent: the smell of them was heavy on the air. The pack began their downhill run, with Sgian and Dileas abreast behind Saighdear, flanking him but not at his flank. Their tails went up as the odour of deer and deer urine became thicker on the air, and they knew their quarry was not far away.

A roebuck, with antlers in fraying velvet, leaped from a thicket and broke uphill, taken by surprise because the pack was coming on to him upwind and he had no warning of them before he saw them. The temptation to follow was there, and Sgian cast a glance over his shoulder, but the three held together, bounding downhill in gouts of snow into engulfing deer-smell like an invisible cloud under the trees. The hinds had not been alerted by the roebuck's flight, and the pack was in view before their ears went up and they broke away in a stampede of plunging bodies and snowbursts from flying hooves.

The deer bounded diagonally down towards the open hill and the Tarf – eight hinds with five calves crowding their mothers.

With fur flowing and breath misting the pack pressed hard on the rear runners, floundering where the snow was deep, but still closing because the hooves of the deer slotted deeper. Sgian ran the left flank of the stampede, with Saighdear and Dileas on the right. As the deer broke from the forest into the straggling trees on the fringe, a gathering of blackcocks, resting thigh-deep in snow, burst into the air with whicker of wings and fled in down-curved flight, flap and glide, to pitch on a mound among birches on the other side of the Tarf. Saighdear and Dileas cut out an old hind and calf from the right flank of the herd and pulled her down before she could reach the river; she died in an eruption of snow, with the pair on her back and rump.

The calf bounded on in wild panic, trying to join the herd before they crossed the river, but Sgian turned him, forcing him to leap into the water where it was running deep and billowing under the bank. Struggling and bleating the calf was carried away by the strong current, but he might well have got a grip on it, and swum to safety, had not Sgian plunged in after him and killed him. The wolf was also carried away; but not far. Still holding on to his prey he struck out strongly for the bank, with the current trying to pull it from his jaws. Dog-paddling with all the power of his tireless muscles, he reached the exposed, undercut roots of a big alder, where he rested for a moment in a simmer of foam before clambering on to them, dragging the heavy prey. Once clear of the water he tugged at the body until he had it on the roots beside him. Then he backed up the bank with it, tugging and straining and skidding in the snow until he had it on the flat top. On the slope he left a gashed trail like an otter slide.

Panting, but not taking time to rest, he bit and slashed into the calf's groin, ripped back the hide from the rump, and lay down to gorge. Saighdear and Dileas were already feeding on the dead hind, a quarter of a mile uphill from him. The hind herd, with their calves, had come to a halt two hundred yards beyond the far bank of the Tarf, looking back with flanks heaving, tongues showing, and nostrils flared. The lead hind was fronting the herd, her calf at her side, and stamping with a forehoof. The hind killed by the wolves had been her grand-daughter.

With his stomach full, and a bloody slab of rump point in his jaws, Sgian left the kill and set off at a swinging trot on the long

40

run back to the den, not waiting for his pack mates and breaking new ground below their outgoing trail. His pack mates, also gorged and carrying meat, took the out-trail back, shadowed by the An Sgarsoch eagle, now hunting again after delivering a white hare to his mate on the nest. He came down to kestrel-height to view them, gliding above them and glaring, before banking away westward to his forest boundary to hunt the low ridges above the Tarf for the hares swarming there.

On his first sweep from the tree fringe he saw the torn body of the hind on the blood-stained snow, and circled down to look it over. Forgetting about hares he swooped in low, uphill, and pitched on it. With wings half-closed he stood tall to glare right, left and around, as though expecting to be driven off. But his fierce, hazel eyes could see nothing moving on the snow, so he folded his wings, changed his stance on the carcass, and began to tear at the dark flesh. He filled his craw with venison, clawed his yellow beak and whetted it on the flank hair of the hind. Now he could hunt hares for his mate. He had to go hunting because, unlike the wolves, he could not cut out a hare's weight of meat to carry away in his talons. The raven who followed him had no such problem. He pitched, stabbed with his beak, ate his fill, then flew away with a pouchful for his mate on Ben Dearg, more than two miles to the south-west beyond the Tarf.

Sgian was not in the clearing when Saighdear and Dileas arrived; he was up in the timber, dozing in a patch of sunlight, close to the place where he had cached his meat. Saighdear padded to the flat rock that had become his lookout and resting place, dropped his meat and threw himself down beside it. Dileas ran to the walkway entrance; there she dropped her meat and whimpered, and Alba came out. Ignoring the offering, she trotted down to her drinking place, and this time she did not return at once to her puppies: she sat down and clawed her ears, rose and clawed her flanks, then went down on a hip to lick her belly and vent. She rose and shook herself, shedding a few coarse hairs, early sign of the moult to come. Next she rolled in the snow, then put a shoulder to it and furrowed it, thrusting with her hindfeet. She returned to the clearing wearing snow-burrs like ectoparasites, touched noses with Dileas, picked up the meat and disappeared into her den.

The sun was warm in the clearing and the trees were

41

beginning to drip; within an hour the pines lost their mushroom crowns. Dileas moved into the pine cover above Saighdear and lay down, muzzle on outstretched forepaws, to sleep; but she had hardly closed her eyes before she was on her feet again, shaking snow from her face and ruff. A squirrel, leaping from one branch-tip to another, had dislodged it. Later on, Saighdear opened one eye questioningly when a bird pitched noisily in the tree behind him. The bird was a cock capercaillie and the clearing was his strutting ground during the spring display season. With head tilted sideways he peered down at Saighdear with one bright eye, knowing he would not be going down there while the wolves were in possession: the capercaillie in the trees is a warier and more wideawake bird than the capercaillie on the ground. When Saighdear moved his head, he crashed from his perch and racketed away through the forest.

That night Dileas remained in the clearing while the dog pair returned to the kills. It was a calm night of big-bellied clouds in slow drift, with an egg-shaped moon bathing the white silence in spectral radiance when it appeared in the clearways. The pair returned from their eighteen miles round trip with stomachs full and meat in their jaws. They cached the meat in the timber. When they were bellied down on the flat rock above the den, Dileas left to visit the kills, not returning until daylight when the sun was a pale gleam on the misty horizon and the An Sgarsoch eagle was already on the wing. She was full of meat. Eagle and raven by day, and fox at night, had eaten from the carcass, but their eatings had made little difference to it: at one gorge Saighdear could have cleared more than all the scavengers together. The kills lasted for four days, at the end of which they were reduced to skin and skeletons.

The thaw warmed and quickened, and the hill streams rushed white-crested down to join the surging Tarf. The hares, patchy in the moult, began to move up, following the retreating snow-line, and the wolves hunted them, not in pack but singly. Sgian killed many on the slopes of An Sgarsoch, catching them easily on foot, or at the entrances to burrows or other hiding places, and eating them down to claws and whiskers. Saighdear surprised a party of three bucks hopping along after a doe who kept kicking at them to fend them off. He cut out a buck and ran it uphill to the snowline, where he killed it on the turn. When he stood back to watch its convulsive kicking, he had fur fluff on his muzzle and forepaws.

Ten days after Alba had whelped, the pack of three killed another deer near the Bynock water, less than three miles from the den. The beast was a wasting stag, shaggy in the coat, with declining antlers and no fat on his ribs, and they pulled him down after a short run over ground clear of snow. Although all three had meat in them, they tore into the warm body, licking blood as it flowed, and filled themselves to repletion on haunch and entrails. When they returned to the clearing Alba was out on the flat rock above the den, licking and scratching herself in the sun, for the first time taking a half hour away from her puppies, who were huddled together in a moleheap at the back of the den, warming each other in the absence of her body heat. The homing trio heard the thud of her hindfoot on the rock before they could see her.

After that Alba left her puppies for a short spell each day, and sometimes two or three times a day. When they were a fortnight old their eyes opened, and they began to make short forays at a toad crawl into the walkway, bracing themselves with their forepaws. They became conscious of the light at the exit from the walkway, and it attracted them more and more each day, although they had no idea what it was. Within a few days of their eyes opening they had another experience: they could hear the whimpers of their mother when she suckled them and mothered them.

But their seeing eyes were of little use to them in the den, and there Alba remained a warm, known presence, a recognizable movement without recognizable form. Towards the end of their third week they began to venture farther along the walkway, but not as far as the source of light, because Dileas was there to turn them about with gentling nose and barrier paw. Saighdear and Sgian were curious, but Dileas held them off with a low growl of warning when they tried to look into the entrance. Their time was not yet.

At the age of three weeks, in the half-light of daybreak, the puppies followed Alba along the walkway and huddled together at the entrance, blinking their eyes and peering furtively into their strange new world – five round-headed, podgy, dusky, smoke-eyed balls of fur, droll innocents, not afraid because they knew nothing about fear or what to be afraid of. When Alba stood over them they swarmed about her feet, yelping and whimpering, wagging their tails and falling over each other: for the first time they were seeing, as a wolf, their known comforter, nurse and source of warmth. Dileas came to them to sniff and touch them with her muzzle, while Alba stood by with her eyes half-closed and her tongue quivering over her teeth, showing no hostility. The family did not stay out long on that first morning, and were already crowding backwards into the walkway before Alba entered and led them back to the den.

It was the next day at first light before Saighdear and Sgian, returning from a hunt, saw them at the entrance to the walkway, with Alba crouched nearby, muzzle on forepaws, watching them. Dileas left the rock lookout where she had been lying and ran to greet them, wagging her tail in great excitement. Alba rose and joined them and the pack began to howl their chorus, with her gruff, throaty half-barks in descant, and Saighdear's wild coronach rising to gasping crescendo. The howling session over, the bitches padded back to the puppies, who had shown no reaction to the chorus, and the dog pair followed. They sniffed over the puppies, who neither cowered nor responded, nor realized there were four adult wolves standing over them. But that was the first subtle imprinting of the pack on puppies not yet aware of its existence and only now learning to recognize their mother on sight.

There were three dogs and two bitches in the litter, the dogs already bigger and heavier than their siblings. One of the bitch puppies had a malformed hip, and walked carrying the paw clear of the ground. The others were normal and strong. On the third and fourth days after their first appearance in the open they were rolling and grappling and play-biting with their milk teeth, six feet from the walkway entrance, still with no sense of danger and not knowing what to look out for. Each day they became more venturesome, playing as far as twenty feet from the den, lolloping fat-bellied and awkward instead of toad-walking, and falling over every little obstacle in their paths. By the end of the week they were ragrowstering among the rocks, noisy and rumbustious, and their play became rougher, with the biggest dog pup leaping on the necks of the others, making them yelp in protest, and asserting the beginnings of mastery over them.

44

The crippled pup, unable to compete in the brulzie, suffered much. She withdrew more and more from the play, breaking off as soon as she was rolled over or lifted off her feet. She found refuge on a moss-capped boulder near the middle of the clearing and watched the others from there, joining them again only when it was time to go below ground to sleep. She was four and a half weeks old, and rising ten pounds in weight, when the An Sgarsoch eagle struck.

He knew the pups were there because he was overflying the clearing many times each day, and had seen them from their second time out. To the eagle they were fox cubs, bigger than he was used to seeing at that time of year, and not red, but fox cubs just the same. And he was a habitual fox killer. His problem was that the clearing, with its big boulders and rock jumbles, was not a good place for a strike. The crippled pup invited attack when she set herself up on the moss-capped boulder, for there she was a clear target. That morning, when the eagle drifted over, she was sitting on the moss cushion, on her good hip; when he swung back for another view she was standing, three-legged, watching her litter mates at play, and it was then he came down.

He swooped low over the pines on a downhill strike, a feathered missile, streamlined, a flying wedge of immense power, with talons like the fingers of a man. The pup had no idea he was there, or that she was in danger. He hit her like a thunderbolt, and the thud of the impact brought Alba and Saighdear to their feet on the lookout rock where they had been lying. They leaped down and ran to the boulder as Dileas came rushing from below. But they were too late to help the pup, and there was nothing they could do about the eagle. He swooped from the boulder in a clear downhill take-off, with the pup crying in his talons and the wolves running below in a frenzy, looking up. For a moment it seemed that he might not have enough lifting power to clear the tops of the trees, but he made the height in time, and sailed away with his feet down and the body of the now dead cripple dangling from his talons.

The three wolves bounded down into the timber and clear to the open but the eagle was now well away, losing height and out of sight, and soon he was on the ground dismembering the body of the pup so that he could carry it to the eyrie, fore end and haunch, in two flights. Alba weaved about whimpering;

Saighdear and Dileas stood staring towards the twin headwaters of the stream, but it is unlikely that they associated them in any way with the eyrie or the eagle. Alba turned back to the edge of the timber, where she raised her muzzle to the sky and howled like a dog whose puppies have been taken away. The others loped up to join her – no ritual chorus this time, but a coronach rather, and who is to say it was not?

When they returned to the clearing the four pups were in the walkway, and Sgian standing tall and alert on the lookout rock. He had been away on a maverick sortie, hunting hares, when the eagle struck. Alba rushed into the walkway, sniffed the pups, and stood for them while they suckled her. They did not follow her out, but remained in the walkway while she slept a waking sleep near the entrance, with ears alert and nostrils twitching. Perhaps she had already forgotten the crippled one. Perhaps she knew that the pup would never have been able to run with the pack or hunt for herself. What she surely knew was that the eagle would be back, and the next time the pups came out she led them into the timber above the clearing, where they could romp and play out of his reach. The eagle did come back, drifting over on motionless wings, but there was nothing for him in the clearing and he stopped looking.

The pups accepted the change, and maybe because of more than pack discipline, for they had seen the assault of the eagle and heard the cries of their litter mate. They very quickly learned their way over a half acre of the forest, treading out trackways which they could use instead of always blundering through the ground cover of blaeberry, heather and juniper. They also trampled out small clearings where they could grapple and roll in a turmoil of legs and waving tails, nipping, gurrying and flashing their baby teeth.

From the day of the eagle's attack they never played again in the clearing by day.

4

About the time of the eagle's attack Alba's milk was dwindling and she was beginning the process of weaning her pups, suckling them for ever shorter spells with longer intervals between, shaking them off when she walked away, and lying down when they followed her trying to reach her nipples. Her milk could no longer satisfy their hunger, and she responded to their pleadings by bocking up for them a gruel of partly digested meat, which they licked from the ground. Soon they were devouring her vomits greedily, and more and more, as the days passed and their appetites grew, the vomits replaced the milk. Sometimes she vomited several heaps, so that the pups could feed singly over many instead of bickering and fighting over one. And the gruel thickened with the passing days until it became raw meat at blood heat.

By the time the eaglets hatched on An Sgarsoch, the pups were feeding entirely on regurgitated meat, and begging from all members of the pack, who bocked for them almost on demand. Dileas became like a second mother to them, her interest in them growing as Alba's waned, and she licked and fussed them affectionately, as though they were her own. Saighdear bocked up as soon as they mobbed him, sniffing at his mouth, nuzzling his face, licking his teeth, and yelping with sterns wagging. He accepted their rough play and mock assaults without display of annoyance; indeed he seemed to like being hustled and having them among his feet. Even Sgian, the often maverick of uncertain temper, bocked for them when they pleaded, although they had sometimes to run after him, round and round the clearing, before he would lower his head and spill the bock from his mouth. Thus the pups were being bonded with the pack. At the same time they were establishing, among themselves, an order of hierarchy.

The dog pup Luath, the swift one, was the biggest of the family – strong and well muscled, fast on his feet, fast on the turn, and fast to pounce, and not slow to bite or mount the others to show his dominance. He was a dark wolfling, pale only on the throat and lower legs. The other dog pups, Laidir and Boidheach, were lighter in colour and body, and about matched for weight and growth. The bitch pup Geal was the palest of all, showing a lot of silver through the grizzle of her back and flanks; she was also the smallest of the four. She was the lowest in the hierarchy, in which Laidir and Boidheach had to settle for second place.

Alba was hunting again with the pack, sometimes leaving Dileas at home, and on some nights remaining by the den herself to let her run with the dog pair. Sgian regularly trotted off on his own, but was not hunting for himself alone; when he returned he always had some meat to bock up for the pups. On such nights Saighdear ran with one bitch, or two.

One midnight, when all four were running, they killed a staggie, a young male red deer, with a broken foreleg; he had broken it when his group was being harassed by the An Sgarsoch eagle. It was an old injury, and he had managed to live with it, putting on flesh and casting his antlers with the most forward stags in the group. But the wolves knew, the moment they put the herd on foot, that the staggie, despite his power of running, was the weakling among them and would soon fall behind. So they launched to the pursuit at a gallop, with tails level and fur billowing. They cut him out, turned him uphill, and pulled him down within a quarter of a mile, beside a small pool where frogs had spawned about the time Alba's pups were born. He fell with his face in the shallows, stirring up torpid tadpoles and gulping water as he groaned. The pool was less than half a mile from the den in the forest.

The wolves killed him quickly, and after they had filled themselves with warm meat they sat down and howled in chorus, which made the eagle stir over protesting eaglets and set the ravens talking four miles down the glen. A dog fox, picking his way cat-footed round the headwaters below the eyrie, carrying a hare for his mate and cubs, stopped to listen to the pack-song, which he now recognized and feared. The pups in the clearing heard it too, and answered with a chorus of their own. They had howled before, about the time they were weaning; but this was real wolf-song, making up with variety what it lacked in volume. The pups knew each other by sight and scent; perhaps they were now learning to recognize each other by voice.

Before dawn the pack returned to the clearing. Alba bocked for the pups and, when they had eaten, called them to follow her. She led them down through the forest on their first foray, and to their first sight of a kill. They crawled over it excitedly, with tails wagging furiously, licking, biting and tasting, and growling low in their throats. Alba sheared off meat for herself, and tossed aside vole-size morsels, and bigger, for the pups. They chewed the morsels and bolted them, gasping and choking on bigger than vole-size chunks, and were barrel-bellied before she turned about to lead them back to the den. Laidir carried away with him a shred of deer hide, chewing on it as he followed last in the line.

Day was breaking when they reached the clearing. The An Sgarsoch eagle was already scouting on the wing, with a raven underflying him from behind, like a moss cheeper following a cuckoo. Cinnamon and purple fish-scale clouds were banked on the horizon, with the sun's rim rising rayed like a dandelion. Curlews and oyster catchers were calling down by the Tarf. A crested tit flew from a rock as the wolves entered the clearing. The pups ran straight to the walkway and lay down to sleep, not in a bourach now but separately: their huddling days were over. Laidir curled up with his shred of deerskin muzzled against his flank. Saighdear and the bitch wolves mounted the lookout rock and settled there; Sgian moved into the timber above to sleep alone.

The raven flew down and pitched on the moss-capped boulder from which the eagle had snatched Alba's pup. He bowed to the wolves on the lookout rock, raised the feathers of his crest, bristled his beard, and said: *Kronk!* The wolves watched him for a moment, then lost interest in him and closed their eyes again. He was not there to chivvy them; he was looking for leavings. Foxes he knew, and at dens with cubs there was often something to scavenge. And maybe, like the eagle, he was thinking this was a fox den. But he could see at a glance that there was nothing for him in the clearing, so he leaped from the boulder, banked steeply, and swooped in mock threat at Saighdear before lifting over the pines and away.

That night the pack returned to the kill, with Alba leading her bouncing, boisterous puppies on their second foray. The adult wolves let them push through to the carcass, with only Sgian grumbling low in his throat, but not threatening. The pups could make little impression on the solid meat with their baby teeth and had to chew on raggles of flesh. The pack fed until the staggie's carcass was almost stripped clean, and when they stood back the pups mobbed them, begging for bocks, pawing and nuzzling their muzzles, and yelping. The four wolves put their heads down and disgorged part of their heavy meal, and the four pups gobbled with tails wagging in pleasure. The next night the adults visited the carcass to pick over the bones, then went out to hunt in pack, leaving the pups to themselves in the clearing.

Sooner or later the wolf pups had to meet the badger cubs, for three were born where Alba had first prospected for a den and met the sow face to face. Being a badger, and a mountain one at that, she had stayed on, not to be driven out even by a wolf. Until now she had seen nothing of the pack, although she had heard them without knowing what they were, and their paths had not crossed. But her cubs had to surface some time, and this was the night; they were two days older than the wolf pups. It was Luath who found them when he was prowling round the east end of the clearing, and his yelp of excitement brought Boidheach and Geal scampering to join him. Laidir remained at the walkway, fully occupied chewing and tearing at his deerskin.

The badger cubs were as naif and innocent as the wolf pups had been on their first day at the walkway entrance, and the three crouched with striped arrowheads pointing at three wolves looking at them with ears cocked and tongues a-loll. Neither trio knew what to make of the other. Boidheach, becoming impatient with curiosity, bellied down and yapped, and the badger cubs closed flanks and darted their arrows at him. When Luath skulked to one side, with his head down, they shuffled round to face him. Geal flattened, scraped with a forepaw, and began to inch closer; the cubs darted arrows at her.

50

The wolf pups were curious but not afraid. The black and white faces intrigued them, but were somehow off-putting. The badger cubs were not intrigued by the wolves, and were more scared than curious about them. Luath and Boidheach yapped, and the cubs crouched lower. Then all three began to howl and the badger cubs backed into their den. Laidir dropped his deerskin and gave tongue from the walkway.

After the howling session the three pups stalked to the rock hole into which the badger cubs had retreated. It led far into the rocks and branched into tortuous alleyways. A wolf could have bellycrawled for several yards from the entrance before being blocked by the narrows; but the pups did not enter. They were marking at the hole, sniffing and scratching half-heartedly, when the sow badger arrived to suckle her cubs and bock for them; they were still not weaned and she came to them at least once in the night. When she saw the wolf pups on her doorstep she rushed at them, snapping at their pads, and they scattered, yowling in protest and fear, crashing through heather and lichened birch scrub until they were at the lookout rock. They mounted it and stood tall to look back, with their ears up and their nostrils sifting. The sow badger lumbered to the den and met her cubs near the entrance, where she suckled them and disgorged for them. The cubs remained in hiding after she had gone, and the wolf pups did not return to the perilous doorstep of the den.

So a mutual tolerance was born in the clearing, with badger cubs and wolf pups out at the same time but not mixing. The adults hardly knew each other, if at all, because the boar and sow badgers were usually quietly away on their regular runways before the wolf pack gathered to hunt. But one morning, close to dawn, Sgian met the boar. The badger was homing along his own trail at an inswinging trot, and Sgian was following it up to his day-bed in the timber. The wolf held to his line, but the boar did not step aside; he kept coming on and crouched only when he saw his way blocked. Sgian took another step forward; the badger snapped at his pads, not following through, and crouched again, Sgian growled, showing his powerful teeth, but the badger was not impressed. He moved forward, spring-footed, and Sgian stepped aside to let him pass. Wilful he was, but he had more wisdom than to quarrel with a mountain badger for no reason. He might have killed the badger, but the badger could have crippled him.

Ring-ouzels, the mountain blackbirds with breast crescents of white, were back on the hill; wheatears were feeding young; crested tits and crossbills were nesting in the pines. Red deer and roe were fat with young; the hares, living high, had leverets running, and next litters ready to be born. Eagle, fox and wildcat were hunting hares. The wolf pups became more and more active. They leaped and chased; they reared and grappled; they tore heather and blaeberries, ripped bark and lichens from scrub birches, wrecked seedling pines, and chewed on branches blown down by gales. Laidir joined in, forgetting his deerskin, which by now he had ripped to tatters.

Later in the day they went mouse hunting, stalking smell or movement then rearing and pouncing like foxes, and at first they missed more than they caught. They wandered farther and farther from the clearing, always downhill, and met their first roe deer, fox and capercaillie. They also met a big wildcat, who hissed at them and climbed into a tree to wail his war-song with ears flat and teeth bared to the gums.

Although they played with obvious delight, and were engrossed when stalking and pouncing, they fretted and whimpered if they were left too long on their own, and greeted the adults effusively when they returned. They did not fret when the adults were lying up near the den, even when they were out of sight, because they could always run to one or other of them to fuss and be fussed over.

But there was a growing restlessness in them, shared by Alba, and one evening, when the sunset was like a forest fire in cloud-smoke, trailed by a gilded moon in a starless sky, she led them from the clearing, down through the timber into the open, and across the stream, below the fork, to the other side of the glen. And there she found a place for them, below a low cliff – a half acre hollow of rocks and seedling pines and birches, fronted with heather, tormentil and bedstraw, with a threshy flat on one side and a screen of alders on the other: a bosky place of wheatears and whinchats, with kestrels nesting on the cliff and a pair of pine martens in the uphill pines. Here the pack would

52

keep tryst with them as before, and feed them.

The lip of the hollow gave them a wide view of all the low ground, down to the stream and across. But from the hollow they had no view at all, and that was where they were lying two mornings later, warming in the sun, when they met the human animal for the first time in their lives. The adult wolves were up in the timber, sleeping. Alba was bedded where she could see the hollow, but not the ground below.

The humans were Alan Roy Stewart and Angus Robertson Murray, youths from the houses of thatch across and down the Tilt. They were plaided in tartan, bare-legged, shod in worn brogans, and had dirks at their belts. They were strong youths, with the first flush of beards on them, and they had been to the shieling above the Tarf, ten miles from home and three from the old wolf den in the clearing. Now they were keeping to the north side of the river on a wide circuit back to the Tilt. Their circuit included a visit to the An Sgarsoch eyrie. When they crossed the forked headwaters of the stream they walked along a deer path below the forest, talking quietly in the Gaelic which southrons called the Irish Tongue, seeing without conscious looking, and they were at the lip of the hollow before the wolf pups knew they were there. The pups bolted, but the youths saw them, and bellied down, with their faces screened by heather, to wait in the hope of another view.

'A den of foxes,' whispered Alan, who had an interest in such things.

'They do not look like foxes to me,' said Angus. 'They're big, and not very red of the plaid. They're dogs of a kind surely?'

'Dogs? Out here? And nobody yet at the shielings? I have never seen hound pups like these. They're too short in the legs for one thing. Unless they're of the Irish breed maybe ...'

'Maybe they're Sasunnach pups,' Angus laughed in a whisper. 'Lost by the redcoats maybe from one of the Posts and running wild.'

'If it's dogs they are,' Alan said, 'there will be a bitch with them somewhere. Some bitches run off to have their pups, just like a pig sometimes, or old Fiona Robertson's goats.'

Angus whisper-laughed again, for they had both tramped many miles, and expended a lot of energy, chasing after old

53

Fiona's runaway goats. 'If we could see the bitch we might recognize her,' he said. 'But maybe she'll be away hunting Fiona's goats for the pups.'

'Let us look in this place then,' Alan said, and rose.

They walked slowly among the rocks, taking care not to trample the pine seedlings, and probing with their sticks. The hollow was already cris-crossed with trails where the pups had played and chased. The youths worked through systematically, casting the width before moving forward, still probing and turning heather aside with their sticks. Laidir, Luath and Boidheach had found hiding places under rocks, where they could not be seen, but Geal was above ground, head in below an overhang, her rump screened by heather, and the youths found her. When they stopped over her she turned her head and looked at them sideways, showing the whites of her eyes.

Alan touched her gently with the tip of his stick, but she did not move; her only reaction was to show still more white in her eyes. When he bent over her, and touched her rump with a hand, she trembled, still unmoving, with no show of teeth or growl of threat.

'It's a wild thing, and afraid,' said Alan, without realizing the significant truth of his remark. 'And no fox to be sure. It's a dog all right, but the like of it I've never before seen.'

'Nor I,' Angus agreed.

'Maybe we should take it home to see can we find out who is missing a bitch dog. Anyway, it would be best if all the pups were brought in before they grow any bigger, as they will surely.'

'You have taken the words from my mouth,' said Angus. 'I wonder if it would bite if you tried to gather it?'

'If you held it down with your stick I could try to get a hand round its mouth.'

'Yes, and bind it with a bit of rag.'

'If we had a bit of rag,' Alan laughed.

'I have the very bit flapping on my plaid.'

Alan knelt beside Geal, and stroked her rump with the lie of the fur, then began to move his hand lightly up towards her neck. Still Geal made no move to rise or threaten; instead she crouched more tightly into her wedge under the overhang. 'It's a quiet one and sorely frightened,' Alan said, and moved his hand to her skull between the ears. 'Now I'll try to get a grip on its muzzle. It's not very old and if it bites the bite won't be much.'

He spanned her muzzle and she made no move to resist or bite. Angus tore the strip of tartan from his plaid and handed it to him. It spanned Geal's muzzle but was too short to be tied.

'You should have torn off a longer bit,' Alan said. 'This is no good at all. I'll keep my hand on its mouth and try to lift it. Then you can help me wrap it in my plaid, and we'll—'

At that moment Alba called: *Ow-ow-ow-ow-owoo-owoo-owoo-owoo!* and on the lip of the hollow Saighdear appeared, whimpering.

'That'll be the bitch now I'm thinking,' Alan said. 'So let us be away from here before she finds out we have her pup. And by the arse of King George it's heavy! We'll have to take turns carrying it. It must weigh more than twenty pounds.'

They hurried from the hollow down to the stream, intending to take a direct line to the Tarf. When they looked back they were not greatly surprised to see Alba two hundred yards behind; but they were taken aback when Saighdear appeared and the pair began to howl. So there was a dog with the bitch after all. They made slow time along the bank of the stream, even when they took turns at carrying twenty-four pounds of wolf pup. Every now and again they stopped to look back, and there was Alba still following, with Saighdear a little way back, both of them whimpering and sometimes howling.

'This is a strange matter,' said Alan. 'If we had a rope we could tie the pup by the neck and make it run with us on its own legs.'

'We have no rope,' replied Angus. 'We didn't come out pup hunting remember.'

After they had gone a mile downstream they noticed that Alba had closed the distance to a hundred and fifty yards, and they became uncertain about what to do next. She was so big, the one behind her bigger still, and they began to wonder if she might attack them to recover her pup.

'I think we should leave it here and let her get it back,' said Angus. 'We couldn't handle two dogs that size if they took it into their heads to go for us.'

'You're right,' Alan agreed. 'Anyway the thing is too heavy to carry for eleven miles, and two rivers to cross.'

He unwrapped Geal from his plaid and put her down, then the two hurried on downstream. When they looked back after two hundred yards Alba had Geal on foot, following her back uphill, and when they arrived back in the hollow there was great excitement in the pack, with much whimpering and displays of affection between adults and pups.

Three hours later the youths were in the house of thatch where Alan lived, speaking to his father, a tall, rugged Highlander who had been out with Mar in the '15 and taken a ball in the shoulder at Sheriffmuir. He listened with grave politeness to what they had to say, and the smile on his grey-bearded face was tolerant.

'If the pup was as heavy as you have been saying,' he told them, 'it must be a hound pup of some sort. We can ask around to discover if anyone is missing a deerhound.'

'But they were not deerhounds, father,' Alan insisted. 'Of that I am sure.'

'I haven't seen their like hereabouts either,' Angus supported. 'Perhaps they're of an English breed, lost by the military.'

'Or Irish maybe,' said the senior Stewart, fingering his beard. 'The Irish hounds are very like our own.' Then, with a mirthful gleam in his eyes, he asked: 'You heard them bark and howl you say? What was it like?'

The youths did their best to mimic Alba's yowls and the howling of Saighdear. Alan's father laughed and said in mock-serious voice:

'They can't be English hounds then. The dogs down there now bark and howl in German. I've no idea what kind of dogs you have been seeing, but they must belong to somebody, no matter how long they have been running loose. We can ask in Blair tomorrow after church. We can also ask of the military, although they have no Gaelic and I have little of the English as you know.'

But they learned nothing at Blair, not from the minister or the blacksmith or anybody. No dogs were missing from the castle, where lived the Hanoverian duke. In the end they sought out the bodach, a man of eighty-six years, and wearing them like the oak its winter leaves, who had been at Killiecrankie with

56

Claverhouse, first Viscount Dundee, the debonair soldier remembered by the clans as *Ian Dhubh nan Cath*: Black John of the Battles. The bodach was white-haired, with not a patch of the balding, and his mind was still as bright as a glisk of sunlight on a salmon pool. He listened to them with much civility, rubbed his white-bearded chin and said:

'When you are hearing what I am going to tell you, you will be thinking I am out of my sense and talking foolishness. Only two years ago a man from Moy was telling me that a black beast was killed there that very year which was said to be a wolf, and—'

'A wolf!' his listeners exclaimed in chorus.

'Yes, a wolf, so they said. And seemingly it had killed two children before it was killed by one Macqueen, who was a tackman of the Mackintosh; and I can remember – I can remember because I was a young man of . . . oh . . . twenty at the time – Cameron of Lochiel killing a wolf not far from here, at Killiecrankie.'

'So you are saying that what the boys saw were wolves?' said Alan's father. 'I cannot believe it. There have been no wolves here in a lifetime . . .'

'They've been here in mine,' the bodach reminded him, 'and don't forget the Mackintosh one only two years ago.'

'Yes – but if the boys were carrying a wolf pup why did the wolves not attack them? It is well known what dangerous beasts they are.'

'How can you well know something that does not exist?' the old man replied. 'I said you would think I was out of my sense, but I have said it. I don't know whether a wolf is dangerous or not. Lochiel did not seem to have much trouble with his. But you can leave what I have said, or take it, as you wish, though I would have these pups looked for anyway, whatever they are.'

'I agree with you there,' said Alan's father. 'It will be better to be sure.'

It was unlikely that Saighdear and his band would have escaped discovery for much longer, because the kyloes, the hardy black cattle, were being pushed to the hill, and men would be appearing at the shielings. The bodach made discovery a certainty, and brought it sooner.

57

5

Nobody cried wolf. Alan Roy Stewart, the father of Alan, and Ewen, the father of Angus, decided that night to go to the hill with their sons in the morning to find the pups and make sure what they were, instead of risking being thought out of their sense by asking the help of others to hunt wolves which nobody believed still existed in Badenoch. So they did not ask for hounds, and would be going without dogs, because they had none of their own.

The mother of Alan said to his father: 'My God, Alan Roy, you are not about to be taking the boy with you on this ploy?'

'And why not?' he asked. 'We will need him and Angus to show us where they found the beasts.'

'Since when did you need to be shown a place you could find by the telling about it?'

'That's wild country out there, and the place might be hard to find.'

'But it could be dangerous,' she insisted. 'Did not the bodach say the pups might be wolves?'

'The bodach is a wise man, but he could be wrong about this. If I had believed him I would be asking others to come with us, and for dogs from the castle.'

'He is seldom wrong,' she said, knowing young Alan would be agreeing with his father, 'and never opens the mouth until the thoughts are clear in his head.'

'Alan will go with us: there will be no danger I am sure. Now look you at this that I am taking with me.' He produced a left-handed steel gauntlet, the *lamhainn chruaidh* once commonly used by the Highlanders and Irish. 'This I was given by the

58

bodach himself, to use if need be. He is a great collector of things of the kind.'

'Father,' young Alan spoke for the first time, 'I have been thinking. Might you not take the gun with you? It would a better thing than a stick or spear, or that fancy glove you are holding.'

Alan Roy Stewart looked sternly at his son. 'I have told you before that you must never mention gun in the house or anywhere else. Is it in prison you would see your father, with your talking about guns at a time like this, and the rumours flying about like wild geese?'

There was indeed a gun – a Brown Bess hidden away, with ball and powder and sword, in a secret place, where it had been since the time of the Disarming Act, after the failure of the Rising of '15. And these were not things a man spoke about openly.

'I am sorry, father,' the boy said. 'I must be out of my sense.'

'That is all right, my boy. Now go you to bed to sleep, for we must be up and away early before that rooster of yours crows reveille.'

It was a sullen morning of low clouds, and the sky not to be seen. The grass was soaked with dew, and the four had wet feet before they crossed the Tilt, leaping from stone to stone and splashing through shallows. Mist webbed their faces with gossamer wet. A lark was already singing above the river mist, and ducks were quarking and splashing on dark pools upstream. The men strode out for the hill, with the boys following. All had long sticks of hazel, and were carrying rawhide to make spears of them with their dirks if need be. The rawhide would also make leashes for any pups they might catch. On the first ridge above the Tilt, Alan the father of Alan halted and spoke:

'In an hour or about the sun will be up. It is a tidy step to the place and it will take about three hours to get to it. But we'll have a lot of daylight after that to do what we have to do.'

When the sun rose clear from its kindling the morning became warm, with the sky blue and the flies out, and the An Sgarsoch eagle flying. A group of stags, in early velvet, bounded uphill when surprised by the men, then stopped, bunched on a knoll, looking back to view them passing below. They were about a half hour's slow-walk from the hollow when they stopped suddenly to listen, and what they were hearing was the howling of wolves. Alba, for some reason, had not moved her pups.

'That's the howling, father!' Alan exclaimed excitedly. 'How clear it is too, and we nearly two miles away.'

'I do not know what the howl of a wolf is like,' said Ewen the father of Angus, 'but I have not heard hounds singing a song like that. What think you, Alan?'

'I am puzzled, Ewen. But I am beginning to have the feeling that perhaps the bodach was not talking foolishness after all. Now we have to stop and think about what we are going to do. We will be in full view if we keep on up the glen at this level. The wind is for us but there is nothing to hide us, so I think we should move up into the first trees then go on under their cover.'

'Let us to the trees then,' Ewen agreed, 'but before we go on I think we should make ourselves the spears. If the beasts are wolves we could be in great danger.' When the four were seated in the cover of the trees, he added: 'Indeed, would it not be wiser, now that we know what is up there, to go back and have himself at the castle call a gathering to hunt them with hounds?'

Alan fingered his beard reflectively. 'We still do not know whether they are wolves or not. We do know that the boys were not threatened, even when they had a pup stolen. Let us make the spears by all means, but I think we should go on for a closer look. The beasts might yet be dogs, and I hope they are, and the bodach could be wrong and I hope he is.'

With their improvised spears they set off in file through the lower forest, with Alan the father of Alan leading and Ewen the father of Angus at the tail. Light of tread, they walked with the stealth of wolves, their eyes alert for movement ahead or on their flanks, and Ewen looking over his shoulder from time to time to watch their rear. The forest was quiet except for the trickle of birdsong and the whisper of the trees. Neither men nor boys spoke a whisper on the walk, and all stopped as one, frozen in posture of movement, when a goshawk – mightiest of the hawk kind, yellow-eyed and fierce – leaped from the torn body of a hare and swung out, mounted, and flashed back over their heads, screaming angry abuse: *Gek-gek-gek-gek-gek-gek!'* In a pine tree, not far uphill, his mate was sitting on eggs in a nest of sticks and twigs, decorated round the rim with fresh green sprays of rowan, and she was more interested in the chicks now tapping on the shells than in the vociferations of her mate. The goshawk, a smaller bird than his mate, but still a hunter of immense power and disconcerting speed, followed the men for a hundred paces before turning back to tear away the haunch of the hare and carry it to the nest.

Alan the father of Alan stopped and whispered to the others: 'When whatever they are up yonder hear that they will surely know we are coming.'

But Alan Roy Stewart was wrong. The wolves did not hear the goshawk's screams because the wind was carrying them away: nor had they warning of the approaching men, nor sight of them among the trees. So the hunters were almost at the hollow before the pups bolted for cover and the adults up in the timber rose to their feet. The wind was still telling them nothing, but they could now see the plaided figures on the lip of the hollow. Alba skulked away with head and tail down, up and around until she had the man-scent on the wind. Saighdear padded after her, and when they were joined by Sgian and Dileas the four sat down, with tongues out, waiting. They still could not see the men, who were now in the hollow, but they knew from the wind that they were there, and Alba began to whimper.

The plaided four quartered the hollow, walking in line abreast, with their makeshift spears held firmly, forward pointing and down; but there was no pup in sight. All they could see were the pathways they had trodden, and they recognized them at once for what they were, because they had seen the like often enough where fox cubs had played after being moved from the den to outplaces on the hill.

'There is sign enough of feet running about here to be sure,' said Ewen the father of Angus, 'but not a pup to be seen anywhere. I am thinking that the wolves saw us coming and have taken them away.'

'You are still having them wolves, Ewen,' said the father of Alan, 'but there is no way we can yet be sure. You are right about one thing though. We should have brought along dogs of some sort, for we are lost without the noses of them.'

'The pups could still be here, father,' said Alan. 'When Angus and I came on them they all ran into holes, except the one I caught hiding under a rock. That is how I was able to catch it. We should search a bit more, and look in all the likely hiding places a pup might squeeze into.'

They quartered the hollow again, like setter dogs in slow motion, in the end going down on their bare knees to peer into the likely places, and became so engrossed that they forgot about the danger of wolves and laid down their spears to free their hands as forepaws. Of the adult wolves they saw nothing, which is a common experience of people who live in wolf country for a lifetime without ever seeing a live one on foot. For the wolf is one of the shyest and most withdrawing of wild animals, shunning man and his works, a beast of menace and mystery, an unseen chorister in a chorus of invisibles, until seventy or eighty pounds of him are lying dead at someone's feet.

Suddenly, Alan the younger called out in an excited voice: 'Come here, father! Quickly! There is something here in a hole in the rock.'

The men came running and knelt beside the boy. The hole, overhung by heather, with trampled ferns at the entrance, led into a tunnel not unlike the walkway to the den where Alba had given birth to her pups. Half in and half out of it was a deer trotter, which had been brought to the hollow by Saighdear and was the plaything of the dog pup Boidheach, the beautiful one. The men could see nothing, but Alan was certain he had seen a shadowy movement and heard breathing. And he was right. The tunnel was a dead-end, nine feet long, and Boidheach was at the end of it, flattened and terrified, facing away from the light. Alan threw the deer trotter aside, wriggled in to the waist, then wriggled out again.

'I can see nothing now, father, because when I go in I shut out the light. But there is a pup in there I am sure. Let me go in and catch it. I will not go in too far and get stuck. The three of you can watch out for the parents.'

'Indeed you will do nothing of the kind, boy!' his father said. 'There could be a big wolf in there. It is too dangerous. I will have a look for myself.'

'It will have to be me, father,' Alan insisted. 'The hole is too small for a big man like you to squeeze into. I will be careful.'

'Even if it is a pup, it could make a mess of your face, boy.'

'The last one I handled was quiet, father, not even showing its teeth. I can edge a spear in with me and hold my dirk forward. Please?'

Two men and the son of one of them turned their backs to the hole, while the son of the other elbowed his way into a wolf den with a dirk in one hand and the neck of a spear in the other. His bare feet were hardly out of sight when Alba appeared on the lip of the hollow. She stared towards the men for a moment, then began to pad along it, with her tail slack and her head skewed. She turned at the end of the lip and padded back again. On her second turn she was joined by Saighdear, who lofted and then lowered his tail before following in her tracks at a spring-footed slow lope.

The men and the boy standing guard by the hole readied their spears and drew their dirks, not knowing what to expect but prepared to stand to any onset. Alan Roy Stewart was a strong man, and brave, but his heart beat faster at the sight of two big wolves prowling in front of him while his boy was in their den. All he knew about wolves was the folklore of his people, and that was enough to make the stoutest heart quail and the blood of a man run cold. He had to get his son out of the den.

'Keep watch,' he said to the others, 'while I try to get Alan out.'

But even as he bent down to call into the tunnel he heard the muffled voice of his son calling to him: 'I have a wolf by the tail, father!'

His father pushed his face through the heather screen and shouted back: 'You have what?'

'A wolf by the tail, father! But I cannot budge it because of the grip of its paws on the ground. Catch me by the feet and pull me out.'

Alan Roy Stewart swore under his breath. Now had he not only two wolves at his back, but his son out of sight in the ground with a wolf by the tail, and the tellers of stories had never told a story like that. He looked at the wolves as a raven swooped over their heads and soared away; then he laid down his spear and reached into the tunnel with his right hand. He gripped Alan by a foot and began to pull, moving him a little, but not enough to please him, so he shouted in to him : 'Leave go of the pup! There are big wolves out here. If they attack we will all be in trouble. So leave go!'

'One more pull, father,' Alan called in a voice muffled by his plaid, 'then its forepaws will be loose and I shall manage myself.'

Alan Roy Stewart realized that it would be better to keep pulling than to keep arguing, so he thrust his right shoulder into the entrance and gave another long, steady pull, and in a moment there was half of his son out, with the kilt of his plaid over his shoulders, and one hand of him still holding the wolf pup by the tail. With his shoulders clear, the boy took hold of the tail with both hands to drag the unstruggling Boidheach into the open. But before he had the pup's head out, and before he knew what was happening, Ewen Murray struck down with his spear. The dirk went through the pup's ribs to the heart, and the yowl and dying wail of him were heard by Alba and Saighdear, who padded faster along the lip of the hollow, to the far end and back, to the far end and back again, then a third time to the far end where they sat down and howled. They stopped howling when the raven came back, and swooped at them, and this time Saighdear leaped at him, snapping.

'Let us get the hell out of this, and quickly,' Ewen Murray said to Alan the elder. 'We'll leave the dead pup to keep the pair of them busy and let us get away. If there are more than two of them we could be in a lot of trouble.'

Alan the younger wanted to carry away the body of the pup, but was allowed just long enough to cut off the tail, which he stuffed inside his shirt. Then the four backed away, all with spears presented and Alan Roy Stewart with the *lamhainn chruaidh* on his left hand. They were on the edge of the hollow before the raven lifted away, and Alba stalked slowly, almost fearfully, towards her mutilated pup. There she sat down, pointed her muzzle to the sky, and howled. Saighdear, still on the lip of the hollow, howled too, and presently the men heard the voices of Sgian and Dileas joining the coronach.

Alba stopped howling when the men had disappeared into the trees, staring after them with a faraway look in her seemingly say-nothing eyes, yet maybe a wolf could have read in them something a man could not, unless perhaps a poet-man sensitive to nuances of sorrow. And maybe she was having no thoughts at all, being a wolf after all, and not a Christian man.

The men were well into the trees, hurrying at a pace that would have killed a lowlander, when the pack, now gathered round the body of Boidheach, sat down to howl in chorus, while the flies settled where spear and dirk had struck. When they were crossing the stream, scaring a dipper from a stone and a heron from a pool, Alan Roy Stewart found breath to say: 'If that is not a lament we are hearing I have never heard pibroch played.'

6

Alba could not, and did not, know that within days everybody would be crying wolf; her sanctuary had been discovered, and one of her pups killed by men, and that was enough for her. She had to get her remaining pups away from the killing place, to which men would surely return. But although there was a great fear in her, a frenzy almost, she waited until late in the day – when the forest was hushed as a cathedral, the sky barred with indigo clouds lined in gold, and the stream pools aglow with sunfire – before she decided it was time for her to go. The pups, excited and wagging their tails, mobbed her, nuzzling her muzzle, and followed her boisterously when she trotted from the hollow, with Dileas, Saighdear and Sgian in line behind. They left the body of Boidheach for the flies to buzz over on the morrow.

The pups were not yet fit for a marathon run, and Alba knew it. Without them the pack could have been thirty miles from the hollow by morning; with them the distance would be decided by the legs of the pups and not by the stamina of the adults. She led them down to the stream, and they followed it to the right tip of the fork, where they were viewed by the eagle on her nest and her mate perched on a pinnacle above. The indigo clouds had now lost their edge of gold; the fire was dead in the pools. The gloaming in the corrie was like mole's fur, although overhead the last of the light was slow to fade. Alba led her pups right out over the top of An Sgarsoch, then turned west, into a stirring wind, below the dark bulk of Sgarsoch Bheag. Five miles by their tracks from the hollow of the killing she let them throw down to rest, panting with their tongues over their teeth and dripping sweat.

But she had them on foot again before daybreak, for there was anxiety in her, and she wanted more miles behind her. Tired and leg-weary they were, and this time they padded after her without boister or fuss – round the many-forked headwaters of Allt a Chaorainn, a tributary of the Geldie, to the east face of Carn an Fhidhleir, the Fiddler's Cairn, behind which a fan of light was spreading from the risen sun. Above the brightness six ravens were flying. Alba found a wooded gully on the north-east face of the Fiddler, near the headwaters of another hill burn, and the pups found hiding places among the rocks and trees.

There the adult wolves bocked up the last of their meat for them. The pups devoured the warm vomits, then drank from a cold seep of water before lying down, exhausted after nine miles of running. Alba, being on ground she had never travelled over before, did not know whether she was leading her pups towards men or away from them, so she padded to the top of the Fiddler for a view. The farthest view was across the rugged, broken wild country to the north-east. Elsewhere she was ringed by mountains, peak after peak, girdled with mist in the sunrise.

Saighdear, Sgian and Dileas were already lying at the top of the gully when she returned. She picked a couch lower down, closer to her pups, and curled up to sleep, not tired by running but wearied by anxiety. The morning was warm and the pups slept soundly, breathing slowly and deeply, with flanks gently heaving, and ears twitching now and again to fend off venturesome flies. Butterflies, blue and brown, were fluttering where the trees thinned at the bottom of the gully, and voles were moving in the tussocks, with a bitch stoat hunting them to feed her kits in their nest of dried grass and vole-skins under a rock only two hundred yards away. Redpolls and siskins were flittering among the pines and birches. Below Alba's couch a buzzard was brooding small chicks in her nest in the crown of a big rowan growing horizontally from a rock fissure, with only her head showing through the leaf screen of twigs brought in by her mate. For minutes at a time she tilted her head to peer upwards, for she had seen the wolf arriving and knew she was still there. Deer in small groups were moving to windy ridges to escape the flies, and a few of the hinds had calves at foot. This

67

was still the range of the An Sgarsoch eagle and he came over twice in the morning, with the wolves not seeing him and he not knowing they were there.

Cloud tufts like bog cotton, followed by mushrooming drifts of white, came over in mid afternoon and their shadows were a running tide across the hills. From one shadowy wave a vixen appeared in the light, to hunt voles where the stoat had hunted earlier. Her fur was threadbare and her breasts shrunken; she had five weaned cubs in a cairn two miles away, and she was hunting for them. Like the wolves she could bock or carry, or both, and she knew, none better, how to hunt the fat, short-tailed voles, rearing, pouncing in parabola, and pinning them down with her forepaws, before chop-clicking and bolting them.

She had three inside her and was stalking a fourth when the eagle came over on his third foray of the day. And he saw her. Whether he meant to strike, or merely to chivvy her as he sometimes chivvied deer, only he knew; he was a killer of cubs and halflins, not adults. The vixen did not wait to find out. Rarely caught off guard, she was in her stride when he banked to come down, and in the first tree cover when he swooped. There he could do nothing about her, so he lifted over the tops, turned steeply, and glided across the glen.

The vixen watched him to the limit of her seeing, but did not leave the shelter of the trees; she waited on in case he came back. It was then her fine nose wrinkled on the taint of wolf, which to her meant dog, and that sent her light-footed out of the gully. But the eagle had brought Saighdear and Sgian to their feet, and they were running when she broke from the trees. After her ...

Wolves are not usually fox hunters; they tolerate or ignore the lesser dog. But sometimes a wolf will chase one and kill it. Saighdear and Sgian chased the vixen, perhaps because they were still keyed up by what had happened the day before, perhaps because they saw her as another threat to the pups. They ran her wide, one on each side, then closed in to head her. Saighdear turned her uphill, then lost interest and loped back into the trees. Sgian bounded on, cut in on her and caught her by the middle of her back. His powerful, rending teeth almost bit her in half. He tore out her entrails, exposing the voles she had eaten, and sheared her hind-quarters from her trunk. Then he

68

tossed the bloody bits and pieces of her aside, for the ravens to croak over on the morrow, scavenging what the wolf chose not to eat. When he returned to the gully he was greeted by the pups, nuzzling and begging, but he had nothing in his stomach to bock up for them and they padded back to their hiding places.

That night Dileas remained with the pups when the other three left to hunt. It was a clear night of pale moon and unseen stars, with a soft wind from the west, oyster-catchers fretting far down on Allt a Chaorainn, and a thin line of light creeping behind the dark mountains to meet the sun again at its rising: a night of moth wings, water music, hooting owls, and spectral hares grazing. Five miles away a kyloe bull bellowed, and his bellowing was heard by Dileas and the pups, and the pack out hunting.

The pups played with Dileas, scrambling over her belly when she lay down on her back for them in submissive posture, mounting her when she stood, and mouthing her throat and neck, gurrying and growling in mock savagery. She was patient with them, like a mother, licking their heads and sniffing at the roots of their tails, and pinning one or another of them down with a friendly paw. They were fit again and hungry, but not famished. After their play session Dileas took them from the gully, downhill, where they joined with her in hunting voles, pouncing on tussocks as the fox had done. They lost many and caught few, and the few went little way to satisfy three big wolf pups, any one of whom could have eaten sixty.

They were still vole-hunting when Saighdear led his band over the watershed and down to a fast-flowing tributary of the River Feshie. They reached it where it was flanked by oak, alder and willow, with pines on the uphill, and crossed where it was shallow and rippling, following their own distorted moon images. Before them was the dark steep of Cairn Meall Tionail, stark and treeless above the glen bottom, with wild screes on its north face and snow still lying in deep clefts above.

The wolves trotted down the west bank of the stream, and turned the north face below the scree, on to a ridge where red deer hinds were moving. The wind brought the deer-scent to their noses, and they became excited, fidgeting, wagging their tails and rubbing shoulder to shoulder. Then, quietly as cats, they began to stalk into the wind, crouching, with their bellies brushing dwarf juniper and deer grass, bearberry, crowberry and mountain azalea. When they were close enough to hear the small-talk of calves at play, they sat down to ponder.

One hind was grazing below them, with three calves playing around her; five were above her, straight ahead of the wolves, with a single calf following. The wolves knew they had to separate the hind playing watch-nurse to three calves from the five with one following, and stalked in closer. The hinds, most alert and wary of beasts, were slow to react when they first detected movement. Instead of breaking at once, they faced about with ears up and nostrils asking questions of a wind that was telling them nothing. Not until the wolves were on their feet, and leaping into their stride, did they turn and run, and by then it was too late. The pack, with Saighdear leading the others in line, bounded forward to cut out the nursemaid hind and calves. She was a strong beast and wise, and broke downhill with her own calf following, turning the rear of the pack and leaving two calves stotting and bleating in blind panic. She came round close to the scree and galloped after the five, now well away in headlong flight.

The two calves left behind tried to follow, but for them there was no escape. Saighdear caught one and Alba the other, and they died after a brief wail of terror, one with its head almost sheared off at the shoulders and the other with its spine torn out close to the haunch. Sgian, leaving the killing to his pack mates, chased after the fleeing hind and her calf, but she had made so much distance that he broke off after a quarter of a mile and returned.

Saighdear lofted his calf to one side and began to tear it up: Alba and Sgian shared the other, and she was not put off by his token growls of threat. When they had eaten the calves down to the spine, hindlegs and trotters, they left on the four-mile up and down trail to the gully. Sgian left them on the watershed and turned south to hunt alone, while the pair returned to the trysting place and bocked up their meat for the pups, responding at once to their mouthing and whimpering.

Saighdear did not linger for long after he had emptied his stomach, and Dileas followed him from the gully, leaving Alba with the pups. They were back on the watershed, running flanked by their elongated shadows, when they heard the wolf

70

howl three miles to the south-west and knew it was Sgian. They stopped to howl their reply, then changed course and loped downhill side by side, through dark hollows and over moonlit ridges, to answer the call, and twice, before they came up with him, they paused to squirt urine on dwarf junipers which he had already marked with his own.

He was in the shadow of a long rock outcrop, on a meadow flat of blaeberry and crowberry, sheep's fescue, hair grass and saxifrage, where he had surprised a hind at the calving and killed her as she tried to rise, with the calf's head showing and its nostrils sneezing gleet. Saighdear ran to him with his tail up – the clan chief sure of his station. Sgian greeted him with head down and tail slack, and nuzzled his mouth like a pup seeking meat – the clansman showing respect to the chief.

The three began to tear up the warm prey, and soon had it stripped of half its meat, including the calf that had drawn only a few breaths of life. When they left they had blood on their masks and ribs rounded with gorging. Each carried meat to be cached, led by Saighdear who was hefting a half-stripped shoulder with the trotter dangling. At the trysting place they cached what they were carrying and bocked up part of their meal for the pups. Saighdear cached the shoulder of hind below the rowan where the buzzard was nesting and she, not alarmed, craned over to watch him. Alba bolted down the meat brought to her by Dileas and Sgian.

Seven wolves, replete with venison, slept in the gully until the misty daybreak, when the four adults left again to the flyting of greyback crows. They returned to the kill, and after driving away five ravens – two parents with three flying young – they crouched beside it to clean it of meat and crunch some of the bones. When they had finished there was little left for the black birds of Odin to croak over, although they flew down to probe and croak after the pack had gone.

And still the pack remained undiscovered and unsought, for the human animals in their far off dens were slow to believe in its existence, and the bodach held his quiet in the face of their unbelief. Not even the tail of Boidheach, handed about by Alan Roy Stewart, would convince the most doubting, who were most of them, because there were those who had seen its like on dogs from the north country of the Vikings. So the days passed

71

peacefully, with the cry of 'Wolf!' not yet like the war pipes sounding, and the pack hunted in the quiet nights and lay up in the gully by day, while the buzzard carried prey to his mate and downy chicks, siskins like green-laced canaries chased each other in carefree flight, ring-ouzels fed fledglings gaping on lichened rocks, and a dog fox coursed hares for big hungry cubs made motherless by the whims of a wolf.

For whatever reason of her own, Alba moved the pups to a new trysting place in the high scree of Meall Tionail, a rock fortress where a thousand soldiers might have hidden with not a red coat showing. The pack killed hares, two goats, and a sickly stag, and by day and night they howled in chorus, unheard by human ears because the nearest ears were out of hearing. Then Sgian, hunting alone at the midnight of the year's shortest darkness, found a herd of kyloes, the black cattle of the Highlandmen, and after refusing the head-down challenge of the bull, and ignoring the threats of the nursing cows, he coursed a heifer who broke away in panic and pulled her down. And the sight of her, with the massive wolf surgery plain to see, was something that not even the unbelieving could ignore.

When word of the killing came from the shieling many doubters became convinced, but as many still refused to believe. The unbelievers had history and good reason on their side: nobody in all Athole had even whispered wolf for the lifetime of a man, and they were not ready to make a slogan of it now. The killer of the heifer would likely be some big dog, they argued with much reason, or a pair running wild with pups, or dogs of the Irish kind maybe, or wolf-like cross-breeds, from one of the garrisons or military posts; for was it not well known that the soldiery sometimes had big fierce dogs with them? Nevertheless, a hunt there would have to be, whatever. On that they were all agreed, and their agreement meant that the days of peace for Alba were nearly over.

Nearly, but not yet, for they had to plan a hunt, with only their native wit to guide them. They knew only the wolf of folklore, which was rich in stories of wolves hunting men, and men killing wolf pups in the den, but short on instructions for men hunting a pack on foot and running. A wolf pit, baited with the remains of the heifer, was out of the question, for a man could not dig down two feet on the ground where she had been killed. Even the bodach had no wisdom to offer, but he could tell them, just as though he had been there, of the great day in the proud past when Queen Mary – she who lost her head in England's green and pleasant land – hunted this very ground, with dogs and two thousand red-legged kerns, and by the day's end they had killed five wolves and three hundred and sixty deer.

Even a fraction of that number of Highlanders assembling now, with redcoats coming and going, and carts and ordnance rumbling on the roads built by Marshal Wade, and the rumours being whispered about the coming of Tearlach Mac Sheumais, would have been looked upon as an army, even without the arms denied them, and the idea of them as mere wolf hunters would have raised eyebrows to the height of Meall Tionail and a laugh that would have been heard at the court of King George.

Such a gathering would not have been permitted, even if it could have been raised. Rumour, fear and suspicion were flighting like migrant birds north and south of the Great Glen, and the redcoat soldiery were more interested in the movements of the Highlanders than in some rigwoodie kyloe killed by a whatever. The story reached the unholy trinity of Forts William, Augustus and George, where it was received with derision, but there were officers who opined sagely that it had been put about by the bare-legged, plaided savages as a screen to cover some more sinister ploy.

So the Athole men were left to go hunting with home-made spears and dogs who had never seen a wolf. Some of the men, like Alan Roy Stewart, had firearms hidden away, but they dare not carry them, for bearing them was against the law of the Sasunnach. Two days after their meeting the hunters set out for the hill: fifteen men and seven youths, with oatmeal cake, goat cheese and salmon in food packs and six hounds leashed in couples. They went out in the late afternoon by way of Glen Mhairc, which they left after four miles, climbing out over the steep eastern slope before they reached the big scree, then through the glens to the shieling across the Tarf, where they meant to spend the night. The shieling was close enough to An Sgarsoch for them to reach, within an hour of first light, the hollow where Ewen Murray had killed the wolf pup Boidheach, the beautiful. Even if the bitch wolf had moved her pups, it was still the obvious place for them to start.

Although the hound handler was with the party, he was a hunter of deer who knew no more than the others about wolves. Should the hounds be hunted in couples, or as a pack? Nobody knew any more than the man next to him. Alan Roy Stewart wondered if the hounds would hunt wolves at all. They were big, fast and strong, but they were deer hunters, and generations of their forebears had never seen a wolf. Yet their line stretched back to antiquity; their kind had hunted wolves for a thousand years, and in their veins ran the blood of Luath and Bran, Fillan and Ryno, the hounds that Fingal bred. Maybe the atavism would kindle the fire in them when they viewed a wolf.

'We'll find out when we come up with the wolves,' the handler said to Alan Roy.

'We will if we find them,' Alan Roy replied. 'But we won't if we don't, will we?'

In the night there was cannonade of thunder with sheeted rain that filled the gushes and sent the hill streams leaping white-crested down; but the morning sky was clear, with larks rising, and the men were up before the ravens. They singled the hounds, one to a man. Alan Roy had the bitch hound Tarf; the handler kept in hand the dog hound Dearg, an enormous smokey dog, a thruster of great courage, yet gentle, like the rest of his kind, with people. When they reached the hollow they encircled it, with the dogs evenly spaced round it. A homing badger, taken by surprise, turned back with a *woof* of alarm and porpoised downhill, raising a whimper but no indiscipline among the dogs. A pine marten peered down on the gathering from a high pine branch, then retired discreetly into hiding. The first day birds were calling. But of wolves there was no sign, except the bones of Boidheach. The men assembled below the lip of the hollow, considering what to do next, for the hounds were showing no interest in the ground, and clearly there was no recent wolf scent there to rouse them.

'What now, Alan Roy?' the handler asked. 'I would think to the north myself. The beasts would hardly come down nearer the Tarf after having a pup stabbed to death here before their eyes.'

'I agree,' replied Alan Roy. 'Such is my thinking too. I am for going out over An Sgarsoch and lining out as far as twenty-two of us can stretch, maybe fifty yards apart, and a dog to every three of us. Then we will drive in the direction of the place where the heifer was killed.'

'The dogs do not know what it is we are looking for, and might easily cross a fresh wolf trail without telling us about it.' The handler looked questioningly at Alan Roy. 'That is what worries me. If they get a view that might be different.'

'I have with me this.' Alan Roy took the tail of Boidheach from his food pack. 'It might help if I give them all a sniff of it. And there is something I have noticed about it.' He pointed to the precaudal gland: a dark spot near the root of the tail. 'Maybe this has something to do with smell – a kind of gland maybe, as in the fox or the badger.' He presented it to each hound in turn, but they were more interested in worrying it than smelling it.

The men started up to the headwater fork on An Sgarsoch, climbing in file and six of them leading a dog. Two eagles appeared and circled overhead, watching them. Alan Roy pointed to the eyrie where twin eaglets, within a week of flying, were wing-flapping on the edge: grown birds now, and powerful, in lack-lustre black and brown plumage, with white on their tails. The hunters turned the east shoulder of An Sgarsoch, well below the peak where dwelt ptarmigan, dotterel and snow bunting, then followed the stream on the high plateau between it and the lesser top of Sgarsoch Bheag. They lined out along the bank of the stream, and waited while the handler spied out to the Fiddler with his telescope.

The rising ground ahead hid the lower ground between, and he knew he would have to get to the next ridge for a view. This was not like foxhunting in the fat lowlands; the wolves might be anywhere in a hundred square miles of mountainous country where a man had to get to the highest top for a commanding view. He was beginning to think the day would bring them nothing more than the exercise, which none of them needed, and asking himself what twenty-two men and boys with six dogs could do on the ground where it had taken two thousand to kill five wolves in the presence of their queen.

The line moved to the forward ridge, from which the handler spied again, north and south of the Fiddler and the many-forked headwaters of Allt a Chaorainn below. All he could see were two eagles soaring and a red kite gliding low. The line moved forward at a slow walk, on a thousand yards front, with the dogs still held, and none straining at the leash. They strained when a parcel of stags bounded from a hollow, and the handler was almost lifted off his feet by the thruster Dearg. A jack merlin, the pocket peregrine, flashed across their front, with a fledgling wheatear in his talons. Golden plovers rose to circle, piping in alarm. Three more stags broke from behind a rock outcrop when the line was on the way down to the forks and the handler halted with a wave of his spear.

He spoke to Alan Roy Stewart: 'If we slip the dogs before we have sight of a wolf the damned things will likely go hunting after deer.'

'Then we won't slip them until we find what we are looking for,' Alan Roy replied.

When they were on the south face of the Fiddler, and still not a wolf seen, Alan Roy said to him: 'This is no good at all. We might as well be fish trying to climb a tree. Stay you with the dogs and the others and I will make to the top to see what can I see from there.' He took the glass from the handler, and handed over Tarf on her leash.

He went up the Fiddler like a pilgrim, using the shaft of his makeshift spear as a staff, but not at pilgrim pace. Gone was the Highlander's deceptive slow-walk that covers so much ground without seeming effort: now he was striding up, with shoulders forward, at a speed no soldier in the Great Glen could have matched or kept up with, as General Hugh MacKay learned when he met Claverhouse's clansmen at Killiecrankie, and he thinking they were still in Lochaber. Soon Alan Roy was near the top, where the snow beds of yesterday were now starred with saxifrage, and the hair grass waving and emerald mosses in pristine variety. On the summit ptarmigan were croaking and crackling, and a cock dotterel brooding newly hatched chicks. Two hinds, with spotted calves, trotted away when they saw the man approaching, and vanished over the rim.

Alan Roy sat down on a flat, grey boulder and spied around him, using his home-made spear as a prop. He spied back and down to the web of the Allt a Chaorainn headwaters, round leftwards to scan, to the limit of the glass, the ground stretching away to the Feshie and the Cairngorms, then left again to the big scree of Cairn Meall Tionail, where he held it steady. There was nothing to be seen there; but in such a fortress what might there be that he was not seeing? He swung the glass slowly to the south, probing wooded gullies and sweeping the glens with their remnants of the ancient forest. Eagle, raven and kestrel he could see, and a blackcock flying, and farther down black kyloes and some sheep, but the only other beasts moving on the ground were hinds with calves at foot.

Alan Roy Stewart knew nothing about wolves, but he knew Athole better than any deer or eagle, and the more he looked at the scree the more he thought of it as a likely place for them to hide in, unless they were already away, heading for the Cairngorms or the heights of Mar. Instead of signalling to the others to come up to him, he hurried down to rejoin them, with a plan already taking shape in his head.

'I can see nothing anywhere,' he told them, 'and what I am going to say is pure guessing. But the scree on Meall Tionail looks as likely a place as any. It's about six miles from where Ewen killed the pup and the same from where the kyloe was killed, and a wild place whatever. I think we should go over and take a closer look. But we'll come in from the south. We can be there in an hour.'

To send hounds through the scree would be risking their legs, so wolves, if they were there, would have to be forced out to run. But there was no way of smoking them out, and here was no tract of forest to burn down over their heads as was the custom in olden times. With their puny resources they knew there was only one way open to them – to post each hound with a handler, and drive the scree with men. That meant twenty-two men, with six dogs, to cover at least twelve square miles of rugged, broken country – two men and half a dog to the square mile, as Alan Roy put it – and not to be compared with Queen Mary's two thousand, with more *rachis* than the Athole men had ever seen together in one place. But they had to try, knowing there would be no great hunt, for men had more on their minds these days than chasing after wolves that were more than likely dogs anyway.

'It will take about two hours to sort this out, don't you think?' the handler said to Alan Roy. 'We will put a man and dog on the Fiddler, and you Alan Roy will stay here with Tarf. The blacksmith will take a dog to Coire Creagach yonder' – he

77

pointed to the cairn a mile away to the southwest – 'and I will go with Dearg to the Feshie along with two others with dogs. That will leave sixteen men to drive the scree from the top. And let us hope the beasts are there and will run from the shouting and the beating of sticks.'

'And what if a wolf comes out and attacks somebody?' one of the younger men asked.

'If anyone does not want to go,' said Alan Roy, 'he can stay here with me, and no one will think the less of him.'

No one said he did not want to go.

Within two hours men and dogs were in place – three on the tops, facing north, and three along the south bank of the Feshie, the man on the east at the gap between the river and the north ridges of the Fiddler. Alan Roy Stewart nodded to the sixteen who were to go down through the rock field and they strung out to form line, with spears held level and forward, their tips flashing in the sun. Each man balanced on the first rock, hoisted his spear to signal readiness, and the line began to clamber and stumble down.

They tap-tapped on the rocks with the end of their sticks and poked the dirk-tips into holes and crevices, some laughing, some shouting slogans, and others making no more than noise; none knew what to expect, and more than one or two of them wondered what to do if a wolf appeared suddenly in front of him, and his nearest neighbour forty yards or more away to right and left. But they kept up their beating and their shouting as they worked down the treacherous scree, and the hidden wolves heard and wondered, not knowing whether their hiding place was a refuge or a trap.

And suddenly there was Saighdear on a rock below the left of the line, taut, with his weight on his hindfeet, looking up, down and around. The beaters raised their spears and the slogan cries of battle, and there were those with a mind to charge down on the wolf. But the wolf did not wait. With a cat-footedness incredible in a beast of his size and weight he picked his way across the scree to the left of the line and a hundred feet below it, intending to turn it and run for the high ground. The voices raised to pitch a second time when the dog pup Laidir surfaced, and hesitated before scrambling after the leader, less confident on the rocks and not cat-footed, and it was then one of the beaters called out: 'With a Brown Bess at my shoulder I could have him!'

Saighdear ran uphill at a tireless lope, a beast of flowing hair and rippling muscle, with Laidir plowtering behind in leggy, halflin awkwardness. The big wolf could not see the man on Coire Creagach, but when Tarf was slipped by Alan Roy Stewart he turned downhill, at a flat gallop, with fur billowing and tail level, heading for the Feshie and leaving the plunging Laidir farther and farther behind, falling in the heather, slowed in the peat saps, and tiring. The leftmost man on the river bank turned loose his hound, and she left him, prancing, leaping and turning, seeking sight or smell of deer, and not knowing what she was expected to hunt. Then she saw Saighdear and came at him like a giant greyhound, which indeed she was, to intercept.

At the same time the handler, who was the centre of the line, waved Dearg out, and the big dog hound, seeing the running wolf, needed no further telling about what he had to do. Tarf was coming on too until she put up a knobber and two hinds with calves and broke off to hunt them. She pulled down the knobber and killed him, then went striding back to Alan Roy, to be received with ancient Gaelic curses instead of the commendation she expected.

The two hounds converging on Saighdear could not close in time to cut him off from the river, but they were in time to meet the lolloping Laidir, and it was Dearg who took him in his stride, turned him, threw him, savaged him, and left him torn, bleeding and dead before cantering back to his handler. The bitch hound sniffed over the body and savaged it further, then began to cast about for deer. Instead she roused a big lanky fox cub and broke him up before padding back to her handler. By then Saighdear was across the Feshie, running north, settled now into his marathon stride, untiring, breathing with mouth slightly open, the fear gone from him, but distressed because he did not know what was happening to the other members of the pack.

The beaters watched him crossing the river and halted to await a signal from the hound handler, who was walking with Dearg towards the left-hand man. The right-hand man, who had been guarding the gap between the Fiddler and the river, started walking up towards the beaters, with his dog still

79

leashed. And at that moment Sgian broke from the rocks.

The right-hand man could not see him, because there was a low ridge between them, but the hound handler did and waved Dearg back. At first the big hound cast about, whimpering with his nose to the ground, not knowing what he was looking for; then he saw Sgian running flat out for the river, and knew. Sgian was two hundred and fifty yards away when Dearg leaped into his stride – the fiercest thruster in the hound pack hunting the maverick of the wolf pack: the man-made dog of ancient lineage hunting his wild-dog ancester of ten thousand years before. They were matched for weight, but if the hound was perhaps faster over a short distance he had not the staying power of the wolf. And the wolf was well away, running at full stretch, with two hundred and fifty yards of Athole between them.

Ahead, the Feshie turned north, then west, forming a loop, and Sgian leaped and splashed across half a mile from the turn. Within three seconds he had shaken the water from his coat and was heading due north, sometimes hidden by the contours, sometimes in view. Dearg had won some yardage by the time he reached the Feshie, but once across it he was slowed down by Sgian's disappearances, for he was a sight hunter, needing a fleeing quarry in view to keep him running true. He was hunting blind, and faltering, when he loped on to a knoll and from there saw the wolf crossing the Feshie again, near its junction with the Eidart. The sighting keyed him to renewed eagerness and he leaped from the knoll in pursuit, breathing hard now, with his long tongue showing, but before he reached the river the quarry was once more out of sight. The hound handler, a mile and a half behind and following on with two dogs leashed, was sure that Dearg had lost the race and the wolf clear away.

And he should have been. He was across the Feshie for the second time, running for the Eidart, when Dearg appeared in view and saw him. The big hound came on, his pace slackening after three miles of hard going on killing terrain; but so long as he had a view he would run. Sgian plunged into the Eidart without checking, rashly, not reading the water, and landed on an axe-blade stone, not showing on the surface, which almost slashed the heel-pad from his left forepaw. The water was immediately stained red, and he left eddies of blood behind him. He yelped once in shock and pain, and when he scrambled on to the far bank he was carrying the paw. Blood was seeping freely from the wound. He put the foot down to follow a deer path above the river, and was not at first noticeably slowed down by his injury; but the rough ground soon began to irk, and heather to snag in the cleft, and he was limping before he reached the waterfall half a mile ahead. By then Dearg was over the Eidart, running blind again and fading, but still following on, and perhaps he was owning the smell of blood.

Sgian sat down beside the waterfall to lick his wounded paw: blood was still seeping from it, staining his tongue. A grey wagtail flew up from the fall to a rock, where he alighted to flirt his long tail and peer bright-eyed at the wolf: behind the thin cascade of water, on a moss-fronted ledge, his mate was feeding five near-fledged chirling young. The bird flew down again to hunt the pebbly shallows below the fall, and Sgian looked over his shoulder to his back-trail. Minutes passed, and he bellied down, the more easily to lick the paw, which he raised, turning the heel-pad to his tongue. More minutes passed and he rose to stand three-legged and look back again before leaving. And this time he saw the big hound Dearg trotting towards him.

Dearg came on with a rush, not knowing the wolf was wounded; but Sgian knew he was now unfit to outrun him. There were no big rocks at hand where he could hide, and he had few seconds to think. He started to cross the head of the waterfall, but when Dearg leaped after him he turned about to meet him face on rather than offer him his unprotected back. There was no hesitation in Dearg's attack, and he clashed head-on with the wolf. They closed, slashing at each other, with only two wagtails to witness the strange spectacle. They sheared muscle from each other's necks as they grappled. In the grapple they reared together and Sgian threw the hound. But Dearg held on and they went over the waterfall together, separating as they fell, to crash on the rocks below.

One and a half hours later nine men arrived with five hounds leashed, Alan Roy, Ewen Murray and the handler approaching from below and the others from above. Alan Roy pointed to the body of Dearg, lying with his face on the edge of the shallow where the wagtails had dabbled. He was dead, with a shoulder smashed, some ribs through his lungs, and gouts of blood dried on his mouth.

'A sad day at the end of it,' Alan Roy said. 'A fine dog dead and one wolf pup to show for it.'

The handler, wiping moist eyes with his knuckles, nodded and said huskily: 'And the wolf away. I wonder how the dog managed to fall over here.'

Alan Roy, casting about in the way he had, suddenly shouted from lower down: 'He didn't fall. They came over together. Come here and have a look at this.'

They hurried down to him, and there was Sgian, with his front legs broken and his breastbone smashed, staring at them with expressionless eyes, helpless and hopeless, and wagging his tail like a dog.

'I'll do it,' said Ewen Murray, and he speared Sgian through the heart. Yet there was no elation in him when he left with the others, rather a vague feeling of regret.

7

Pack loyalty in the wolf runs deep. Rooted in infancy – about the time the pups first appear at the den mouth – it blossoms with their growth into powerful, emotional ties with the adults, who play with them, feed them, and show great affection and solicitude towards them. Long before they are able to run with the pack their loyalty is unshakably bonded, and even strange wolves are shunned: no animal takes longer than a wolf to accept new friends. A pack member, returning after an absence of a day, is greeted with ceremonial welcome, as though he had been away for a month – a form of demonstration well known to a respected owner from his dog, itself the descendant of the wolf ten thousand years removed. The wolf was the first wild animal domesticated by man, who made it into a dog and exploited its loyalty, knowing it would not attack him when his back was turned, because it feared him, which is as true today as it was a hundred centuries ago.

After the trauma of his encounter with men and dogs at the place of rocks, Saighdear was tense and nervous, trembling when he stopped to check his back-trail or forward; and twice, while running, he voided a foul-smelling, porridge-like mess the colour of peat. The place of rocks might fade from his memory; what had happened there would stay with him for the rest of his life.

Fear drove him on after he had crossed the Feshie, until he reached its westerly course, six miles from the loop near which Sgian had died. Panting, from heat not exhaustion, he came to a green place of trees and coolth, above a waterfall, and trotted through until he reached a second fall, spilling from a hill burn leaping and bickering to the Feshie. Below the fall he threw himself down on a cool, damp moss cushion beneath a slanting, crow-stepped rock freckled yellow with tormentil and crusted with lichens. On the other side of the rock, in the full glare of the sun, fat bees were crawling over blaeberry and cowberry. In the old pines crested tits were calling. Saighdear sighed and closed his eyes, then fell into a resting half-sleep, with ears and nose alert for footfall or scent of man.

The green place of trees was two miles long and a quarter of a mile wide – another relict of the ancient Wood of Caledon: a still place of pine and birch and scattered juniper, with a straggle of oaks on the lower flats and alder and willow along the banks of the river. Here lived pine marten and wildcat, roe deer and red squirrel, and on shriving days in midwinter red deer sheltered in it. Young pines, from seedlings to wolf height, were growing where the deer had trampled and where feral pigs had rooted out the ground cover.

Many eyes had watched Saighdear on his passage through between the waterfalls, and some were curious about him; but a roebuck, finding the taint of him on the air, drew quietly away downwind without waiting for a view. One of the watchers was a pine marten – the cat-size weasel of the trees, brown-furred with orange throat patch – whose curiosity drew him on for a closer look at the stranger. He came down to the lowest branch of a pine tree, tilted his head, and peered at him with bright, questioning eyes. Saighdear moved an ear, opened his eyes, and yawned, displaying his enormous teeth, and the marten fled to the crown of the tree, pulling himself up the main stem like a bear.

Saighdear slept through the long hot daylight, sometimes curled nose to flank, and sometimes with muzzle on forepaws and a hind leg outstretched, disturbed only by flies walking over his ears and nose. At sunset he awoke and mounted the slanting rock, to stare across the darkening mountains into the glowing amber of the western sky with its rash of purple cloudlets. An owl hooted, and moths flew in the blue-violet dusk. When the afterglow was fading Saighdear lifted his muzzle and howled – a long drawn-out cadenced coronach, broken by half-barks and sobbing gutturals; a voice with loneliness in it, and perhaps a kind of anguish; and who can say there was not?

84

For ninety seconds he called, then he stood, facing the south-west, statuesque and motionless, like a dark sculpture, with ears forward, listening. There was no reply, and he knew that if wolf ears were not hearing him they must be more than four miles away, if there were ears to hear at all. What he did not, and could not, know was that Alba was back on the Fiddler – the only real sanctuary she had known since she moved her pups from the den – howling in chorus with Dileas, Luath and Geal to make contact with him. But the Fiddler was more than six miles away, with high ground between them.

Now he was the lone wolf, in distress, not knowing which way to go; but he had come from the south-east, and from the rock he trotted away in that direction, across the waist of the wood to the open hill, where he halted to howl again. Again there was no answer. Holding true to the south-east he trotted and loped along the west shoulder of Sron na Ban-righ, then climbed to its highest knoll, and there, for the third time, he stopped to howl into the night. By then Alba was moving down towards the Feshie, with the pups following in line and Dileas at the tail, and this time she heard him, faintly, and knew that the caller was Saighdear. The four howled their reply in chorus, and were heard by Saighdear on Sron na Ban-righ.

They met in an area of many lochans north of the Feshie, where it flowed north-east before running on to make its loop. It was an excited, emotional meeting, with much tail-wagging and whimpering. Alba and Dileas rubbed shoulders with Saighdear and licked the sides of his mouth, while the pups leaped round him, yelping and imploring him to bock for them. He had little to bock, but the little he had he bocked, and they licked the meagre vomits greedily. Alba and Dileas had already emptied their stomachs for them, and all were hungry, for they had eaten the last of the cached meat on the day Sgian killed the heifer, on which none but he had fed.

Alba wanted to be away, but she knew the pack had to kill first, if only for the sake of the pups, so she put them down on a rocky hillock, overgrown with heather, rowan and birch, and surrounded by boggy ground, and left them there. They knew they had to stay there, and were grappling in play when their mother trotted away after Saighdear and Dileas. They sent out no rallying call for Sgian, but ran mute into the dark.

All the year's crop of red deer calves had now been born, ranging from one week to four weeks old, and Saighdear had winded a number of hind groups on his way from the wood to Sron na Ban-righ, and from there to the lochans, so he knew where he was going. He led the bitch pair through the scatter of lochans, keeping to the dry ground and ignoring the craiking of ducks in the rushes and the big dog polecat hunting frogs and voles, who hissed at them from a hole under a sallow and filled their nostrils with the stink of his funk smell. Nor were they lured into chasing after the shadowy shapes of hares bolting uphill along well padded trails on the slopes of Sron na Ban-righ. Hares they would hunt if they had to; but it takes many to feed five hungry wolves, and more effort to kill ten than one hind the weight of twenty. Calves were easier to kill than hinds, and a strong stag calf, running with the hind, was the equal of five hares. Saighdear and his band had their mind on calves.

They were running at a spring-footed trot along a ridge on the west slope when they winded deer – five hinds with four calves and a yearling, in a corrie below a low cliff draped with ferns and woodrush. The deer had no warning of them because the pack was downwind. They were relaxed and off guard, with no experience of wolves and knowing that deerhounds did not hunt at night. The pack, in line ahead, split the small herd with a rush and cut out two calves, while the hinds bounded from the corrie, followed by the others and the yearling stotting behind. Saighdear pulled down a stag calf, which screamed before his massive teeth sheared through its loins. Alba killed the other. Dileas coursed the yearling for two hundred yards then broke off, knowing she was losing the race, and the hinds stopped and faced back, with ears up, all stamping with a forehoof. They knew, as deer know, that the pack would not be hunting them again that night. Two hinds snorted their groaning calf-call, and one minced forward a few paces, with the spring in her knees. Then all turned about and trotted away, not looking back and two hinds knowing that their calves would not be returning.

Saighdear ripped the spine and back flesh from the stag calf, and spilled out the paunch and entrails: Alba and Dileas squatted face to face and shared the other, which they presently pulled apart. They ate all that was eatable, including the skulls and skins, and scraped and crunched bones, leaving only the shoulder blades and trotters for the carrion birds to squabble over in the morning. Before the trio were back at the hillock, woodmice were nibbling at morsels of flesh on the shoulder blades of the carcasses.

The pups greeted Alba with ears pinned back, eyes slitted and tails sweeping the heather. They nuzzled the sides of her mouth, forcing her head up, but she pushed past them into the scrub and bocked for them in a small clearing among brown flower spikes of dwarf cudweed, where lizards scurried or basked in the heat of the day. With half the contents of her stomach between them, they ran to Saighdear and Dileas, who both bocked part of their meal. And then they curled up under a twisted rowan and wanted to sleep.

They slept while the old wolves dozed, but Alba had them on foot within an hour, and was ready to go. The hundred square miles the wolves had hunted over would have maintained any pack of five for as long as they wished to stay; but Alba could not forget the past week of harassment and killing by men and dogs, and she knew the days of wandering had returned. The urgency in her was sensed by Saighdear, who rose suddenly, shook himself, and led his band from the hillock.

A crescent moon was rising when he left, with Alba close behind and the pups between her and Dileas at the tail. They followed the lower ridges to the Feshie loop, running most of the time in full view of eagle, raven and red deer, for here were only scattered scraggles of shriven birches and aged unfruiting pines slow to die. They waded and swam across, with the pups plunging and snorting, and shook the water from their fur – a mile and a half from the place where the skinned body of Sgian lay, as yet missed by the ravens and still sheathed in shrinking muscle, with flies glossed like beetles crowding on it. They held away to the east, with the moon's crescent at their backs, and reached the Geldie a mile from its source.

For many miles it flowed in tight loops, like an old spring uncoiled, and Saighdear led his band straight along the ridges to cut them out: answering no summons of place, knowing only that he had to keep travelling into the mountain vasts, along no remembered trails, probing for space, avoiding the human animals, yielding ground wherever they pressed and occupying it where they were not. Thus has the wolf had to live since men gave up hunting and gathering to become stock rearers and tillers of the soil. The wild dog made tame – the fellow worker and companion of its creator – became a malign beast of mystery and menace, calling unseen in the night, with every man's hand against it.

Below the hill known as the Duke's Chair the Geldie unlooped to run straight and Saighdear changed direction down to follow its north bank. On pools where the moon's reflected crescent gleamed and shuddered, goosander ducks were dipping and plashing, while their ducklings scooshed and scuttered across the surface, snatching midges. Sandpipers rose in the path of the pack and flickered away, flashing white, to pitch, piping plaintively, on boulders. Deer on the far bank, owning the wolf taint on the wind, rose and spring-trotted to higher ridges where they stopped and turned about to stare back, with ears up and nostrils flared: to them, wolf-smell was dog-smell, and therefore dangerous.

A dog otter, oily sleek, with the moon glint in his water-dimmed eyes, sat up tall in weasel pose on a rock in mid-pool – an ebony silhouette with a salmon smolt at his feet – to watch the strange dogs running the bank. He knew nothing of dog-smell, and the scent of wolf was new to him; but he disliked it, and snorted on it, and twitched his whiskers, and slipped noiselessly into the pool with the smolt in his jaws. He surfaced below the far bank, and climbed out to crunch on his smolt after the pack had passed by. The bitch otter, playing with twin cubs in a pool downstream from her mate, also saw and winded the wolves, and dived with her family to seek shelter among roots in the undercut bank. Unlike her mate, she knew dogs by scent and sight, for she had been rousted by a brace of hounds, who drove her through a pool and bayed her in her holt before reluctantly leaving to the recall of their handler.

Three hours and twelve miles from the place of lochans the pack reached the low ground below Cairn Geldie, with the pups leg-weary and beginning to whimper. Saighdear turned uphill, leading the pack at a steady lope; the pups might be tired but he wanted them out of the glen on high ground. Fifteen hundred feet of extra height could mean greater safety than twenty miles of extra running. Daybreak was not far off; mist was creeping up the Geldie and swirling in the corries. Ravens began to fly over;

then a pair of yarring hoodie crows. The sky was cloudless, speedwell blue overhead, with waves of violet, rose-pink and saffron lapping over the peaks.

Saighdear slowed to a dog-trot on the steep, but his pace was still too much for the flagging pups, who began to fall behind. Alba and Dileas held back for them, licking their muzzles to encourage them, and they found new strength and came on, panting, with tongues flacking, sleeking their outer fur with dew from heather, deer grass and bearberry, and snagging stems in their toes. High on the Cairn they found Saighdear among grey rock outcrops, and threw themselves down, exhausted after twelve miles of running and a climb of a thousand feet.

The sun was coming up plaided in fire, and the ground mists flushed in the glow. The An Sgarsoch eagle, with his mate and two young, were flying at wolf's eye level above the Geldie, which was the limit of their range. Saighdear found a flat-topped rock with moss stars in the cracks, and crouched on it to stare into the vast grandeur of the morning. From his seat he had a commanding view of the glen, down to where the Geldie was joined by a lesser stream before flowing on to the Dee, with its teeming salmon and forested banks, and black cattle grazing on the down-river flats and ridges.

He was now in dangerous country. Although there were no human habitations in sight, there were thatch houses, bothies and hutments farther down and all the way to Braemar, hardly more than twenty miles from where he was lying. Down there on the braes, thirty years before, the Earl of Mar had gathered five thousand men in guise of a hunting *tainchel* and raised the Stuart standard, proclaiming James VIII king of Scotland, England, Ireland and France.

That night, before moonrise, the adult wolves left the pups among the rocks and headed north and down towards the Dee, with a light, warm wind ruffling the fur of their left flanks. Below them and ahead was a great oakwood, with pines along its uphill length and pine, birch and aspen on its lower, above the river. The wolves followed the near edge down to where the oaks thinned out, then turned into the trees with the wind again on their left flanks and the wood in their noses. Saighdear, in the lead, stopped suddenly after a quarter of a mile, and faced into the trees with nostrils sifting. Alba and Dileas stopped close behind him and sniffed their questions to the wind. And the wind's answer was pig. Up there somewhere, in the dark under the whispering oaks, a shaggy sow was rooting in the ground litter, with five half-grown piglets rooting and squeaking around her.

But they were not true wild pigs, the fierce tusky boars of olden times 'whose tusks turned up whole fields of grain, and rooting raised hills upon the level plain'. The wild pig, taken young, tames easily, and the Scots of old tamed it. They let the herds roam on the hill and in the forest like their wild ancestors, and like their wild ancestors they remained through the centuries, without admixture of domestic blood, leggy and hairy and swift, heavy forward and lean behind. They harvested the acorns, and rooted in the oakwoods. They uprooted young trees and damaged the roots of the established, but like the jays and squirrels they buried acorns to replace them. They scavenged in the villages. They hunted the hill, devouring the roots of plants, the eggs of birds, and the birds themselves if they could catch them. They hunted voles and mice, and were in their turn hunted and eaten by man. They remained wild pigs tamed, not man-made domesticates running wild.

Although smaller than their long-ago ancestors they still resembled them closely, and a pig that looks like a wild pig, behaves like a wild pig, and survives like a wild pig, is a wild pig for all the practical purposes of wolves and men, so it is impossible to say when the real one became extinct and its niche was taken over by its tamed, identical kin.

The wolves became highly excited at the smell of pig, nuzzling muzzles and wagging tails before moving, in line abreast, to the stalk. The sow was a dusky, bristling, long-legged razorback, with erect ears and shoulders layered in hard muscle. Roused to a fury, she could have charged down a man or bitten the leg off a dog. Rooting in the oakwood she was placid and happy. She had a good nose, and there was no scent of wolves to warn her because she was upwind of them; her hearing was acute, but she would not have heard their stealthy tread even if she had been downwind of them. Maybe she belonged to somebody, and maybe to nobody or anybody, and maybe she went back to forage among the human animals from time to time.

To the wolves she was a wild prey to be hunted. Their rush took her and her piglets by surprise, and they were surprised by the speed of her when she turned about and galloped downhill, outflanking Dileas on the right. All three chased after her, and she had almost reached the river-flats, two hundred yards from her rousting, before Saighdear and Alba leaped on her back and pulled her down on her face. She squealed as she fell, and was gnashing her teeth, trying to reach round at them, even as they were tearing gaping wounds on her rump.

The five piglets had scattered in panic flight when the pack broke away after the sow; now they were crashing, hooves drumming, at incredible speed, on converging course to the river. Dileas spurned away in pursuit, choosing the laggard of the five, which reached the river ahead of her and was swimming when she plunged in from the bank. She overtook it in deep water, and it squealed when her massive teeth closed on its back. She shook it and broke its spine, then dog-paddled sideways, using her tail as a rudder, hauling against the pull of the current until she reached water she could stand up in. The piglet was heavy, not to be hefted, and she dragged it to the bank, where she bellied down to shear flesh from rump and loin. She stayed down to strip meat and gulp the small pieces, but rose to swallow the choking chunks. There was much remaining after she had gorged. She trotted back to join Saighdear and Alba, who were rib-taut with feasting. Then the three padded up through the oakwood, into the pines, and on to Cairn Geldie where the pups were lying.

They were greeted effusively by the pups, who tongued their teeth begging for bocks. Alba and Dileas disgorged half their meat for them, while Saighdear trotted away to his lookout rock. Digestion in the wolf is rapid, and in the meat bocked up by the bitches it had already begun; but it had not gone far enough to make the chunks easy eating for the pups, who still had their milk teeth. They bolted the pieces up to choking size, then squatted to chew on the chunks. Without any signal to Saighdear the bitches left to return to the kill; and this time they both fed on the carcass of the sow, stripping it to the ribs and spine, and even rasping off flesh with their tongues. They scraped the haunch clean and ripped away the massive shoulders, spitting out bristles and rubbing their faces with a forepaw. They left the head and trotted the mile and a half back to the rocks, where they found the pups couched apart and asleep.

This time there was no greeting from them. They opened their eyes, sighed deeply, and closed them; they were belly-happy. Saighdear appeared, and the bitches touched muzzles with him. Then for three quarters of a minute they howled in chorus: *wow-wow-wow-wow* and *oo-oo-oo-oo* to a high-pitched wail, with the *wow-wow* from Saighdear and the *oo-oo* from the bitches. The pups opened their eyes, howled faintly and tiredly for two seconds, then fell asleep again. The howling was heard, and listened to, by the red deer on the hill, the martens and roe in the oakwood, and by hunting fox and wildcat. It started sleepy crow-talk in a tree near the place where the bones and head of the sow were lying; the greybacks were awaiting first light to scavenge. Ravens at roost two miles away heard it, and croaked brief guttural comment. But the pack song was not heard by the man-enemy because the nearest human ears were too far away.

An hour before daylight Alba rose and padded downhill, followed by Saighdear and Dileas on the short run back to the kills. They cleared the carcass to the bones, scraping with their incisors and rasping with their tongues. Saighdear tore away the strong jaws for the tongue and bolted it whole. From the sow they went to the piglet, and knew from the musk taint that a fox had been there thieving not long before. They cleaned it of meat, and again Saighdear ripped off the jaws to reach the tongue. Dawn was not far away, but instead of turning back to the trysting place with the pups they began to prowl in the oakwood.

They found no more pigs, but they put on foot a roebuck, a strong beast beginning to warm up for the rut. He was downwind and could smell them, and was bounding through the wood, boughing in alarm, before he could see them. He was waywise in the wood and they were not. Despite this, and their full bellies, and the ground cover, they ran full stride to the chase, hunting by sight when they could see him, and by the crashing of him in the undergrowth when they could not.

They ran him, seeing or hearing, for half a mile, by which time he was showing his tongue and snorting from flared nostrils. Then, suddenly, he turned sharply to the right at the bound and stotted downhill towards the river, open-mouthed and gasping for breath. The wolves lost yardage when he made his sudden turn, as a greyhound does with a jinking hare, but they quickly made it up and were on top of him when he half-stumbled from the bank into the water. They killed him there, and lapped the bloodied water before dragging the body ashore, where Alba took sole possession.

At first she tried to haul it by the neck; then she changed her grip to a hindleg where there were no sharp antlers to annoy her face. She backed away, with the fore-end of the prey furrowing the ground litter, and cached it below the roots of an old windfall, nosing and pawing it into position before scraping ferns, sticks and mouldy leafage over it with her hindfeet. Once she had it completely covered she ran to Saighdear, wagging her tail, and touched noses with him, before taking second place in the file when he led them from the wood to tryst with the pups. Saighdear went to his lookout rock and bellied down, chin on forepaws, to stare with pale say-nothing eyes into space across the Geldie. Alba and Dileas curled up, nose to flank, and slept beside the pups.

Nothing came to disturb the trysting place by day, and each night at darkening the adults left to hunt, returning in the morning before first light. And still their howling chorus did not betray them. They killed two big deer calves and a goat, running eight miles to Glen Luibeg for the calves and five to the north-west for the goat. These kills and the cached roebuck kept the pack fed for four nights.

On the fifth night, facing the red glare of sunset, Saighdear went hunting alone, and travelled twelve miles to the Tarf water, where he killed a four-horned, dark-fleeced sheep in the light of a half moon gleaming in a clear sky. He gorged on it and left carrying the skinned hind-quarters in his jaws. He cached the hind-quarters under an outcrop below Cairn Geldie, and scraped heather and rubble lightly over it. At the trysting place he was met by the begging pups, and bocked up half his stomach contents for them. He had made a round trip of twenty-four miles between the setting and rising of the sun. Presently Alba and Dileas arrived and went to sleep without bocking because the fed pups did not beg. They had hunted and lost two parcels of stags, then killed a fat knobber in a corrie and cached there

93

what was left of him after they had filled their stomachs.

But discovery was near, and the cached hind-end of the four-horned sheep led to it, for Saighdear had not hidden it as carefully as he should have done, and it was discovered by the greyback crows. Two mornings later he was on his lookout rock, staring across the glen, when he saw two plaided figures on the other side of the Geldie, with a hound casting in front and two squat, rough-haired, cattle-hustling messans padding behind. Saighdear stared at the distant figures, and who can say what thoughts or feelings arose in him at the sight? The men were of Clan Chattan, a Farquharson and an Erskine, the one a tackman of Mar, the other a smallholder and hound handler, both wearing the philibeg and carrying long sticks. They saw the crows flapping and squabbling across the river and, being hill men and knowing that where crows gather there is meat, they splashed to the other side to see what was afoot. The hound bounded ahead, with the cattle tykes following, and scattered the crows, who lifted away cawing harshly. The three quickly found the hind-end of the sheep, snatched at it, and pulled three ways on it, snarling and snashing until the men came up and threatened them with their sticks, when they released it and slunk to heel.

The Erskine turned it over with the toe of his rawhide brogan.

'No fox did this,' he said. 'No fox could lift the weight, let alone take it from the rest of the body.'

'No indeed,' agreed Farquharson. 'Only a big dog could do this, a real big one like Fingal there.' He nodded towards the big deerhound, who turned his head away, knowing he was being spoken about.

'But what dog? Whose dog?' Erskine said, scratching the back of his neck. 'Nobody has said anything about sheep being killed or a dog seen on its own.'

The two men searched around not knowing what they were looking for or if they were looking for anything, and they let the dogs cast about with them. Suddenly, Fingal put a shoulder down and began rubbing his neck on the ground.

'What now?' Erskine said rhetorically. 'Leave it, Fingal!'

The hound came to command and Erskine picked up a wolf scat, fatter and longer than his middle finger. Saighdear had deposited it there after his gorge on mutton. The two men examined it together.

'No fox passed this,' Farquharson said, 'and it hasn't got any whisker ends whatever. Looks like dog shit to me, and a big dog too.'

Erskine teased out the scat, which was dark matter and bone fragments wrapped in hair.

'This isn't deer hair,' he said. 'It's goat hair. Now where are goats from here?'

'In the glen to be sure. But nobody is missing a goat.'

'I mean the wild ones.'

'On Ben a Bhuird for sure, and that's a tidy step from here. And out towards Cairn Toul, and that's just as tidy.' Farquharson reflected for a moment, then added: 'Why should a dog eat goat away out there, then come down to the Geldie to drop his load?'

'It's a strange matter surely,' said Erskine, throwing away the scat and wiping his hands on the grass. 'The hind-end there is sheep, not goat, and if we find the dog we'll find his next shit wrapped in wool.'

They went home thinking of dog, and it was dog they spoke about when they arrived, for they had heard nothing of the wolf talk in Athole, forty miles away for an eagle flying and a wilderness of mountains between. Everybody talked dog for a day, and nobody was missing a sheep, and nobody could know that the hind-end found by Farquharson and Erskine was from a beast killed far away on the Tarf. So, with the rumours being whispered and everybody with more than enough to do with the clipping, and the tillage, and the cattle herding, there was no fiery cross calling them to hunt a killer dog which nobody had seen or heard about anyway.

Although Alba was nervous, she did not move the pups, which she would be doing soon for her own reasons without hostile promptings by men, and likely she would have waited for that time if she had been left undisturbed. But a wolf pack is a wolf pack, not understanding the difference between the wild creatures of the hill and the sacred cattle of men, and not knowing that actions lead to consequences. Two days after the Clan Chattan men had discussed a wolf scat with remarkable acuity, the young herds were pushing black cattle farther out to the hill, and the same night, by the light of an egg-shaped moon, the pack killed a stirk beyond the Geldie, near its junction with the Dee. They ate to repletion on it, and shared it with the pups, but did not return to the carcass. The herd found the body in the morning, and it was clear for anyone with eyes to see that no one dog had removed so much meat from a stirk. So they began to think of several dogs in a pack running wild. No one cried wolf, because the thought never entered anyone's head.

But the find brought out the clansmen as surely as the summons of a fiery cross, and next morning at break of day the muster took place – fifteen men with two dogs with noses and five hounds including Fingal – and the wolves heard the barking of the dogs when they were more than four miles away. That prompted Alba, and within minutes she had the pups roused on foot. Saighdear left his rock and loped away down the north face of Cairn Geldie, with Alba in his tracks, followed by the pups with Dileas at the tail of the file. They were six miles away when the hunters crossed the Geldie, and ten when they came round the Cairn on the west side where there was no scent of wolf. They were twelve miles away when the dogs found the place where they had been lying. So they were clear away; for not even Highlanders, with the lungs and legs of a deer, could match running wolves, and no deerhound yet born could hope to catch up on a pack with a twelve-mile start.

Saighdear held the pack high, following the ridges, and had them above the Eidart where its tributaries formed a fork below Tom Dubh, with eighteen miles behind them and the pups exhausted.

8

Next morning the pups were leg-weary, foot-sore and stiff. Twice in nine days they had been taxed beyond their age and strength, covering distances that no bitch wolf, with free will, would have forced or expected them to travel. Short journeys of three or four miles, from site to site, are the rule in the days of trysting, until the pups are grown up enough to run with the pack. Alba had no freedom of choice. Men and dogs were a threat, and she knew that their will, not hers, had to be done. She would move her pups again, and yet again, for her own reasons, mostly to keep them within easy reach of the hunting pack; but she would move them at any time when the man-threat loomed, for she had not forgotten the killing of Boideach and Laidir, or the pups dirked to death in Kintail.

Daylight came with a camstrairy wind stirring leaf whisper in the gully and fretting the pools in the burn below. White clouds, domed and peaked, filled the southern sky like a mountain range in snow. Out of the north-west crawled others, black and big-bellied with rain, to engulf the overhead blue, and the early brightness became twilight again. Rain purred down and the pools simmered. It dripped from the trees and rocks, and the drips became trickles, and the trickles veined into snakes of water, darting and probing and winding down to the burn, with flotsam of leaf skeletons, drowned flies and drowning beetles. The pups shook loose water from their fur and padded stiffly up to dryer ground among the rocks and scrub, where they lay down on their sides and fell asleep, breathing deeply and wagging their ears against the itch of wet.

When Alba appeared, with her belly crammed with venison

and a blue hare in her jaws, they were too tired to run to her in greeting. Instead, they beat the ground with wagging tails, turned their heads, and showed her the whites of their eyes. She put down the hare and bocked meat for them. She padded to them, whimpering, and licked their bellies when they rolled over on their backs. But they were not to be coaxed to their feet. They yawned in her face, with their long tongues at full stretch, and their new ivory front teeth showing between discolouring baby tusks. They needed rest more than food, and Alba knew it. So she backed away to let them sleep and, after sniffing the hare and her vomits, trotted up the gully to where Saighdear and Dileas were already lying among ferns and woodrush, with their eyes slitted and the hindlegs of a deer calf lying downhill from them in open view. The pack had killed the calf above the Dee near Devil's Point, and Alba had snatched the hare as it leaped almost from her feet on their homeward run.

The sky cleared in the late afternoon, and in the hot sun the flies came to buzz. Luath and Geal rose, yawned, stretched their legs and gulped down the bocks, now cold, left by Alba in the morning. They tore open the belly of the hare and ate the entrails, but they needed more than the fluid in them. Their thirst was now commanding and they skulked down to the burn, keeping to the shadows, and lapped from a shallow pool beside the cast antler of a stag, bleached and chewed, which Luath pulled from the water and carried away.

Flies were walking on the hare when the pups passed it on their way back to the scrub-shade among the rocks. They groomed themselves and each other with their new front teeth before lying down, facing the open, with chins on forepaws and branch shadows like zebra striping on their backs and flanks. Unmoving, they were invisible in the broken light and restless shadows under the scrub, and were missed by the kenning eyes of two greyback crows who pitched in the top of a rowan to talk crow-talk about the hare, long-necking and upending as they peered down at it and around. Seeing nothing to put them off, they hopped to lower branches for a closer look, suspecting nothing but wary by habit, and it was then that Luath raised his head to stare at them with expressionless, amber eyes.

They saw the movement at once and *kwarped* their discovery in duet. The discovery led to more crow-talk, and the pair perched there for some minutes, uttering hoarse comment and snipping off rowan leaves in anger. The pups watched the leaves eddying down, and the crows watched the pups. Luath lowered his head again. One crow flew down and swivel-swaggered round the hare, then began pecking at an eye. The second pitched beside it and stabbed under the fud. But these were mere preliminaries, and presently both began to work on the bloody cavity opened by the pups, with one foot on the hare and the other on the ground.

Luath and Geal were no longer tired. They were fresh, fed and wideawake, and the aching stiffness was going from their muscles. At first they were no more than intrigued by the crows. Then, perhaps because he suddenly realized that what they were eating was his, Luath rose to his feet with the hair of his back on end and his tail in the air. The crows flapped back from the hare and stood tall, with their crown feathers hackled, to watch him. Luath stared fixedly at them, with his left forepaw clear of the ground and his weight on his hindfeet. The crows, in the taunting way they have, swaggered back to the hare, and one stepped on to it. At that moment Luath rushed at them.

His rush did not take them by surprise, but the speed of it did, and the second one to rise heard the snap of his teeth at its tail. Both flew into the rowan, where they *kwarped* and cawed, and performed more defoliation. From there they watched him licking in the bloody cavity, then tearing at its edges, before snatching up the carcass and carrying it into the scrub. Knowing they had lost, the pair lifted into the air without further comment and disappeared up the gully in rising flight.

Geal hustled her brother for a share of the hare, but was warned off by his low growls and the look on his face, for the wolf's is a saying face and what it says is understood at once by others of its kind. Luath carried the hare deeper into the scrub, and there ate it down to the last toe nail and the last wisp of fur. After he had licked his fur and his forepaws he returned to Geal, and found her playing with the antler he had carried from the pool. He snatched an end of it in his front teeth and they played tug of war with it, growling and gurrying in mock ferocity; but they tired quickly of the game and began to chase each other instead – through the scrub, into the sunlit open, then back into the scrub, crashing and stumbling, sometimes falling, and yelping from time to time in their excitement. But, like all pups everywhere, their attention was not held for long by any single ploy, and they turned to mauling the scrub – ripping off leafage and chewing at bark; scraping at roots and biting them; tearing at ferns and woodrush; and cracking dead, dry sticks as they would one day crack the bones of a prey. And likely all the biting and chewing would be helping their teething, for they still had their adult tusks and back teeth to grow.

They were panting, at the peak of their wrecking, when Alba and Dileas appeared. They had left Saighdear on his morning seat, near the top of the gully, from which he had a commanding view of the ground down to the Eidart. The pups greeted the bitches excitedly, with sterns wagging in pleasure at the sight of them. Geal ran to Alba, and Luath to Dileas. When Alba turned away, Geal followed her, neck to neck and soliciting; but Alba had nothing to give. Luath fussed Dileas, shoulder to shoulder, reaching up to lick her muzzle; then, over-excited and bold beyond his age, he tried to mount her, in the assertive way he had mastered his litter mates. She threw him off, ungently but not threatening, lofted her tail and glared at him.

Although a born spoiler of pups, she was also the ranking wolf next to Saighdear and Alba, and Luath had to learn his place. He turned his eyes away from her stare, and read the sayings of her face and tail. The wolf has an aversion to fighting, and avoids it most of the time by the sign language of face, ears, teeth and tail. It took man to instil a love of it in certain breeds of dogs. Luath was learning the signs, and when Dileas lowered her tail and her face relaxed into its usual placidity, he ran to her and grappled with her in rough, intimate play. That kind of roughness she accepted with calm and indulgent dignity and when in the end, she pushed him away, there was camaraderie in the paw.

At darkening the pack left to hunt, travelling north with the wind on their left flanks, and the pups spent the next few hours chasing after mice and scraping where they found mouse-smell. They expended much effort catching few mice, but they were learning coordination of eye and muscle. Saighdear and the bitch pair were seven miles away when the moon, now nearing its full, came up in a clear sky with pale stars, flooding the gully with light; and the night was silent except for the whisper of leaves in the wind and the small-talk of water refreshed by rain.

The pups went to the burn to drink, and lapped from a pool where the moon's image rippled like a jellyfish in the tide. Instead of turning back they splashed across, and stalked low into the wind, slowly and cautiously, with their noses asking questions and their ears listening forward.

Here were big outcrops of rock, crowned and fronted with heather and blaeberry, with scrub birch and aspens in the clefts. Below a lichened column the pups found the smell of cat, but there was nothing else in the pressed-out bed. The cat was on top of the rock, as they suddenly realized when they heard his explosive hiss. There was no way they could reach him, which was as well for them, because he was a mighty wildcat in his prime, with luminous moon eyes, teeth more powerful than theirs, and clawed fists and hind feet that could have taken their eyes. He knew that, and they did not. He also knew that he was not coming down while they were there. Doing nothing would leave him with a whole hide, and he had the patience to wait them out. So he sat there, with an armed forepaw upheld, behaving like any of his kind trapped on a rock, which is to make threat display and no move to attack.

The big cat made his display, with ears flattened and teeth bared to the gums, and the ringed tail twitching, and the moon eyes glaring, and the menacing war pipes of him wailing; and the magnificent catness of him, with all his weaponry arrayed, was wondrous to behold. Each time the pups leaped up at him he spat and sizzled, and cuffed the air with the forepaw. They were curious about him simply because he was there to be curious about, although if he had come down it is likely that they would have chased him, for something running away is as tempting to wolf pups as to any pup of the man-made dog.

Before long Luath and Geal lost interest in him, and he calmed down; but instead of leaving they took over his bed, turning round and round in it, and enlarging the press-out before lying down on it, and he was left to fume in silence. A half hour later he was wondering what had become of them, because he could hear no movement, although the smell of them was still there. Being neither reckless nor a fool he craned over to discover where they were and what they were doing. He knew they were down there somewhere because they could not have left in the bright moonlight without his seeing them. When he

101

realized that they were asleep, he climbed warily down the other side of the rock and bounded silently away. And the pups knew nothing of his going.

While they slept, the pack, led by Saighdear, came round the Wells of Dee and ran the low ground below Cairn Toul to Angel's Peak, where they turned south-west to work back to the trysting place with the pups. In eleven miles of running they killed only a nanny goat, well fleshed of her kind because she had lost her kid early in the year, but hardly prey enough for three big wolves with two four-months-old pups to support. Twice they winded deer – a parcel of five hinds and four calves, and one of seven stags well forward in velvet – and tested them. But the hinds were well away with their calves before the trio could make contact, so they did not run them: the stags were equally alert, and Saighdear broke off the chase after three-quarters of a mile. Now the pack was homeward bound, warmed up but untired, with only a goat to three bellies, and most of that would be bocked for the pups.

The following night the pack hunted out to the Dee, running south then east, not waywise and without plan – three wolves probing into the unknown, in line ahead with Alba on point, and all with ears, noses and eyes alert for movement, scent or sight of prey. The wind from the south-west was almost directly behind them, ruffling the hair of their right flanks, so their noses could tell them nothing of what might lie ahead. Although the moon had not yet risen the light was good, as it is at that latitude in the month when golden eaglets fly, and the pack kept up a steady lope. They were at a thousand feet on the south face of Beinn Bhrotain when the wind brought them the scent of deer – a parcel of three hinds, all with calves at foot. Alba halted the moment her nose owned the scent, and the three faced about with nostrils plotting distance and location. All the advantages were with the wolves, and Saighdear moved to lead the band on the upwind stalk at a running walk.

This would be a surprise attack, with the deer filling the attackers' nostrils while their own were receiving no wind-borne tidings of wolves. Nor were they helped when a curlew, rising almost at Saighdear's feet, startled the night with its warning cries: *cu-cu-lu – cu-cu-lu – cu-cu-lu!* The clear signal put the hinds and calves on foot, alerted but not alarmed, because they were not hearing, smelling or seeing threat of danger, and they knew that the bird's warning might mean no more than fox, or wildcat, or marten, or stoat, and of such they had no fear. They stood with ears swivelling, and nostrils flaring and closing, until the curlew fell silent, but there was nothing from upwind and all they could hear was wind-whisper and the hooting of an owl in the forest below. So the pack was almost on top of them before the leading hind broke away on an uphill slant almost across Saighdear's front.

The others tried to follow her, but Saighdear cut them off and bounded after her while Alba and Dileas turned a hind and calf downhill. The hind escaped across their front, but they cut out her calf and coursed him like a brace of greyhounds coursing a hare. He was a strong calf, fast and waywise, but panic made him run wild, crying for the hind, and they killed him in a flat of rushes below a trickle-fall of water. They had the body torn apart, and were bolting gobs of flesh and crunching bones, when they were joined by Saighdear, who had followed his hind uphill for half a mile before breaking off, realizing she was a strong beast that he had no chance of catching. On the way down he had passed her calf going up in search of her mother, and had missed her although they were only a hundred yards apart, because this time the calf was down-wind with the wolf-scent in her nose and her own not in the wolf's.

When the trio had eaten the kill down to the trotters they were ready to hunt again. They had to go, although the kill was enough for three, because the pups would demand most of what they had in their stomachs – a demand none of them would resist or refuse. The moon was coming up and they still had the greater part of the night ahead of them.

They followed the Dee upstream then turned west into Glen Geusachan, padding in file under the cliffs with the wind almost full on their muzzles and their elongated shadows flanking them on the right. In a corrie two miles from the Dee they roused five stags from the cudding, and gave chase, pressing them hard, probing for the weak, the laggard, the disabled or the sick. But there were no falterers or weaklings in the group, and after half a mile the five stopped and turned about, fronted by a big-bodied six-pointer, with budding tops, who would be a royal when he cleaned velvet and would come early to the rut. When the wolves arrived they were faced by five stags with antlers at the present, fronted by the six-pointer scraping the ground with a forehoof.

A stag in velvet is careful about his antlers which, at that stage of growth, damage easily, as well as being sensitive, living bone and tissue. In quarrels with his fellows he rears up and boxes with his forehooves. Not until they are cleaned of velvet, when they become dead, insensitive bone, does he use his antlers as weapons. What five stags would have done in a confrontation with a wolfpack was not put to the test. However much or little, if anything at all, the wolves knew about antlers in or clear of velvet, they were daunted by the fearful array of weaponry.

Saighdear stopped, facing into the wind, with tail level and a forepaw lifted, like a pointer dog standing to game. Dileas sat down behind him, to his right: Alba bellied down, behind and to his left, and began to bite between the toes of her left forepaw, completely ignoring the deer. The stags kept their heads down, and hardly moved their antlers when Saighdear stalked a few stiff-legged paces to his right, with his tail in the air. They held their threat posture when he stalked to the left, back to his starting point, bristling and still with his tail hoisted. He was testing their mettle. He tested them further by stalking a few paces towards them, but they were not to be stampeded into flight.

No wolf ever born would have made a frontal assault on five strong stags prepared to stand to the onset, not even the wilful Sgian. Saighdear turned about and trotted back to Alba, who leaped up to fuss. Dileas trotted over to join them, and the three held a short session of tail-wagging, with their heads together, nuzzling each other, sniffing ears and licking faces, and a mere man might have been forgiven for thinking they were discussing the problem of five unscared stags who refused to run and whose flanks could not be turned.

Whatever the meaning of the brief ritual, it ended with Saighdear turning away uphill at a spring-footed trot, with tail hanging slack and the bitch pair running in his tracks. When the wolves were directly above them, the stags moved sideways round to front them, with antlers still at the present. When the pack padded downhill on a slant to come behind them, filling the air with wolf scent, they threw up their heads and ran downstream, not in panic flight but at an easy canter, and not stopping until they reached its junction with the Dee. They had the wind behind them now and knew, without looking back, that the wolves were not following. And likely they knew that they would not be hunted again, for they soon kneed down and settled to chew cud. The pack watched the shadowy shapes until they were out of sight, then turned about and trotted upstream.

At the head of the glen Alba turned south, and after some whimpering and tail-wagging her pack mates fell in behind her. They rested on a cliff four miles from the Eidart, licking flanks and vents, or squatting with forepaws forward and tongues flacking with no drip of sweat. The sun came up like a dying ember in purple smoke, and the moon was gilded at its setting. Soon the day birds were calling: mountain blackbird and wheatear, golden plover and pipit, and in the sky the mewing of buzzards and the croaking of ravens. Deer were moving between the cliff and Beinn Bhrotain, beyond the limited vision of the wolves, and on the wrong side of the wind to be owned by their acute noses. A dog stoat, big of his kind, with rump fur erect and a nose like a ripe elderberry, appeared from the rocks and sat tall to wrinkle his nostrils at the taint of wolves he couldn't see until Alba rose, shook the dew from the flat summer fur of her belly, and yawned. He saw that and whisked away like a leaf in a gale.

Alba soon found a way from the cliff and led the band to the western slopes of Beinn Bhrotain, five miles from the Eidart, where mountain hares were swarming at one of their peaks, more than half of them yearlings and spring or summer leverets of the year, and all of them heavy with health and good living. Two thousand acres of the slopes had recently been fired, leaving the scattered trees brittle, carbon skeletons; but the firing had left the grass green and the heather patches leafy, and in the heather grouse were calling.

The nearest hares showed little concern when they saw the wolf trio, and reacted slowly, some sitting tall, some crouching, and some ambling away; but when Alba leaped to the attack there was upheaval and panic flight, spreading over five hundred acres when Saighdear and Dileas joined in. Then, when it became obvious that each wolf was chasing a chosen hare and ignoring all the others, as a stoat does with a rabbit, the commotion subsided, and the unchased settled again to graze, or sit, or stand tall to watch. Six stoats of the year and their dam were also hunting hares, but the wolves ignored them.

Each chosen hare wanted to go uphill, and uphill it went, and only Alba succeeded in turning hers and forcing it into a downhill run, which handicaps any hare, mountain or brown. She closed with it in mighty bounds, rolled it over, and killed it against a boulder, where she stood to tear it apart, and squatted to crunch bones and bolt it down to the whiskers. Saighdear and Dileas had to run their quarry to the top of the first ridge, where they killed after much jinking and changes of direction. Like Alba, they ate the prey where they had killed it.

For an hour afterwards they hunted hares, from the smallest leverets to the heaviest does, catching them on foot or running them to ground and killing them there, working over two thousand acres, coursing singly or in couple, always trying to force the quarry into a downhill run, not losing pace despite the prey already in their bellies, and caching what they killed until the hunt was over. Then they padded from cache to cache, gorging, followed by grey crows looking for leavings; and leavings there were, for the wolf, like any other predator, can be choosy in face of plenty, discarding morsels it would clean up in face of commanding hunger.

When the trio joined up, with flanks bulging and tongues dripping, Alba and Dileas pressed excitedly against Saighdear, licking his raised muzzle and sweeping the ground with their tails. Among them they had over fifty pounds of meat in their stomachs. Although they had put twenty-two miles behind them in twelve hours, with an hour of strenuous coursing at the end, they could have covered the same distance again, despite the loads they were carrying. The trysting place with the pups was barely six miles away. But Alba chose to rest, perhaps because of the hot sun burning her fur, perhaps because she felt exposed in the wide open, although she had seen no sign of men since the run from the Geldie. The pups would be hungry, but they could wait a few hours longer.

So she led the pair along the slope of Beinn Bhrotain to a mossy place in a small corrie where a trickle of water was the beginning of a burn, and the three threw themselves down in the moist coolth, groaned in a kind of ecstasy of meat-sate, stopped

106

panting, sighed, and fell asleep. They lay on their sides, with legs outstretched, motionless except for the heave of their breathing, or the twitch of an ear or wrinkle of a nostril against a prospecting fly. A family flight of six ravens saw them as they were passing overhead, and one bird turned back and pitched on a rock to say so. The say-so cocked three pairs of unsleeping wolf ears to listen, but only Saighdear opened an eye. He could neither see nor smell the sayer, but could recognize and place him with his ears.

The raven was an earock, a young bird with the active curiosity that leads to greater wisdom or death, and Saighdear was a wolf who had helped many lesser crows to both since he was a yearling. The earock made several low flights round the corrie, and while he was flying Saighdear moved to the belly position with forepaws forward and hind legs gathered under him. When the bird came down to strut and swagger near the sleeping wolves, Saighdear watched him through slitted eyes, waiting patiently, cat-like, for the rash moment of over-confidence. The rash moment came when the raven turned his back at twelve feet. With a mighty thrust of his hindfeet Saighdear leaped, taking the bird in the air, and it died croaking in his jaws without knowing what had happened. Alba and Dileas leaped to their feet and rushed at Saighdear, snapping for a grip on the wildly flapping dead thing he was holding aloft in his jaws. Although he had his eyes closed against the sting of wings and the spasmodic clutch of claws, he knew they were there and growled them off. When the flap and clutch were over he lay down, tore wings and body feathers from his capture, and ate the body except the head and feet.

The sun was halfway between its height and its setting before Alba left the corrie, which was now in shadow, but instead of running in direct line to the tryst she led the way at an easy lope to the Eidart and followed it upstream to a small side pool where the three stopped to drink. They were now four miles from the tryst. Legged frog tadpoles were wiggling in the pool, prodding at the bottom and making mouth bubbles on the surface. Alba pawed at them playfully and speculatively, seeing them only in movement, then turned away and sat down to howl, with mouth open and muzzle pointing to the sky. Dileas, then Saighdear, joined in, and they sang in chorus for a minute, before Alba turned away and led the way home.

Luath and Geal had heard the singing and were expecting them. Instead of waiting patiently for them to come on, they left the tryst and rushed in gawky gambol down to the river fork to meet them, greeting them with much stern wagging and fuss, and licking muzzles and teeth, begging for bocks. All three wolves disgorged for them, and stood by with tongues a-loll watching, not impassively, but with near-smiles of pleasure, while they gulped and half-strangled bolting down the already much pre-digested meat. When they were replete, with even their elastic stomachs bulging, they trotted back to the tryst among the rocks, leaving two untouched bocks in the open. Saighdear threw down a few yards uphill from the bocks, on a brown and grey rock spur from which he had a clear view down the Eidart. Alba and Dileas moved into the shade of boulders above the sleeping pups.

Saighdear, with chin on forepaws, dozed in the sun, which was now throwing long shadows across the low ground. He slept in short naps, with ears and nose unsleeping, waking four times within the hour to rise, stretch, yawn and stare down the Eidart. How far he could see, or how critical or selective his seeing, only a wolf can know, but likely he had not the shrewd, kenning eyes of the red deer, and certainly not the sharp-edged vision of the eagle or falcons. But he had the ears of an owl and the nose of a fox, high-tuned to nuances, hearing the distant and smelling the stealthy, forming clear pictures in his brain, even when his eyes were closed and himself asleep. So he heard the flight of ravens before he opened his eyes, and when they came down as indistinct blurs they were ravens clear as life in his head. He knew what they were and where they were before he set eyes on them. When they were there, five of them, swaggering about twelve feet below the bocks, he watched them with ears pricked and chin on forepaws, alert but not hostile. Or friendly. He could take ravens or leave them: crows too for that matter. He could kill them or be tolerant of them, as he had shown on Beinn a Ghlo in the spring and on Beinn Bhrotain that morning.

There were three young ravens and two adults, and almost certainly there had been a sixth – the earock he had killed that day and which was now in the stomachs of the pups. The birds clearly wanted to feed from the bocks, but they were dubious about the big wolf staring at them from twenty-five feet away. They had never seen a wolf until that day, but they were ready to play the age-old game of camp follower and scavenger. They had him in sharp focus. What their eyes could not tell them was whether he was in hostile or tolerant mood, or if he was in any mood at all. But they were determined to test him, as he tested deer.

The adults were robust birds in sheened black and purple, bearded like capercaillies, with years of wisdom in their heads: they had played camp followers to foxes, and tormented them, as well as scavenging after men, since before Saighdear was born. While the earocks flapped and skipped at their backs, stabbing at the ground with their beaks, the adults came on with hen-toed swagger, not directly but slantingly, poised for the turnaway if Saighdear attacked. His say-nothing eyes were saying nothing, and they were not at once reassured by his relaxed display of indifference. They turned away, retreated, pecked tauntingly at the ground, then came on and retreated again. At their third approach Saighdear closed his eyes and they took their first peck at a bock, snatching a beakful and whisking away to swallow it. They came on a fourth time, and a fifth, pecking a beakful and skipping away to swallow it, while Saighdear watched them through slitted eyes. And soon all five were hen-toeing forward, snatching a beakful and retreating, never once standing to swallow beside the bocks. Saighdear became bored and fell asleep, ignoring them while they stuffed their craws and pouched what they could carry away. When they left he rose, yawned, and went to sleep again between the bocks.

At sunset, when the river pools were plated with fire, Saighdear left his seat and roused Alba and Dileas at the tryst. The pups joined them, and after they had licked the faces of the three with great display of affection, the five sang in chorus, starting the ravens croaking in the cliff below the river fork and grey crows *yarring* in query from waterside trees. When the pack left the tryst on their night hunt, the pups trotted down to the bocks and cleared them, leaving not a morsel for the ravens in the morning.

9

For a fortnight Alba kept the pups at the Eidart tryst. Although there was little tree cover, except along the river banks far below, the rocks hid the pups by day and the pack hunted only at night. She knew there was forest cover east and west of her, in Mar and Feshie, but had no urge to move to either. She was remembering how dangerous a forest could be, with the axes ringing and the woodmen's brush fires rising like incense, and not forgetting the run from Mar after the killing of the stirk.

South of her were five hundred square miles of mountainous wilderness, with scattered trees and wooded glens remaining, where men were to be seen only rarely in summer and not at all in winter, and in that trackless vast there were deer to be hunted, and goats and hares, and sometimes a hairy razor-backed pig, and sometimes a bit of young carrion to be found by following the flighting of the scavenging birds, just as the ravens sometimes followed the pack. And there was smaller prey, like mice and voles, and even frogs, not to be sniffed over and rejected by any wolf with an empty niche still left in its belly. She was a forest wolf longing for trees, but she was also a frightened wolf longing for an absence of men.

The pups had to be left somewhere, and the Eidart was as safe a place as any, until they had all their adult teeth and were fit to run with the pack, and that day was still some way off. Likely she would have kept them there, or somewhere near it, for more than the fortnight; but on the morning of the first day of August she walked into history ...

In the grey-dark of the early morning the pack had hunted hares on Beinn Bhrotain's eastern slopes, and when the sunrise

110

came sunless, with the ground mist like a glacier along the course of the Dee, they were lying on a spur above the river, lazing and digesting, in no hurry to return to the tryst because the pups had gorged on most of the rump of a knobber the night before and were left with the hindlegs to chew on.

They dozed while the sun blazoned in the mist, blinding with its glare, and the ringlets frayed like wool, and wisped, and dispersed, from the dark-veined crown of Creagan nan Gabhar across the river. The sky cleared. Four buzzards drifted into the overhead blue and the wolves, lying on their sides, could hear the cat-calls of them as they glided and soared. Goosanders flighted down the Dee, breasting pools rippled by sun-fishing trout and salmon. It would be another day of furnace heat, and lazy butterflies, twittering twites and pipits, golden plovers whistling, buzzing flies, stags in velvet bouraching on knolls in a micro-forest of their own antlers, fat bees drunk with nectar in the heather, and nothing left for a wolf to do except sleep until darkening. Saighdear was rolling over to offer his other flank to the sun when all three were brought suddenly wideawake by a single gunshot and a wild stampede of six stags heading for the spur on which they were lying.

The hindmost stag, a big eight-pointer, well fleshed and rounded with good living, was hirpling behind the others flapping a shattered hindleg. Incredibly, the .753 musket ball, fired from a weapon that was useless at more than three hundred paces, had hit him on the leg at a range of eighty yards, breaking the bones above the hock. The stags veered away from the wolves as nine men appeared on a knoll below, gesticulating and shouting, but they made no attempt to follow up the wounded one, who was running only a little way behind his fellows. Perhaps they knew that a three-legged stag, unless he is bleeding to death, can outrun any man.

Presently the men disappeared below the knoll, where they had been bivouacked all night, out of sight, scent and hearing of the pack, without camp fire, and making no noise, for they were a scouting party seeking out Highlanders carrying arms without licence from Marshal Wade, or unauthorized gatherings plotting against King George in the guise of a hunting *tainchel*. They were in red coats, wearing white gaiters halfway up their thighs, and carried Brown Bess muskets, ammunition pouches

111

and bayonets of fluted steel. That they were Hanoverian mercenaries of the army of occupation, hunting men, not wolves, was something Alba could not know. They were men, and that was all she needed to know.

The wolf is a simple creature, respecting the frontier signs and boundaries of other wolves, avoiding conflict with neighbours, averse to fighting, devoted to its young, and loyal to the death to pack and kin. Always in awe of the human animal, it has no way of understanding him – his wars, genocide and murders, his desertion of family and young, his cruelty, his killings in the name of religion or what he calls political necessity. Alba reacted to the Hanoverian presence in the only way she knew: she fled from the spur and loped homewards round the middle height of Beinn Bhrotain, with Dileas in her tracks and Saighdear bringing up the rear, his hackles raised and his tail hoisted. There was a great and growing fear in them, greater than their age-old awe of men, perhaps because they had slept while the arch enemy was so near.

They covered the fifteen miles to the tryst in under two hours, their pace betraying their fear, and were greeted joyfully by the pups, who begged for food although their ribs were still taut with feasting. Dutifully, the three bocked up part of their stomach contents for them, and the pups bolted the bocks, grimacing and choking until filled to repletion. Now they wanted to sleep, and they slept, and Alba knew they would not be fit to travel until nightfall. She was under stress, nervous and uneasy, keyed up to run, knowing the fugitive days were back again, and maybe even realizing they would never be over. In the place in her head the picture was forming of where she wanted to go, and it was fifteen miles away by the direct flight of a crow, and closer to twenty over the contours the pack would have to travel.

The hot day cooled as clouds came over in the late afternoon, and before darkening rain began to fall in a steady drizzle, purring like a cat where the wolves slept, soaking their fur, and sending the water singing again in the runnels. The pack would not have hunted in such rain, but Alba was prepared to travel through it. She let the pups sleep until long after dark, then rose and trotted from the tryst, with Luath and Geal at her flanks, Dileas behind her, and Saighdear, still hackled up, at the rear.

She knew where she was going, and perhaps Saighdear and

Dileas knew it too, for the wolf, like its descendant the dog, can hear sounds of frequencies inaudible to the human ear. If it can hear such sounds it might well be able to say them, so maybe members of a pack can communicate with each other in this way. Pack members have to be able to communicate with each other in some way other than howling; otherwise a pack attack on a big prey would be an unorganized rabble of individuals, which it is not.

The picture Alba had formed in her head-place was of An Sgarsoch, and likely Saighdear and Dileas knew it, for they followed her without question down to the Eidart and along its east bank at a steady six miles an hour – the pace a wolf pack can hold hour after hour without tiring. But Alba had to think of the pups, growing in stamina and strength but still a long way from peak, and after eight miles she called a halt beside a tributary burn of the Eidart to let them rest. The rain was still drizzling down, wavering now and again in stray flaffs of wind, and the wolves' fur was dark with wet.

The pups rested by the riverside, under dripping alders, while Saighdear and Alba padded away on a short foray up the tributary burn, and whatever gods watch over the destiny of wolves must have been overseeing that night, for within minutes their noses were thrilling to the hot scent of deer. And not just any deer. They were the six stags roused on Beinn Bhrotain that morning by the redcoats, and still with them was the beast with the broken leg, which was now an acute anguish, hard and swollen, making it difficult for him to lie down, or rise.

He was down when the wolf pair began their stalk into the group. When his fellows broke away at the sight of the onrushing wolves he was floundering, trying to rise, and before he could struggle to his feet Alba and Saighdear were upon him, reaching for him with their massive teeth. Saighdear leaped on to his rump and took hold, locking his teeth while Alba closed hers on his neck, ignoring the back-rake of his velveted antlers, which could do her little harm. The stag was a bit of time a-dying, because two wolves can't perform the massive surgery of four or more, and his pelvis was exposed before Alba broke his neck. The pair tore steaks from the body and gulped them down, before returning to Dileas and the pups. After five voices had howled in chorus by the river, the pack trotted upstream to the

113

kill, which was a godsend to beasts who had not expected to hunt that night.

The eight-pointer was a heavy beast, nearly thrice the weight of Saighdear, and the five wolves fed on him to bursting point. The pups, with their upper tusks almost fully grown and their lower back teeth through, were able to chew off some of the meat for themselves, but they would have been all night eating without the generous bocks from the adults. Alba had to change her plans, because no wolf pack would leave such a kill unless under extreme pressure. They would stay with it until they had cleared it, bones and all. But in the meantime they had to find a place to lie up in during daylight.

As it happened the wounded stag had been lying in a saucer hollow, backed by a rock wall with rowans and ferns growing in the clefts. The hollow was sufficient to hide the wolves, and the lip would give a view down the Eidart. The pack curled up below the rock wall, unsheltered from the rain, and before daylight they fed on the carcass again, gorging as before.

They stayed with the kill for three days, at the end of which they had reduced it to antlered skull, pelvis and trotters; the rib cage and spine they had devoured completely. Each day the mountain scavengers came to visit: buzzards, ravens and crows, and once a fox which Saighdear coursed and almost caught before it went to ground under a rock slab where it was out of reach of everything except a man with a stick with a knife on the end of it. Saighdear tolerated the ravens – his ambivalence being in one of its spells of tolerance – but he killed a greyback crow on the first day, and another on the second, choosing the moment of their over-confidence and catching them in the air when they were just clear of the ground. When small birds came to peck on the bones he ignored them, and he was good-humouredly impressed by the antics of a pair of pygmy shrews wrinkling their trunk-snouts in his face, as though challenging him to mortal combat.

On the third night, in gusting, intermittent rain, with the moon appearing and disappearing above drifting clouds, Alba led the pack back to the Eidart, which she followed until it turned west to join the Feshie. There she left it and took the direct route to An Sgarsoch, passing within a mile of the place where Sgian had died. The darkness was greying to morning,

114

and the rain slackening, when she settled the pups in the old trysting place below the eagles' eyrie. They were tired, with their tongues flacking; but they were not worn out, and that was a sign of their growing strength. They found their old couches, from which they joined in the pack's morning chorus before falling asleep.

The sky at early light was harebell blue, and cloudless except for a tuft like bog cotton on Ben Dearg's summit. From Tarf to Tilt the mist was a snowfield, with the riverside trees drifted to their crowns. The sun came up in a blaze of gold, flashing spears of brilliance, and the heather ridges purpled in its glow. A wandering wind stirred the aspen leaves, and the wolves sought out sheltered places where they could lie and steam themselves dry in its warmth. Alba lay down near Saighdear, who curled up nose to flank and closed his eyes, while she crouched, chin on forepaws, staring into the south-west. Now that she was at An Sgarsoch she was fretting to be away again. Apart from one assault from the eagle, nothing had troubled her time there; but perhaps she was remembering that she had lost two pups and a pack mate to men and dogs not far from where she was lying. In her head-place she had no new pictures, but she was drawn to the south-west where Ben Dearg was still wearing its bog cotton tassel of cloud.

Three cuckoos flew low over the dozing wolves, who pricked their ears and opened their eyes to slits. The birds were adults, moving out to begin their migration to Africa or Arabia, leaving behind offspring they had never seen, to make their own way, unguided, later in the autumn. They were out in the deeper air, with eight hundred feet of space below them, flying in triangle, hawk-like, when the peregrine tiercel came down – down – down, in the grand stoop, streamlined, with the sun's gold on the blue and ermine of him – the king of all the falcons – and the leading bird was broken in an explosion of feathers. The falcon underflew the wreckage and caught it in his talons, then carried it to a rock where he stripped it of more feathers before tearing at the keel with his beak.

With the falcon down the watching wolves lost interest. They had seen the assault of wings as a blurred image, and it held no interest for them. The forest wolf, living in a diversified habitat with a variety of species, was a versatile hunter and an opportunist. It could also play pirate, like the bald eagle with the osprey or the skua with the gannet, when piracy was called for. In the falcon's strike there was nothing for them; so they had no interest. But when Fior-eun came over later in the morning, shadowed by one of her eaglets, she roused the pirates.

Down by the burn fork, hidden from the wolves by the contours, a parcel of hinds was moving, with big calves at foot. Fior-eun, coming round the middle height of An Sgarsoch, saw them and swung down below them to attack. Any one of the calves was a big prey for any eagle but Fior-eun, with two eaglets still learning their trade and dependent on her and Iolair, was prepared to go outside her normal prey range. When the hinds broke uphill they came in sight of the wolves, and Saighdear and Alba rose to their feet. Fior-eun struck at the biggest calf, which bawled in terror, throwing her about and trying to run; but she rode it into the ground, with talons locked fast and wings buffeting. The calf screamed in the grapple, unable to break her hold, while the parcel scattered except one hind grunting for her own, and at that moment Saighdear, Alba and Dileas leaped from their seats and charged downhill. Once more the gods of the wolf were looking after their own.

Whether Fior-eun killed the calf or not, she was going to lose it. When Saighdear rushed at her with teeth flashing she leaped away clumsily, with just enough lift to escape the snap of his jaws. His snap was a mere threat to drive her off, and maybe she knew it; he had too much respect for her feet to press her closer. He was a pirate robbing her, not a predator seeking her as prey. The calf was still alive, but mangled and bleeding, and Saighdear killed it quickly while Fior-eun circled above at kestrel-height, rocking on the air, glaring down at him with angry hazel eyes. When the three wolves were shearing flesh from the kill, and ripping out paunch and entrails, she made a mock swoop at them, with her feet down, threatening without intention to strike. But she was reluctant to leave, and presently pitched on a rock a little distance away to wait for them to go. Her eaglet, black-feathered, with white on rump and cinnamon crown, pitched on a knoll above her, and began to preen. When the wolves left, she glided down to the remains of the calf to peck over the bones, the mighty predator turned scavenger because of the piracy of a mightier. Her eaglet presently joined her, pecking perfunctorily and peeping in protest.

All three wolves bocked part of their stomach contents for the pups, then the five sang to the sky in chorus. At nightfall adults and pups visited the kill to clear up the bones, which the ravens and crows had picked almost clean during the day. In some way Alba must have conveyed to the others that she would not be returning to the An Sgarsoch tryst, and when she turned away to run south-west they fell into line and followed her. An hour later they were splashing across the Tarf and heading towards Ben Dearg by the light of a full moon – five wolves loping at six miles an hour with five shadows alongside and Alba leading. By midnight, with the cool wind full on their faces, they were across the head of Gleann Diridh, coming round to the south-west of Ben Dearg, with its wild screes and rocky fastnesses, where dwelt marten and wildcat, fox and mountain badger. And during the last hour of running, before Alba put the pups down in a rocky place like a fortress, the smell of deer was hardly ever out of their noses.

It was country any wolf might have dreamed of, for it was a sanctuary for deer and forbidden to men. Seven years before, in instructions to his forester, the Hanoverian Duke of Athole, brother of the attainted and exiled Jacobite Marquis of Tullibardine, had decreed:

> 'That no forester except himself upon any pretence what-so-ever kill deer beneath the water of Bruar within any of the bounds of Tarf without a written warrant signed by His Grace. That Ben Dearg, Glen Dearg be kept as a nursery for the deer and that no person enter the said nursery but when the said forester is present, and that he give due information to the Baillie of the Regality of Athole of any persons he shall find in the said nursery, or killing deer, that they may be prosecuted and punished in terms of the law.

Where men feared to go Alba and her band chose to enter, for the instructions of dukes, written or otherwise, do not apply to wolves. And as everyone knew, there were no wolves alive for instructions to apply to. But the pack was on dangerous ground, for down there in Blair, less than twenty miles away, the Hanoverian Duke had more than a hundred and twenty fencible men-servants, shepherds, tacksmen, websters and wadsetters – who might not fight for King George, but would certainly

117

muster for a wolf hunt, or a dog hunt for that matter, at His Grace's command. That is if there was a wolf or wolves to hunt. But who would believe that?

So, in that forbidden place, the pack could kill deer in safety, hunting at night and lying up by day, unless maybe the forester made a visit and found a half-eaten carcass or was guided to the remains of one by the scavenging birds. Then he would know that he was not looking for a poaching man, and think rather of poaching dogs, big dogs, hunting dogs, like the hounds at Blair. But the forester did not come, so his acumen was not put to the test.

For ten nights the pack hunted in and around the sanctuary, killing three calves and a hind, an injured staggie, a fox, and some hares. They tested eight parcels of big stags, now in hard antler, and ran them, but failed to bring down one: three wolves were too few to face beasts with such weaponry when they turned about ready to defend themselves. On the eleventh night Alba and Dileas trotted away due south from the tryst while Saighdear hunted out towards the Tarf. While he was hunting hares a few miles from the tryst, the bitch pair were approaching a wood within an hour's wolf lope from Blair, where there were more people than the pack had ever seen in their lives. They entered a small larch wood, planted only three years before, where voles were swarming, and hunted them as a fox does, rearing, pouncing, pinning down, snatching and swallowing – the first wolves to tread there since Lochiel killed his wolf in 1680, a few miles away down the Garry. And nobody knew they were there.

With a score of voles inside them they left the larch planting, seeking scent of bigger game in the woods stretching from there to the Garry. Here was no smell of brush fires, or charred trees, and no trees lying about or logs piled; for the Hanoverian Duke was a planting man, and new woods were there to be seen from the castle to the river and along its bank. And other things were going on down there too, like houses being built, and bits of road and bridges, and piggeries and stables, with places for fowls and geese and ducks – a fine place for settled people, but an unchancy one for prowling wolves, even at night when men were abed and dogs in their kennels. Wisely Alba and Dileas turned back, and after running a roe deer doe with twin fawns,

118

and killing one of the fawns in a pool, they headed north-west to return to the tryst by Glen Diridh. And at the head of Glen Diridh they made their mistake.

The morning was well on towards daylight, with scattered clouds and a spit of rain, and they were only a few miles from the tryst, when they winded kyloes – a few heifers and cows with some calves – and that brought them to the freeze, with their noses sifting the wind. This was farther out than poor people usually pushed their beasts, even in such fine weather, so maybe the rumours they were hearing were making pictures in their head-places, and they were making sure their precious kyloes were far from prying eyes. If armies were to be marching there would be requisitioning, which is a politeness for stealing, so the farther the kyloes were out on the hill the safer they would be. Then again maybe nobody was thinking anything of the kind, any more than they would be thinking of wolves. Yet there they were, a pair of wolves ready to kill, not knowing that the kyloes belonged to people whose livelihood depended on them.

The black shaggy kyloes, true descendants of the ancient Celtic shorthorn, still retained much of the wildness and courage of their ancestors, and when the wolf pair rushed, with tails up, to test them, the cows with calves refused to run, and faced them with heads down, brandishing their long horns that could have gored any wolf reckless enough to make a frontal attack. The wolves passed them by, their interest being in three heifers running, two with calves at foot. But the two with calves found their courage after a short run and turned about, with their calves against their flanks. The heifer without a calf kept running, and the wolves chose her because she was the one running away.

They pulled her down less than two hundred yards from the herd, Alba locking teeth forward of her rump as she fell while Dileas took her by the nose. The heifer struggled, lashing out with her feet, but could not rise, and because of the nose-grip she could not use her formidable horns. She had to die, and she died slowly, not because the wolves were inexpert, but because they were two. Had Saighdear been there, her anguish would have been shorter.

Two wolves, with no more than twenty voles and half a roe fawn inside them, have a lot of stomach room left for meat, and

119

each bolted about ten pounds of rump and loin, along with some entrails, before they left. They were at the tryst within an hour, bocking for the pups, who licked their muzzles and teeth in greeting. Saighdear had not yet returned. When he did arrive the pups were asleep and replete, and it was well on towards noon before they plagued him to bock for them, and what he put up was partly-digested hare, complete with fur.

The pack stayed at the tryst, sleeping their waking wolf sleep, or grooming their fur, or hunting for fleas, until the sun was westering, when Alba left to lead them to the kill, allowing the pups to follow because it was so close at hand and because she was feeling more at ease than she had felt since they were born. They filled themselves twice during the night, eating into the rib cage, stripping the leg muscles to knees and hocks, and biting up between the lower jaws to reach the tongue. Then, instead of returning to the tryst, or hunting further, they lay down among rocks uphill from the kill, and overlooking it, content to stay there until daylight and clear up the bones. Having the pups with them left them that freedom of choice.

At daylight they drove away two ravens from the kill and bellied down beside it. The birds rose with whicker of wings and circled overhead, *kronking* in protest, the kind of flight and vocal display that would have attracted any hill man within sight and hearing. Luath was halfway into the rib cage, with Geal trying to squeeze in beside him, when Alba rose, dropped the rib bone she had been cracking, and stood taut and trembling, staring to the south with ears pricked and nostrils sifting. She could see or hear nothing, not even the snort or tread of the kyloes, who had moved off the ridge during the night and were now more than a mile below. But she was uneasy with the old unease, vaguely sensing peril, yet unable to form a picture of it in her head-place.

Her unease was quickly felt by Saighdear and Dileas, who also stopped crunching bones to face the south. The wind from the south-west was telling them nothing, except that, far down, deer were moving. When Alba turned away, with tail down, to skulk back to the rocks where they had spent the night, pack mates and pups followed her without question. Crouched among the rocks, out of sight but with a view, they had not long to wait for the cause of Alba's anxiety to appear. Two women, with their long skirts kilted to make climbing easier, and three barefoot, plaided boys, with a cattle dog barking at their heels, appeared over the last rise between them and the wolves, and soon they were walking towards the remains of the heifer, guided by the ravens who had returned as soon as it was left unattended. The women and boys, out to tend the cattle, had missed the heifer at once. They had not passed it on the way up, and guessed it must be higher; and when they saw the ravens they began to fear the worst. They were shocked when they saw what was left of a fine beast fresh from the bull.

The women could not understand what had happened to the beast, but they knew at once that a lot of mouths had been eating from it. In all their lives they had never seen the like. Word had to be got home quickly, so while they walked back to tend the herd they sent two of the boys hurrying away on the long journey to the glen to tell the menfolk. The cattle tyke stayed with the women, but he was eager to be back where the heifer was, and in the end they let him go, knowing he would follow when he had found or lost what he was looking for, which would be a hare likely. He was a strong little dog, and wise, with great courage in him, and he knew there was something up in the rocks, something he had to look into. One cast round the remains of the heifer told his nose where the trails led, and he followed them unerringly to the rocks.

And that cost him his life ...

The pack was already on the move before he reached the rocks, and they would have kept moving, because Alba wanted away; but when he charged after them, barking, they turned about with their hackles on end and their tails in the air, stiff-legged, snarling and growling – a frightening sight for anything smaller than a wolfhound to face. Up to that moment the wolves' display was threat only, not an invitation to battle, and if the dog had turned back they would have let him go. Being the kind of dog he was he chose not to. Instead he rushed at Saighdear, perhaps because he was the biggest, and tried to close with him in a grapple; but when the big wolf slashed him, laying open almost half his face, he turned and fled, howling, realizing this was not the kind of dog he was used to. And Saighdear chose not to let him go. Alba joined him in the chase and they converged on him, like a brace of greyhounds with a

121

hare, and broke him up, and ate him, leaving only his skull for the ravens to pick over. Then they left at their travelling lope, direction west to the Bruar, then north …

It was five hours later before the menfolk arrived – Alan Roy Stewart, Ewen Murray, two other tacksmen neighbours, a shepherd and a sennachie from Dalnacardoch way, who was also a poet man, and a bearer of news about some strange goings-on over in Moidart. His news had been the sole subject of excited conversation until the boys arrived in the glen with the bad news about the heifer beast, which was Alan Roy Stewart's and a great loss, only to be made up to him by the others including his dead beast with the living, and sharing with him what they received from the drovers, for it could have been the beast of any one of them, so why should only one suffer all the loss? That was the way they were thinking, not saying so, and that was the way it would be.

'It's a great mystery,' said one of the tacksmen. 'The heifer killed and the dog missing. How long has the heifer been out?' he asked the wife of Alan Roy Stewart.

'Two days,' she said. 'I brought her straight from the bulling. Why?'

'Well, if she'd been dead a week the eagles, and foxes, and ravens might have cleaned her.'

Alan Roy Stewart was impatient with such an idea. 'All the eagles and foxes and ravens for miles around could never have cleaned her like that in the time,' he said. 'And look at those bones! No fox jaws cracked them for sure. And where is my dog?'

'Big dogs might have done it,' said Ewen Murray. 'Like hounds maybe?'

'Or wolves,' said the sennachie. 'I have been told there was killed here a wolf earlier this year.'

'That was a dog,' the shepherd told him. 'Its skin was examined by an expert. A big northern dog he said, for pulling sledges, and likely with wolf blood in it.'

'Wolf dogs then,' the sennachie smiled with a show of humility. 'Whelped by a hound bitch and sired by the wolf killed on the Slochd two years back. All I can say is that the heifer wasn't killed by the *uruisgean* (spectres) and it looks like wolf work to me.'

And the sennachie walked away, adding the heifer and the dog to his memory bank of the stories that are told.

10

That morning, while Alba was leading her pack north from the head of Glen Bruar, Prince Charles Edward Stuart arrived at Kinlochmoidart with a bodyguard of Clanranald Macdonalds. The London Government, like any Highlander with an ear to the wind, had known for a year about the rumours of another Stuart attempt to take Scotland, proclaim the Old Pretender as James VIII and III, and break the Union. What they did not know was where and when the attempt would be made, if at all. To be on the safe side they had an army of 3800 men in Scotland under the command of General John Cope. But Cope was still at Stirling – a long march away from Kinlochmoidart. So Charles could afford to wait for a few more days while the clans were arming and mustering. The date he fixed for the raising of the Stuart standard was 19 August, and the place Glenfinnan, at the head of Loch Shiel. In seven more days the Rising would begin. And in those days many were saying: '*Thaing mo righ air tir am Muideart* (My king has come to Moidart).'

Alba was resting the pups beside a lochan an hour's running time from the headwaters of Bruar, fifteen miles from the spot where she and Saighdear had eaten the dog, before Alan Roy Stewart and his companions arrived in Gleann Diridh to look at a dead heifer and seek a dog whose mysterious disappearance would be woven by the sennachies into the tapestry of folklore. She had kept the pack moving at a steady trot, over and round the contours, splashing across hill burns without slackening pace, ignoring ring-ouzels and pipits rising from her path, veering right or left every now and again to view her back trail without having to halt and face around. She was still expecting

124

pursuit by men and dogs, and her unease stayed with her until she reached the lochan – a crater of blue on a hill-top, mirroring only clouds and sky.

The pups waded into the shallows, lapping water: they were warmed up, with their tongues hot, but they were not worn out. After Saighdear and Alba had bocked dog for them they lay down to rest, but not to sleep, for they were kept awake by the cackle of laughter of four black-throated divers out in the middle of the lochan. Within an hour Alba had them on foot again, running north, with a squall of rain in their faces and the sun gleaming at their backs. They were on unknown ground, not waywise, running blind into space as they had so often done before, with Alba slowing the pace because she knew she was not being followed and the wind on her face was bringing no nuances of danger. Two hours later they were in a wooded glen west of the Feshie – twenty-four miles from their starting point by the way they had come and eighteen by the direct flight of a crow.

The wood was part of the ancient forest of pine, oak, birch and rowan. Here were old pines that had seen the dawn of the previous century, and young trees burgeoning in clearings where the old had been felled by storms. Alba led the pack through the wood, following a well-trodden trail used by roe deer and badgers, then uphill to a rocky clearing with young growth of rowan and birch, and seedling pines greenly alive on the exposed roots of the fallen. Below the clearing the ground fell away steeply, rock-strewn, to wet flats of bog myrtle, mossed scrub, sphagnum and bog asphodel. Alba bedded the pups below a great cleft rock with a crown of emerald green moss: in the cavity under the crown a pine marten had reared her family of three in the spring. The pups were now tired enough to want to sleep, and after brief play-grapple they stretched out on their sides, making no attempt to follow the adults when they padded away to explore the wood.

They quickly found the bitch pine marten, although they could not see her; there was the scent of her on the ground where she had been hunting, and the clear smell of her on a pine trunk where she had rubbed with her belly gland. So they knew she was up there, without having to see her; and she knew they were below because she was looking down at them. Having no interest in her the pack padded on, with ears pricked, nostrils sifting and eyes alert for movement. They could hear crossbills in the branches overhead and see the movements of crested tits flitting from tree trunk to mossed, broken stump. Their acute ears registered the scurrying of voles among the blaeberries, but they were not diverted to vole hunting. When a blackcock came hurtling through the trees in down-curved, headlong flight, with a goshawk in close pursuit, they ducked and froze momentarily, with ears flattened, startled by the suddenness of it. They were at the far end of the wood, beside a burn flowing through to join a lochan half a mile below, when they heard the barking and stopped, alert, trembling with excitement and with ears harking to place distance and direction.

Bough! Bough!

The barking was gruff and powerful. No dog bark this, or fox yap, but the chesty bass of a full roebuck, with the fires stoked for the rut, and challenging. And the wolves knew what he was; the boughing was transmitting clear pictures to their head-places. The buck was across the wind, thrashing in a juniper thicket, ripping the foliage and scenting it from the gland between his antlers: the master marking his frontiers. He was five years old, with the spring in his knees and the glitter of battle in his eyes. Of course the wolves could not know all these things about him: all they knew was that out there was a roebuck thrashing in a juniper thicket, although likely they would not even know it was a juniper thicket he was thrashing in.

Before they made a move against him all three knew just exactly what they were going to do. Moving to the downwind side of him and stalking from there would drive him into the wood the moment he saw them coming, and in the wood was where they did not want him. They wanted him out of it, to run him in the open. So they worked round the upwind side of him to let his nose know they were there, and the moment he knew, he broke away downhill into the open, with the pack following close behind, Dileas tailing him while Saighdear and Alba ran wide to flank him. They were making a triangular attack, base first, threatening to envelop him, and forcing him to go one way, the way they wanted – forward. And because he was being forced to run the burnside, with a wolf behind and one on each bank, the way forward was into the lochan. And that was where they forced him to go.

When he reached the water's edge he was blowing hard, with flanks heaving and tongue showing from the side of his mouth, and the hot smell of him filled the noses of the wolves. His heart was pounding, and the fear in him; but so was the fire, and he faced them with antlers at the present – a tiring roebuck on a scliff of beachhead hemmed in by wolves. He was an easy prey for three big wolves – from the back; but not so easy from the front, with his ivory dirks presented low and level, ready to strike upwards with eviscerating power. He tried a jink to the right, and was turned by Alba: he tried to the left, and there was the giant Saighdear, staring at him with patient, inscrutable eyes. And there was Dileas, barring the direct route out. So he chose the water. If he could not out-run them he would out-swim them.

He plunged into the water, high-stepped until he was out of his depth, then began swimming for the opposite shore, with only his head showing. Alba leaped in after him, but turned back after only a few yards of dog-paddling to see Saighdear and Dileas galloping round the head of the lochan to intercept him when he came out at the other side. But when he arrived, snorting bubbles, and saw them there, he stopped where the water was belly deep and stood watching them, breathing hard and almost afloat. Saighdear plunged in to swim to him, forcing him to turn back into deeper water and strike out for the shore he had just left. There Alba was waiting for him, and she herded him into the shallows until Saighdear and Dileas arrived to force him out of his depth again. The wolves were not going to out-swim him; they were going to run the shore, dry-foot, until he drowned or left the water.

He was a strong buck, but he was tiring. If he had stood in the water, belly deep and not moving, the wolves might have given up; instead he went swimming again each time they threatened him, which was exactly what they wanted him to do. In the end he came ashore to his scliff of beachhead to find the trio facing him again, and this time he tried to break out. He charged at Dileas, who was again in the centre, with his weight forward, his knees buckled and his deadly antler dirks at the low present. The

127

attack took her completely by surprise, and he knocked her over, ripping open the side of her mouth below the left ear – a wound she would remember for many a day. But that was his last show of fight, and when he was clear of her, after inflicting on her the final indignity of a kick on the head, the fire was dead in him and the devil departed. Saighdear and Alba pulled him down, opening his groin and tearing out his throat, and he died at the age of five so that two wolf pups might have a few more days of life. Death for a little life is all they know on earth and all they need to know. Only the human animal kills more for less.

After the killing of the roebuck the pack found no more deer in the wood, which was good cover for wolves to hide in but too small to hold enough prey animals for them to hunt. So they turned once more to hares, ranging east and west for many miles, hunting by day and returning to the tryst after nightfall. They also hunted red deer. But the red deer were living high, on windy ridges and knolls out of reach of biting flies. Such places also gave them a commanding view, so that they could be away before the pack came close enough to think about testing them.

In six days they put on foot four small groups, two of hinds and two of stags, and hunted them; but the beasts were strong, and they broke off the chase after an uphill run of half a mile. On the seventh day, at first light, on the edge of a strip of the old forest near the Feshie, they stalked into a group of three hinds, two calves and a knobber at a peaty wallow among the bog myrtle and scrub birch, and took them by surprise. There were two hinds and a calf in the wallow when the pack broke cover, and they lost time struggling to their feet and sprackling clear when the lead hind grunted her warning before bolting with the others. They were twenty yards behind her when the wolves flattened into their run, with Saighdear within a few bounds of the yeld hind. The pack ran them for nearly a mile, into the wood and out again, right down to the Feshie and along its bank, and they were on the point of breaking off, with Dileas already slowing, when they found the weakling. On the Feshie bank the yeld hind began to flag and fall back, and the wolves read the signs. She turned away on the short downhill run to the river, perhaps hoping to find refuge there, but she stumbled and collapsed, and the three were immediately on top of her – Alba at her exposed flank, Saighdear at her rump, and Dileas holding her by the nose. The leading hind and her followers stopped two hundred yards away, looking back with ears up and nostrils flared; but within minutes they put their heads down and began to graze, knowing they were safe for the time.

The trio soon had the body of the hind opened up, with paunch and entrails spilled, and great steaks shorn from the rump. Dileas was still stiff about the left side of her mouth, and yelped in self-inflicted pain when she closed her teeth too savagely or pulled too hard on unyielding sinews. The wolf-followers soon arrived to watch and wait – ravens, grey crows and a pair of buzzards, and presently the lordly one himself, the eagle of the place, to pitch on a knuckle of rock and stare at the gathering with fierce jewel eyes. The pack spent an hour at the carcass, stripping it quickly of all the easy meat and scraping every morsel they could from the haunch, back, shoulders and legs. Pickings there would be for the followers, but pickings only, apart from the paunch and entrails, which the wolves hardly touched.

The kill was ten miles from the trysting place and the pack was home within two hours, bocking loads of meat for the pups, after which all sat to sing morning chorus before seeking out shady places to sleep in, with their muzzles buried to the eyes in tussocks of damp sphagnum to escape the assault of biting flies. Although their ears were full of fly-buzz they heard the rush of wings when the eagle came down to pitch on a rock near where Luath and Geal were sleeping.

The bird was an eaglet of the year, down to pant and rest after missing with three strikes at grouse and two at hares. The wolves stared a her for a few moments because she was there to be stared at, and went back to sleep. Then, suddenly, they were brought to their feet, wideawake, by the arrival of another eagle and the far-off bellowing of a kyloe.

This time the eagle was the mighty one herself, the mother Fior-eun, with golden crown, come to drop a haunch of hare to her hungry eaglet, for likely she would be knowing about the hares missed and the grouse not taken. The haunch almost dropped on Luath, who leaped away in fright. Startled, the rest of the pack also drew back, while the eaglet swept down from the rock and ran legged-up and flat-footed, with wings upheld and down-curved, like a crab in haste, to clutch on the haunch and fly with it to another boulder. Only Luath and Geal gave chase, and they stayed with her, pawing at the boulder and trying to jump at her, until she had eaten what she wanted of the hare and flown away with the skin and bones in her talons.

Alba and Saighdear were more concerned about the bellowing of the kyloe, which was closer than the distance from which a wolf howl could be heard by another wolf, so they padded away from the tryst to reconnoitre, leaving Dileas with the pups. Three miles out they were on a spur, looking down on the wooded banks of the Feshie and seeing movement among the trees – two women and three children driving two kyloes with calves at foot, pushing them out far beyond the shieling, putting them out of reach in case the redcoats came plundering, as they likely would if the rumours from Moidart way turned out to be true. The sight of the kyloes kindled no hunting urge in either wolf and, if it had, the presence of the women and children would have put them off. Neither the women nor the children had heard the pack's morning chorus; if they had heard it they might have wondered about it, but it would not have turned them back. Their coming had the opposite effect on the wolves, who turned away at the sight of them, avoiding the skyline and returned to the tryst at speed. The pups were asleep, and Dileas dozing, but Alba quickly had them all on foot, and in line, and led them from the clearing, direction south-west . . .

Perhaps she chose to run south-west because that way she had the wind in her face, for she was probing again, into the unknown, seeking wilderness spaces where men were not, or gaps in their frontier where the pack could infiltrate. In two hours she had put twelve miles behind her, with the pups standing up to the pace and showing no signs of tiring. In a few more weeks they would be ready to run with the pack, adding to its hunting strength and its freedom of movement because it would no longer be tied to trysting places. Their lower tusks were now erupting, and not until they had their full armoury of teeth would a pack of three wolves with two dependent wolflings become a pack of five capable of pulling down even a kyloe bull.

Alba halted in the forest of Gaick, beside a waterfall above a lochan which was a meeting place of many hill burns. All of them lapped from the clear, chill pool below the fall, then lay down to rest. There would be no more travelling that day; nor hunting. They had put safe miles between themselves and the women, and from now on they would travel at night. Saighdear moved up above the waterfall and bellied down with chin on forepaws beside a pebbly pool. When a dipper alighted on a stone near the pool he opened his eyes and watched it until it dived out of sight to hunt the bottom; when it bobbed to the surface again like a cork he opened them wider; but when it dived a second time he lost interest in it and fell asleep. And below him the rest of the pack slept their waking wolf sleep until the sun went down in plaid of crimson and gold barred with clouds of indigo. Then Alba rose, yawned and whimpered, and Saighdear came down from the waterfall seat to join her. Pups and bitches licked his muzzle in greeting, and the five sang their quavering, haunting vesper to the starless sky and dying afterglow. When Alba trotted away the pups followed her, wagging their tails in great excitement, seemingly knowing that they were not to be left behind.

This time Alba did not run them hard. For two hours she walk-trotted the pack until a lop-sided moon rose in a cocoon of gossamer clouds, bathing the wilderness of mountains and glens in soft tranquil light; then she let the pups lie down to rest. The moon was clear of its cocoon, gleaming with cold brilliance in the dark vault of the sky, when she roused them all on foot again, and for the rest of the night they travelled by its unclouded light. But she kept the pace well below normal wolf-time, and the sun was up, and the moon near its setting, before they were across Dalnacardoch, high above Glen Garry – twenty-seven miles from their starting point of the night before, and the pups still fit to run. The morning was bright, with white cloud puffs drifting overhead and the grey threat of rain to the west. In Glen Garry the mists were crawling, with updrifts like pink smoke in the sun. The wolves found a flat rock like a cromlech and bellied down on it to stare across the glen, and when the mists lifted they were looking down on the stark bleakness of Drumochter Pass.

Down there along the Garry ran the road from Inverness to Dunkeld, built by the English General Wade, now a Field-Marshal in the Hanoverian army and Governor of the three forts of William, Augustus and George. He had spent fourteen years making his road through Badenoch and Lochaber to the

Great Glen, and along it to link the forts. He had also built one over the Corrieyairack Pass, linking Fort Augustus with Dalwhinnie on the road south from Inverness. They were military roads, for the easier passage of soldiers and ordnance, for Wade was only too well aware that no Hanoverian army could match the Highlandmen for speed and stamina in the wild glens and mountains where the only tracks were trodden either by human feet or the hooves of cattle on their way to the Crieff or Falkirk markets. General Hugh Mackay had learned all that to his cost when he met Claverhouse at Killiecrankie. Wade had the answer in a word – roads. But besides being a dedicated road-builder, he was also a dedicated Highlandman-tamer, so he formed Gaelic-speaking Highland companies with Gaelic-speaking officers to disarm and oversee the clansmen, who at once dubbed them the Black Watch because of their dark neutral tartan and trusted them not at all.

There was nothing moving on Wade's Glen Garry road that quiet morning, and the wolf pack slept on the cromlech rock until noon, when the sun was a pale gleam in an overcast sky and the Drumochter eagles were flying. Saighdear rose, pointed his nose to the sky, and howled, and the others joined him at once. Seconds after the session was over the adult wolves froze, with ears pricked and tails level. Far away, they could hear the lowing of cattle, the barking of dogs and the voices of men, and the sounds made instant pictures in their head-places. Alba turned away with the pups, but when Saighdear bellied down on the rock beside Dileas, she came back and lay down beside them – waiting.

An hour later the leading beasts of the kyloe herd appeared in view, walking in lines, in pairs and threes, lolloping, bunching, mounting, and engaging in head-to-head combat – a hundred or more of them fresh from the hill, flanked by tough cattle tykes and followed by five men, two of them in Highland garb and all carrying sticks. The drovers were pressing the herd hard, knowing that the rumours they had been hearing for weeks had become reality and that Prince Charles Edward – *Phrionnsa Tearlach* – was somewhere in Moidart trying to raise an army. What they did not know was that he was on his second day at Glenfinnan, with the Standard already raised by the Marquis of Tullibardine and the great war pipes sounding, and Lochiel and

132

his Camerons there, and the Macdonalds of Clanranald, and old Gordon of Glenbucket, and Macdonnel of Keppoch with seventy Hanoverian soldiers taken prisoner near Fort William three days before the Rising was to begin, and all the clansmen throwing their bonnets in the air and shouting: 'Scotland and no Union!'

The drovers had bought their beasts early in the season because of the rumours, and were roaded early because of the realities. Although they knew the Prince's army could not catch up with them, whichever way it came, they could not be sure about going on through Athole where the Duke was a king's man but most of his fencible men were not. So they wanted out of Glen Garry and on to Wade's road from Dalnacardoch to Trinafour and Rannoch, thence over Schiehallion and on to Aberfeldy and Crieff.

Herd and drovers disappeared from view and the pack lay on until they were out of hearing. Then they turned north, letting the pups run with them, and in the course of the afternoon killed a wild-cat and a nanny goat with her kid. They also tested two groups of stags. The first group of five – four in hard antler and one with tatters of velvet still clinging – refused to run. The wolves circled them at a distance of twenty-five yards, sat down with tongues out as though discussing what to do, then circled them again. But they were not to be stampeded. One beast broke from the second group of three and ran, but when he realized that the others were not following he came bounding back on a wide curve to rejoin them, after the wolves were in their stride. Saighdear veered away to intercept him, came in on him behind his left flank, and leaped at him, reaching for his groin; but his snap failed to grip and he was knocked over, winded but unhurt. The running stag set the others moving, and the three bounded away in the opposite direction. The wolves did not follow. They turned back south to the cromlech rock to lie up for the rest of the daylight. And there, in the gathering dusk, came faintly to their ears again the lowing of cattle, the yapping of small dogs, and the voices of men calling to each other in the Scots and Gaelic tongues.

The pack waited until after dark, a black darkness and moonless, but no cattle came through the Pass: the drovers had let them settle for the night after the hard drive from

Dalwhinnie. They had brought them over the Corrieyairack on the advice of the military at Fort Augustus, because the Prince's army might be blocking the road to the south. There were six score beasts in the herd – from Stratherrick on the east side of Loch Ness and the glens on the west – made up of small parcels of three or four or five, each one knowing the others in its own but strangers to all the rest until they were gathered for the drive. They were grazing along the river bank, strung out in their small parcels, upstream and down from where the drovers had their camp fire of heather and dead sticks of birch and alder, when the wolf pack filed along the mountainside high above them, with Saighdear leading. With men so near, Alba would have been away, but she was being outwilled by Saighdear – always the ranking wolf until he chose to let her run point – who was making pictures of kyloes in his head-place and knew exactly what he was going to do.

The wind was south-westerly. Rifts were appearing in the dark cloud ceiling, with a half-moon beaming intermittently in the clearways. The pack waited on while the clearways opened into vaults of sky, unveiling it for longer and longer periods: the hunting wolf prefers moonlight to darkness. Saighdear led the way up the Pass, holding to the high ground until he had headed the tail of the herd. Then he took them down on a long slant, at a skulking walk, warily, with his nose feeling the wind to place the distance and direction of man-smell.

The drovers had pressed the herd hard to keep it out of the reach of a Jacobite army that had not yet begun to march; now they had bedded it down under the noses of a wolf pack they did not know existed. Saighdear came upwind on to the herd, in line abreast with Alba and Dileas, with the pups padding behind on their first spectating foray. The first beasts were slow to move, likely because they were thinking the wolves were dog nuisances to be threatened and kicked. But when Alba and Saighdear pulled down a small stirk, its terrified bawling and struggling set the nearest beasts in motion. When Dileas, backed by Luath and Geal, cut out a calf, there was a turmoil of horns and hooves, one group setting the next on the move, until half the herd was stampeding in all directions, with dogs barking and men swearing, baffled and helpless because they could see nothing in the fitful moonlight except a tidal wave of black bodies.

134

Bellowing beasts plunged into the river and across and away into the night. Beasts were gored in the heaving, plunging mass; others fell and were trampled by oncoming hooves before struggling to their feet to limp or stagger away. One of the droving dogs was tossed and thrown and pounded into a dub of sphagnum. The remaining pair were down the glen trying to herd beasts spread out over miles of country south, east and west, and knew nothing of the wolves feasting in the Pass.

The wolves were taken aback at the way the cattle broke away, without cohesion or direction, and would have been in danger themselves if they had attacked the flank instead of the tail. As soon as they had the stirk and the calf down and dead, they began to eat while the stampede moved away. Luath was now able to tear off large pieces of meat, and managed to fill himself to half-capacity. Saighdear, Alba and Dileas gorged for five, but now there were only four. Geal was not there. Geal was dead. She had been thrown aside when Dileas and Luath pulled down the calf, and battered to broken death under the feet of three stirks running aimlessly, bawling in terror. Alba did not seek her, or look back when Saighdear trotted away, followed by Dileas and Luath. She fell in behind her last pup and followed in line.

All night the scattered beasts bellowed and lowed, and at the flush of dawn the wolves, led by Alba, added their chorus, and who is to say their morning song was not a coronach for a lost wolfling?

The drovers were too far down the glen, and on the wrong side of the wind, to hear the wolf pack's singing. They began to gather the cattle with the two remaining dogs, not knowing what had happened to the third. When they found a partly-eaten stirk and a partly-eaten calf, they blamed some roving hounds for the night's disaster. They found a heifer dead in the river, trampled and drowned after she had broken a leg. They found another two beasts so badly injured that they had to cut their throats and watch them gurgle and choke in their own blood. All the loss would be their own, for they had paid for every beast in the herd with good hard money. It was the middle of the day before they got the frightened, unsettled beasts moving again, and when they reached the first houses of thatch they let it be known that there was beef for the free-taking a few miles up the glen.

Late in the afternoon three men arrived with a pony and butchered first the two beasts whose throats had been cut; then they dragged the drowned heifer from the river, and although its lungs were full of water and it had not been bled they cut it up and loaded the pony to the limit. The rest of the meat, including tongues and hearts, they sacked to carry themselves. They missed the wolf-kills because they did not search far enough into the Pass. If they had found them, the wolves would have been left with the bones, for meat was precious to the tacksmen, and not to be wasted or left for the ravens and crows. Ox blood too was precious, and they thought no more about drawing some from a beast once in a while than they thought of milking a goat. When they left, with themselves and the pony loaded, they had more meat than their families had ever seen before, not to mention the bit they could sell for cash money.

The pack returned to the kills at darkening after a howling session, and filled themselves with meat. Then they lay up nearby until well into the next morning, when they feasted again by the light of a fat crescent moon. They stayed by the kills all day, Saighdear beside the calf and the others with the remains of the stirk. Saighdear had a mind to play the crow game, and when a pair of greybacks came down for a view he backed away a little from the calf to encourage them. They were encouraged, and presently they were swingle-swaggering up to the bait and skipping away again. Then they were making a snatch-peck and leaping away. Then they were putting a foot on it and taking two or three pecks. Then they were standing on the open rib cage, pecking between the bones. For Saighdear that was their moment of over-confidence and he sprang at them. But they were too quick for him. His jaws snapped on air and they were away, crow-swearing, without the loss of a feather. Later in the day he played the game with another pair, and won it. And that night he ate crow, after he had scraped the bones of the calf clean.

Next day the pack had to hunt again. They quartered the many square miles the herd had scattered over and found the bones, ripped paunches and torn entrails of the beasts the tackmen had butchered. There was hardly enough meat left on the bones to keep the crows interested; but there was more than enough for two pygmy shrews eating ravenously inside the rib

136

cage of the drowned heifer. The wolves drove off the crows and sniffed over the skeletons; then they tore bones from them and played with them, lifting them and tossing them, pouncing on them and growling over them, and chasing each other in rings and figures-of-eight, much to the alarm of the crows, who considered it was time to fly, and flew. The bone-game over, Saighdear led the pack to the river, and they splashed and swam across, leaving their wolf taint in the water to puzzle and perhaps frighten for a little while the salmon on the run-up to their spawning places in the chill, pure, limpid waters of the hill burns.

The pack hunted parcels of deer along the north side of Loch Garry without pressing them hard. One group of stags stopped after a quarter of a mile and stood on a knowe, with their ears up, looking back at four wolves sitting on a rock outcrop two hundred yards away, with their tongues hanging out at the side of their mouths as though deer were the last thing on their minds. They rested and panted through the humid heat of the afternoon until Alba rose and began to howl. That put them all on foot, and they howled in chorus. When Alba trotted away they followed her, with Dileas and Luath behind and Saighdear at her flank. Presently he moved to the lead, and they headed north for a few miles to the south slope of the Sow of Atholе, where they surprised a small herd of goats. Saighdear and Alba killed a nanny goat while an old billy, a hairy savage with a great sweep of horns, chased after Luath, likely thinking he was a dog. After they had eaten the goat, the pack padded round the Sow to the north slope and down to the river. Across the river was the other porcine hill, the Boar of Badenoch – *An Torc*.

Round these hills, in the glen, and south to Loch Garry, the pack hunted hares and goats undisturbed. Nobody north or south of the Pass was taking much interest in the strange affair of the killing of the kyloes, for they all had more than enough to think about already. They knew now that a Highland army was on the move, and likely coming their way, so it was even more likely that a Hanoverian army would be coming along the same road from another direction to meet it. If some loose dogs were taking to killing cattle or sheep or goats they would have to wait. And the pack did wait, into the fourth day, hunting in the morning coolth and dozing through the warm, clammy, overcast August afternoons. It was General John Cope who sent them on their wanderings again.

They were bellied down among drooping birches below a rockfall on the east side of the Boar, looking down on Drumochter, when they heard the rhythmic tap of drums in the far distance but coming nearer with every beat. The drum-taps were outside their experience and made no pictures in their head-places. The pictures began to take shape when their nostrils closed on man-smell – the overpowering smell of two thousand sweating, unwashed infantry, growing more nauseating with every step they took. The men were surly and weary, for General John Cope, their commander, was force-marching them to get them past Dalwhinnie before the Prince's Highlanders debouched from the Corrieyairack, which was where they were supposed to be. General Cope was a worried and angry man. Not a single Athole man had joined his force, despite the efforts of the Hanoverian Duke; but they had hampered him, thieving from his baggage, ripping his grain sacks and stealing his horses. He was further infuriated by the desertions from his own ranks. And ahead was the dread possibility of a Highland army blocking his route to Inverness at Dalwhinnie, or the Slochd Mor farther north.

As soon as the van of the army appeared in sight, with drums tapping and bayonets gleaming, Alba wanted to be away. She began to pad about, whimpering and fretting, but Saighdear and Dileas remained down, staring fixedly as the long column of men and horses and carts and ordnance passed below. Only when the last of them disappeared from the Pass did Saighdear rise and lead the way from the Boar, direction west ...

11

It was mid-morning, with a warm, light, south-westerly wind and a thinly overcast sky, before the pack rounded An Torc to feel their way once again into unknown country. Saighdear was pointing west because the army had gone north, had come from the south, and had left a scent barrier like a manned frontier from Drumochter down the length of the Garry to Blair – enough to daunt any wolf with a mind to break out to the east.

The wind from the south-west was bringing only stray tellings of deer and hares, and some spread of carrion which the ravens and crows were squabbling over. Saighdear changed course to run into the wind, and the pack loped at travelling-wolf-time into the forest of Dalnaspidal, down through the pines and birches, then the oaks and alders to the east shore of Loch Erricht, where there was neither taint nor sight of man. They ran the shore south, in and out of stretches of the old forest, with ground cover of blaeberry and juniper and wet clearings of bog myrtle and sphagnum, then crossed the River Erricht, lapping water, splashing, leaping and sometimes swimming. Again Saighdear held to the loch shore, running north through more forest, and at sunset, with a new moon rising, he had them on Ben Alder, following the route they had followed in the spring after leaving Lochaber. They had come full circle, and that day had put thirty miles behind them.

Below the tree-line they found a wooded place, a refuge place or an ambush place, with rocks as big as houses of thatch and crevices like the doors of them, where a whole company of soldiers might have hidden, and here they slept their waking wolf sleep until the night was far gone and the high clouds drifting apart. Saighdear was first on his feet: Luath, still leg-weary, was the last. But he ran tail-wagging to fall into line when he saw the others leaving and took his place behind Alba and Dileas. Rested now, the pack was ready to hunt at daylight, although there was no great hunger driving them.

They were on the high slope of Meall Mor when the sun came up in a haze of gold and to their noses came the warm, wayward scent of deer. Fronted by Saighdear, the pack padded on to a heathery ridge for a view. On that morning of fateful happenings the immense wilderness of towering mountains, purple ridges, winding rivers and calm blue lochans was a great silence of crystal air and singing waters, with only the Ben Alder eagles flying. The wolves saw the deer at once and the deer, above them and about a hundred yards away, saw them, and watched them, with their ears up and forward – five hinds and a knobber with four calves of the year. They were curious but not alarmed, and for a moment deer and wolves were still-life figures in the great silence. Then the deer turned their heads away, and the wolves knew what they were seeing because man pictures suddenly appeared in their head-places.

The deer trotted leisurely uphill and the pack bellied down to view the slopes below. Presently seven men appeared, following a burn flowing into Loch Pattack two miles to the north. This was the land of the Macdonells of Keppoch, and the seven were Keppoch men – with muskets, broadswords, dirks and targes – making wolf-time through the mountains to meet up with the Prince at Dalwhinnie or thereabouts, as Stewart of Ardsheal and Macdonell of Glengarry had done earlier in Lochaber. They knew the Prince's route and that sooner or later the clansmen would be coming by Dalwhinnie on the road south to Blair.

Before the Highlanders reached the forest at Loch Pattack, Alba raised her muzzle and initiated a howling session that lasted for almost a minute; and there are wise men who will say that this shows what a stupid animal the ancestor of the dog is; advertising itself to its arch-enemy. But wolf-howl is for wolves, not men. The wolf has learned so well how to avoid its arch-enemy that there are men who have lived with the howling all their lives without ever seeing the howlers alive and free. The wolf does not know that its singing is recognized, if not understood, by the human ear. It has to sing when the time is for singing; so Saighdear and his band sang their morning song, and the Keppoch men heard it and stopped to ponder over it. But not for long. They were not going to be held back because a few stray hounds were baying on Meall Mor.

The pack did not leave Meall Mor all that day; they prowled round the middle contours, hunting mountain hares. Luath killed his first prey of greater than mouse-size when he chased one into a gravelly bank, under a heather screen, and dug it out. He was now a strong wolfling, big-boned and deep of chest, with his armoury of adult teeth almost complete. While he tore up and ate his prey the others coursed the hares like greyhounds, converging in pair, or one driving to two in ambush. After they had killed five and eaten them, they rested until an hour before sunset, when Saighdear had them on foot again and moving down to Loch Pattack, with five ravens escorting, croaking guttural comment, and the Ben Alder eagles swinging down for a view before gliding home to roost.

Saighdear followed the River Pattack along its east bank into a forest of pine and oak, birch and alder, keeping to the tree cover although the night was dark enough to hide all but the face of a badger, and not being lured to the chase by deer crashing in the understorey or a fox crossing his path. They left the Pattack where it turned west on its loop to Loch Laggan, and soon they were in the great forest of Strath Mashie, a dark wood of ancient pines in gnurly grandeur, with moss-bearded stumps wherein pine martens clawed for crawlies and crested tits nested, and ant cairns the height of a wolf, and capercaillies still holding on to existence, and the charcoal signs bearing witness to long-ago fires that did not kill. In the resinous, brooding dark, with the war-whoop of a tawny owl ringing in their ears, the wolves threw down among junipers to let Luath rest. Alba and Dileas bocked hare for him and then he slept, nose to flank, until they had him moving again.

No wolf in the pack knew where Saighdear was leading them, and likely he had no idea himself; but he loped from the forest without faltering, running west on the high ground above Marshal Wade's road and the River Spey, along which were houses of thatch and hutments, all dark and silent, with not even a dog barking. The pack came down where the smell of cattle dung lay heavy on the night air; here had rested the herd they

141

had harried on Drumochter. They crossed the Spey by a two-arched bridge built fourteen years before by the indefatigable Marshal Wade, now in England's green and pleasant land, an old man still straining at the leash to be marching north to tame some more Highlandmen, waiting for King George to give him an army to teach a forever lesson to the barbaric clansmen and the flamboyant chiefs with their smug erudition and nose for a claret.

Across the bridge Saighdear turned the pack west along the Spey, then north, and by daylight they were high in the forest of Sherramore, bellied down at a meeting place of many waters. And when they howled their morning chorus, they were not heard by the few ears at Garvamore only a few miles away.

At mid-morning the adults left Luath asleep while they explored across the waist of the wood, then to its northern tip and back to their starting place, twice winding deer but failing to make contact with them. Luath joined them, and they hunted the open hill where they killed a dark-fleeced four-horned sheep. They drove another into a burn on the west side of the wood and tore out its throat before it drowned in a pool. On a spur above the burn they lay down to rest and digest their meal, ignoring a buzzard and two greyback crows at the scattered remains of the sheep. The afternoon was warm and humid, and the sky overcast, and they slept their fitful wolf sleep until suddenly Saighdear was on his feet, wide-eyed with ears pricked, while Alba and Dileas raised their heads, alerted, listening west. Faint and far off was the sound, at the limit of hearing, but it made pictures in their head-places because they had heard it many times before in many places – the music of the great Highland war-pipe, this time at the head of a Highland army marching at Highland pace to bring General Cope to battle at Garvamore, where he was supposed to be but was not.

First came the scouts, ranging wide, low and high, on both sides of the Spey, probing for contact – men in belted plaids on foot, and men in tartan trews mounted on Highland ponies. The entire army of 1500 men was already over the Corrieyairack Pass with its tail zig-zagging down the eighteen traverses engineered by Marshal Wade: a Highland army breaking out of the Great Glen along a road built to get Hanoverian soldiery into it. Soon the long column was passing below the watching wolves –

marching men in tartans of scarlet and green and yellow and blue, in kilts and belted plaids, armed with muskets and broadswords, dirks, pikes and Lochaber axes, newly issued or recovered from bogs and thatch where they had been hidden since the Rising of 1715. Men in tartan trews were mounted on the few cavalry horses and Highland ponies the army could muster; and there was the Prince himself in Highland dress on a captured charger presented to him by Captain Scott. But morale was high, and the glens rang to the slogan cries of the clansmen of Cameron and Stewart, Glengarry, Keppoch and Clanranald. And there were the pipers, honoured men like the poets and the sennachies. As Lochiel crossed the Garva bridge his piper sounded the fierce Cameron rant:

You sons of wolves, of wolves the breed,
O come, come here, on flesh to feed.

The pack remained on the spur for the rest of the daylight, with ears and noses alert, knowing fine that men had passed above them as well as below. The army camped several miles down the Spey, and after dark, when their camp fires were like candles flickering, the wolves padded into the heart of the ancient wood and stayed there until the distant rant of the war-pipes sounded reveille. Only then did Saighdear rise and lead the pack into the open by way of the pool where they had killed the sheep, and by the pool they waited until the army was on the march again. Then they filed on a long slant down to the river.

The day was hot and the sun unclouded. The pack followed a deer trail through the heather, owning and ignoring a scent line laid earlier that morning. Foggie bees the size of acorns, golden dusty with pollen, were crawling over the heather, making whine-buzz among the bells. Dragonflies on whispering wings, in gem-like cerulean mail, were hawking insects at wolf height, catching them in their shark-mouths and masticating them like cudding cows. Oyster-catchers and sandpipers rose piping in alarm when they saw the pack approaching the river, and Saighdear halted the line to savour the wind and listen, while Luath backtracked a few paces to sniff and drool over deer droppings. Alba wanted to be across the river and Saighdear knew it. So they waded in and crossed, fighting the current in the glissades and high-stepping where it broke white-crested over boulders. On a gravelly flat above a slack eddy of reaming water they shook themselves and lay down to lick their fur.

Presently Dileas rose, stalked to a big boulder and bellied down in its shade, facing the river, with her face in its damp coolth and only her tail in the sun. Another dragonfly jewelled in blue alighted on the boulder above her head, and she could hear the rustle of its gauzy, transparent wings. A greater glisk of blue, arrowing across her field of view, was a kingfisher flying downstream with a crawful of minnows. The oyster-catchers and sandpipers were back again, running to and fro, probing in wet places, knowing the wolves were still there but no longer heeding. Dileas dozed while her fur dried and buzzards mewed and blue dragonflies darted over the pools. Suddenly she became aware of movement against her right foreleg and a faintness of sound without pictures in her head-place. She pricked her ears, opened her eyes and leaped to her feet. Nine worm-size adders, only two days old, wriggled from under the boulder and glided towards the river. Dileas watched them, with her head cocked like a puppy, then followed them, reaching out tentatively with a paw. With deft scoops she flicked one, then another, into the water, just as Luath came bounding towards her to see what was afoot. He showed no interest in the adders and began to chase Dileas in circles and snake-twists instead.

A little way downstream a big female adder was basking below a boulder in a floss of old river wrack. She was the colour of bronze with a shadowy zig-zag along her back. She was curled up, slack wound not spring-coiled, relaxing in the wide-eyed unblinking daydreaming of the snake, when Dileas came bounding towards her with Luath snapping playfully at her tail. The vibrations from the heavy wolf tread registered peril in the snake's head-place and she uncoiled in a whirlpool of movement to launch away. But she was too late and she knew it. So she reformed a whirlpool, and as Dileas trampled she struck. Dileas yelped when she felt the strike above the dew claw of her left forepaw and immediately sat down to lick the place, while Luath, still full of rumbustiousness, chased after the retreating adder, which was wriggling brokenly away with hind-end crushed. Luath snapped his teeth at her, flicked her over with a paw, then bit her through the middle and tossed her aside to watch her after-death cavortings. She had no defence against him; her working fangs were embedded in the foot of Dileas.

Dileas padded back to the pack, feeling no more than a pin-prick where the snake had struck. But she had received a maximum dose of venom from a big adder with a full sac and strong muscle, and within an hour her paw was swollen and painful, and the pain and swelling were travelling up her leg. When Saighdear led the pack from the riverside gravel flat she had to follow on three legs, and before long she was lurching blindly behind Alba. After two hours she threw herself down in a bosky hollow near the river, trembling, whimpering, vomiting spittle like egg-white, and trying to burrow into the hard earth with her nose. When Luath tried to rouse her with a pat from an affectionate paw she growled at him, and he drew away perplexed. Later, Alba and Saighdear sniffed her over, then backed off with hackles on end when she girned at them through clenched teeth. Luath went to her again and licked her head, but she flashed her teeth at him and drove him away. By then she was glassy-eyed and not seeing. Her pack mates sat around, waiting, not understanding. Before sunset they howled their eve-song without her, and when it was over Dileas was dead.

Alba was reluctant to leave her sibling, yet she wanted to be away, and when Saighdear rose to go she fell into line, with Luath between them. They followed the Wade road west, at an easy lope, with tongue tips showing, and used the eighteen traverses to the Corrieyairack Pass, with man-sign present all the way but no man-presence. Over this pass a hundred years before the great Marquis of Montrose had led a Highland army, in midwinter snow and ice, through trackless wilderness from the lower Tarf to the high shoulder of Ben Nevis, from there to swoop in a blast of trumpets and shatter Argyll at Inverlochy. Saighdear led his band of two round the shoulder of Corrieyairack, from which a wolf pack had viewed Montrose that century ago, and followed a network of burns to the headwaters of the Tarf. And there, in a fork between two burns with forested banks, they waited for daylight, not irked by hunger but suffering great emotional stress from the death of Dileas.

145

At daylight there was gusting wind and racing clouds, with a scatter of sunny rain that rippled the pools like small trout rising. On the open hill, and east and west of the Pass, nothing was moving, as though the army had cleared the ground of deer, cattle, sheep and goats. The wolves rose when the cloud shadows were running like a dark tide race across the heather, and after a brief howling session padded down into a wide strath of lochans and blue water channels. On the first lochan mallards and teal ducks were flapping and splashing. A family of red-breasted mergansers swam away from inshore to open water when they saw the wolves approaching. The pack ran the shoreline, dryfoot through hazels and scrub birches and splashing hock-deep through rushes, bog bean and waving pondweed, rousing moulting mallards to laboured flight. Saighdear snapped one as it rose, in the way he had learned to catch crows. Later, Alba sprang on one hiding in a reedbed, pinned it down with her forepaws, and bit its head off as it *quarked* in her jaws. Luath, after failing with three pounces, came begging to her, but she ate her duck, ignoring his pleas for a bock. It was the first time she had refused his begging.

On the slopes above, blue hares were grazing at a slow hop, or crouched in tussocks, or sitting tall, with ears erect, preening their whiskers with forepaws. The pack hunted for three hours to kill three, then returned to the river fork to rest and digest. Next day they hunted the forest strip along the north fork, and killed a roebuck after driving him into a pool, with Alba and Luath chasing abreast and Saighdear in ambush on the other side. Luath was learning his craft as a member of the pack. For a fortnight after that they denned in the fork, among birches and tall heather below a rock outcrop, and hunted the strath, the woods and the open hill, killing prey enough but not living fat. The absence of the men-animals was worth a little fasting. Even Alba was beginning to settle into the quiet, uneventful routine. Then one day, late in the afternoon, the men-animals came again.

The three were on Corrieyairack, looking down on the Pass, when they heard far off to the west the clink of shod hooves on stone, and the sound made pictures in their head-places: man pictures, not of horses. Soon the men appeared below the Pass – five Hanoverian dragoons on saddle horses, one leading a shaltie pack pony, heading for the link road built by Marshal Wade from the Spey to Ruthven Barracks on the Inverness road. The light was fading fast, with a purple mass of clouds blotting out the westering sun, and the dragoons knew they were not going to reach even the bottom of the traverses before dark, so they decided to bivouac for the night where they were. They were working by map and had never been over the road before. Three men held the horses while two unloaded the shaltie and ran out a picket line. They watered and fed the horses and pony, tethered them, and began to make camp. They made no fire, so after dark the wolves were not seeing them. The men were smoking and talking when an egg-shaped moon came up in a cloud-chequered sky, now hidden, now glowing through, now gleaming bright in the clearways. The five went to bed, posting no sentry. They knew their own troops were holding the east end of the road, and they had Fort Augustus at their backs. The stark loneliness of the moonlit place preyed upon them more than the impossible thought of a surprise night attack by some flying column of Jacobite clansmen.

After midnight the misshapen moon was in a clearway of blue, dark as a rook's wing, with a few stars flickering palely. The men were asleep with knees drawn up against the cold; the horses were asleep on their feet. In the vast, moonlit mountain silence the wind's breath in the heather and the muted chirl of water trickles in the runlets made a greater silence. Alba whimpered when Saighdear started off downhill towards the camp, but she followed with Luath behind her. Saighdear was as much in awe and fear of men as she, but he had learned much about them while avoiding them. In the dark they held no menace, and in daylight they were not dangerous without their great wolfhounds. He knew there were horses down there, and a small domesticated horse, with its wildness tamed, is an easier prey for three wolves than a big red deer stag in his prime of body and antlers is for five. What he did not know was that the horses were tethered and the men armed. But in his head-place he knew what he was going to try.

The picket line was quiet except for the occasional stamp of a hoof: the horses were belly-happy with a full ration of grain. The wolves circled the camp, alert and wary, until the wind was flaffing from them to the picket line. Then the shaltie nickered.

147

His nickering alerted the saddle horses, and they voiced their query with much head tossing. That stirred the soldiers, who listened, muttered something about horses being afraid of the dark, and went to sleep again. Then Saighdear began to stalk into the horses, and as the light wind filled their nostrils with the wolf scent their snickering became more urgent, and the shaltie began to rear and strain at the picket rope. When he saw the shadowy shapes of them, with their glowing green eyes afloat in the night, he began to kick and plunge, almost falling over backwards in his efforts to break loose. The five saddle horses began to strain back on their tethers, a great fear growing in them although they had no idea what they were afraid of. When Saighdear rushed at the shaltie, with Alba closing in on his left flank, the little horse broke his tether at the chin strap and galloped away wildly into the moonlit night. One of the saddle horses broke away before the men came tumbling from their bivouac, half-dressed, with muskets at the ready. Four of them grabbed the tethered horses and tried to quieten them while the fifth fired after the dark shapes of the galloping wolves. The ball grazed Luath's rump, removing some hair and scraping the skin, but he ran on after his pack mates, not knowing what the irritation was.

Now Dileas was being sorely missed; her loss reduced the killing power of the pack. Any wolf pack has to select prey animals within its collective strength, so Saighdear broke off the pursuit of the saddle horse and laid his mates on to the shaltie. The shaltie was an intelligent little horse, with all the smeddum of his kind, and when the pack ran him into a cul-de-sac among rocks he turned his back on them and lashed out with his hindfeet, a kick from which would have disabled any wolf or cracked its skull. The pack sat in an arc around him, with their tongues hanging out, blocking his exit and waiting for him to kick himself to exhaustion. He looked round at them, nostrils flared, breathing heavily, as though weighing his chances. He was tiring but there was still an unquenchable fire in him, and when Alba tried to move in on him he kicked out at her with both hindfeet, squealing in rage. Once again he looked round at them, sitting there jocoe, and he realized they were not prepared to face his flying feet. So he calmed down, to reserve his kicking for any wolf trying to move in to him. And that made it stalemate.

But he had not noticed Saighdear skulking up to the rock above his head, and the first he knew of it was when the big wolf leaped on to his rump, bearing him to the ground. In that moment the other two were on to him, Alba at his stifle and Luath at his nose, hanging on with locked teeth. And that was his war over. He died squealing and fighting – and not quickly, because he was a fighter.

When morning came, sunless and moonless, with sagging clouds and drizzling rain, the wolves were bellied down on the south side of the Pass, their gorge of horsemeat already half-digested, watching the dragoons making ready to strike camp. Four of them rode out to look for the lost horses, leaving the fifth to pack the shaltie's gear. Within a mile of camp they found the saddle horse, a big bay gelding who was as pleased to see them as they were relieved to find him. Of the shaltie they could find no sign, although they cast their search wide, and they assumed that he had kept on running or been lifted and hidden away by thieves from the houses of thatch down the road. The sight of ravens and crows, yarring and croaking, dropping and lifting, chasing and bickering, among rocks half a mile away meant nothing to them: they were southrons and urbanites, unable to read a sign that would have made a picture in the head-place of any Highlander. So they returned to camp, the sergeant leading the bay gelding, and none of them even thinking that the shaltie might be dead.

The sergeant, reflecting on the report he would have to make, said: 'Must have been a raid by some o' them bare-arsed rebels. Lucky we lost only a powny.'

'Strewth!' said the dragoon who had packed the shaltie's gear. 'If it had of been a raid we'd all be fucking dead. Them bare-arses plays rough. And all the horses would've been away for sure.'

'What abawt them fucking great dogs?' a trooper asked the sergeant. 'I've heard abawt the dogs of war but I never seen one before!'

'Anyfink can happen in this god-forsaken country,' said the one who had fired at the wolves. 'I didn't see no bare-arsed

149

rebels but I did see the fucking great dawgs, and I'm sure I winged one of the bastards.'

'Myebe they was wolves,' ventured the man with the shaltie's gear.

'If they'd of been wolves they'd of been in on top of us for sure,' the sergeant replied. 'Anywye, there's supposed not to be any bloody wolves around here, but it wouldn't surprise me none if the cursed country was crawling with them, as well as them other bloody savages in their kilts.'

With an unseen wolf pack watching them from above the dragoons rode away, one man turning back to report and the sergeant going on with three. Before they had reached the last of the eighteen traverses the pack was back at the kill, tearing hide and shearing meat, feasting before an audience of ravens, crows and a single red kite.

The pack stayed with the kill that day and the next, eating until only a few bones were left. On the morning of the third day more of the men-animals appeared in the Pass – Hanoverian redcoats – two mounted on cavalry horses followed by half a platoon of infantry. Only they knew where they were going and why. What Alba knew was that it was time for her to go, and Saighdear in some way understood.

What none of them knew – the wolves, the soldiers in the Pass, or the garrisons at the forts – was that General John Cope's army had been all but annihilated that morning at Prestonpans by a Highland army commanded by Lord George Murray; that the Hanoverian wounded had been cared for, the prisoners humanely treated, and the dead honourably buried; and that the Prince had expressly forbidden all forms of celebration or rejoicing after the victory.

12

The day was windless, with misted rain. The wolves headed
south in line ahead, seeing little except the ground beneath their
feet and halting every now and again to shake loose water from
their fur or rub itching eyebrows with the knuckle of a forepaw.
Saighdear led them in slow-time, reading the ground within
seeing distance ahead, and they were two hours from the
Corrieyairack before they reached the white falls at the
headwaters of the River Roy where they halted to shelter from
the rain, which was now falling in steady downpour, purring like
leaves stirred by a wind. The hill burns, gorged with new water
from rain, rillets and flash floodlets, were gushing down, white-
crested, to brim the pools where samlets were leaping and big
salmon waiting for the spate that would let them continue their
run upstream to the spawning redds.

In the late afternoon, when the rain was slackening again to a
fine drizzle, Saighdear led the pack along the south bank of the
river, which was flanked on both sides by ancient beaches, left
high and dry by the draining away of deep lochs formed by
snow-melt and run-off from the tops after the great Ben More
glacier had dammed the bottom of the glen.

When they were above the second waterfall they were looking
down on a strath with houses of thatch along the river, rucks of
hard-won meadow hay inbye, black cattle on the green and
bleached strips where the glen folk had harvested oats and
barley. Saighdear knew that houses of thatch meant people, so
he turned south, up and across the ancient beach, and through
open woodland of pine, birch and rowan to the tree-line where
he stopped, shook himself and sat down. Alba touched his raised

151

muzzle with her own and Luath ran to him, tail-wagging himself almost off his feet, and licked his face. They found shelter and screen in a patch of juniper where deer and summering cattle had browsed. Dung pats were scattered round nearby pines where cattle had rubbed. All that day and throughout the night the rain purred steadily down and the wolves stayed in the tree cover, moving little, saving energy doing nothing instead of expending it in fruitless questing. Next morning the rain began to slacken and by noon the sky was clear, with the beads of water on the junipers sparkling like sequins in the sun and the heather leafage silvered like frost. And the day became warm with vapour flosses drifting.

The pack left the tree cover and padded over the top of the hill to the south slopes, where they hunted the few hares that were moving. They killed three. Next day Saighdear was the only member of the pack who killed, and he killed one, half of which he bocked later for Luath. They hunted voles along the tree-line, but the number they killed was not worth the energy expended in catching them. Then they found a dead sheep among the trees above the beach-line. Its eyes had already been pecked out by greyback crows but the carcass was fresh, and they gorged on meat, heart, lungs, liver, bones and entrails, leaving only the fleece, head and paunch.

But this was lean hunting for two big wolves and a pup still growing, and after probing on an eighteen-mile circuit of the forest of Braeroy, where the first stags were roaring, warming to the rut, they realized they had to make a big kill soon or move out. They tested three groups of stags and they knew beyond doubt that a mature beast in full headgear was now beyond their powers unless they found one injured, sick or dying. Later they tested a hind group, but broke off the chase after a mile – a long run that betrayed their determination and frustration. It was then that Saighdear, in his head-place, began to make a picture of black cattle in a green strath, and turned the pack back to the trees and down across the beach-line to view the ground below.

Now the picture had changed. Where a dozen beasts had been the day before, there were now more than sixty on the grazing flats, mostly yearling stirks and heifers, round-rumped and big-bellied, and nearly all of them lying down, with full paunches, ruminating. They had been gathered for a drive on the morrow to Spean Bridge, to begin the long journey south to Crieff. The drove roads were safe now, for there were no English troops north of the Border except the fort garrisons and scouting parties, and the Jacobite army was in Edinburgh where the Prince was holding court. Three women and four plaided boys were herding the gathering, gentling the beasts to settle for the night until the first light of dawn. The women and boys would be with the drive, for their menfolk were out with the Prince, serving in the ranks of Keppoch's Macdonells.

The women were home, the stars were out, and frost threatening before the wolves struck. They chose a beast lying away from the herd, a black stirk chewing cud contentedly and already half-asleep, and gave him no time to rise. Saighdear leaped on to his back, sinking his massive tusks to the gums; Alba took him in the groin; and Luath locked on to his nose. He struggled mightily under their weight, bawling in terror and trying to thrust himself to his hindfeet. He lifted Luath clear of the ground and swung him, but could not break his hold. There was nothing he could do about his hind-quarters under the weight and grips of Saighdear and Alba. His bawling put the nearest beasts on foot, but there was no stampede; they formed phalanx to watch. He ceased furrowing the ground with his hind-hooves when Alba hamstrung a leg, and quickly he was dead. The wolves ate fifty pounds of meat from him that night, and in the morning darkness scraped the bones almost clean. They did not return to the kill again.

The three women, four boys and two men puzzled over the remains in the morning. The scuffle marks on the frosted grass round the beast told them nothing, and the going away tracks of the wolves had been obliterated by the hooves of milling cattle. Here was a mystery, with no time to be trying to solve it, for the droving party had to get the herd moving at once and not later. By then the wolves were trotting south-west in slow-time, following a tributary of the Roy, and questing as they travelled, ready to turn aside to chase after any likely prey.

Wild geese were flying over in lop-sided chevron, baying like foxhounds. Ducks were splattering in the burn with a travelling otter watching from the bank where he was eating a fish. Foggie bees with crinkled wings were dying among the fading heather bells. Catcalls of soaring buzzards came faintly from the high blue. Pipits flittered along the ground ahead of the wolves, turning away only when almost trodden upon. Saighdear halted in a small corrie to watch two ravens swooping at an eagle on the flat top of a rock buttress where he was standing on the body of a hare, tearing its belly open with his great sickle beak. Each time the ravens swooped at him the eagle bowed his head; but he was not to be driven off – at least not by a pair of ravens. When Saighdear rushed into the corrie and leaped against the rock face he was taken by surprise and launched away, out and up – without his hare. At kestrel-height above the corrie he banked steeply, then levelled off and circled, rocking on the air, glaring fiercely down while the ravens turned to swooping at the wolves. Saighdear kept leaping at the rock face, seeking a foothold, leaving Alba to make a detour round it and climb up and on to it at ground level. The short heather on top was flattened and pleached, for the eagle had eaten and slept there many times. Alba snatched up the hare and was trotting away to eat it in peace when Saighdear appeared, thrust her aside, and grabbed it from her. And below the eagle's rock he wolfed it down, growling each time Alba or Luath took a step towards him.

The eagle returned to the rock after the wolves had gone, and there strode flat-footed about, perplexed, long-necking, looking right and left and then down between his talons, as though expecting to find the hare still there. When at last he realized it was gone he opened his wings, leaped from the rock and glided away to hunt again. The ravens, too, returned to the rock, where they pecked fluff for a moment before flying after the wolf pack.

They followed for three miles before they turned back. By then the pack was in a wide strath ringed by mountains, with a fan spread of hill burns spilling down to a dapple of blue lochans, and birch woods shimmering gold on the slopes. Here were deer and hares, black grouse and red, and feral goats among the crags: wolf country if left to wolves. The pack killed four hares in an hour, and after resting to digest them they explored twenty-five square miles of slopes and low ground, probing for man-frontiers, testing for him on the wind. They padded into a birch wood, where the sun was polishing the gold, and were immediately harlequined with broken light. Siskins were hopping on the moss carpet gathering birch nutlets, which woodmice also harvested after dark: redpolls were catching

154

others in the air as they floated down on delicate wings like tiny flies swarming. Blackcocks in plumage of blue, purple and ebony beetle-gloss fled from the birches where they had been picking catkins when the wolves passed below, and whirred away over the contours in swift flap and glide flight. On the edge of the wood Saighdear stopped and howled in chorus with Alba and Luath for ninety-five seconds.

Wolves will howl when hunting near the frontier of their territory to let a neighbouring pack know they are there: thus they avoid unwanted confrontation. But sometimes the hearing pack will not answer, in case the answer invites incursion by colonizing rivals. Not since the day he had formed pack with Alba, Dileas and Sgian had Saighdear heard the howl of a strange wolf. But he had to announce that he was there, and listen for reply. There was no reply.

But down near one of the lochans a stag was roaring, and the pack listened intently to place him. When they found him he was in a wallow – a big switch at the height of his powers, with five hinds and three calves standing by watching. The pack approached in full view to within fifty yards, then sat down. The leading hind barked a warning and her followers formed bourach behind her. Her warning brought the switch to his feet and he strode from the wallow, his mane plastered with peat sludge, his flanks dripping black water, and the smell of him thick as a mist on the air. He faced the wolves with lowered head and threatening sweep of his rapiers, showing the whites of his eyes and stamping a forehoof; then up went his head again, the neck of him stretched, and he roared a leonine roar, ending with gasping grunts. The leading hind, stiff-kneed, stamped with a foot and grunted, then trotted away with her group crowding close behind her. The stag, after another threatening sweep of antlers, turned about and galloped after them, and the wolves did not give chase. Saighdear knew he was running to recover his hinds, not fleeing from wolves.

The warm blue and golden Indian summer was nearly over, and soon a ranting gale brought the first bitter skyte of sleet. All the master stags were roaring and rutting, running themselves hot and lean after rivals trying to cut out their hinds. One day the pack left the strath and padded south through the glens, exploring not leaving. After five miles, with the wind in their favour, they surprised two hinds and a calf in a corrie, in possession of a young stag who had cut them out from the harem of a run-out royal. The young stag, in six-point headgear, was not made of the stuff of the big switch and broke away in panic at sight of the pack. He tried to climb a steep face and fell; he tried a second time and fell again; and the wolves left him to his trying. They moved in on the hinds, Alba and Luath kepping like collies working sheep while Saighdear tried to shed the calf. At the second try he succeeded in cutting it out, and was kicked in the ribs by the hind as he swerved away after it, leaping at its flank. Alba and Luath left the hinds and let them run, and the three pulled the calf down before it could reach open ground. They ate while the hinds watched from the top of the corrie, running about, stopping and stamping, then running about again. The stag ran with them, trying to kep them, not knowing what it was all about. The wolves left little of the calf carcass, but the little they left they cached under a rock in the corrie.

They explored south until they reached the barrier of the River Spean, running brokenly with a low head of water, and they followed the bank upstream looking for a place to cross. And likely they would have turned back or gone farther in their search if the wind had not brought once more to their noses the menacing scent of the men-animals. The man-scent was between them and the mountains, and soon they were in view – twenty Highlanders in plaid and philibeg, all of them from Lochaber, waywise in the mountains, making their way through the back country to Blair, heading for Edinburgh where the Prince was still recruiting and Lord George Murray sending frantic letters to old Tullibardine asking for the Athole brigade for the march against England. The men were leading two ponies loaded with supplies, mainly targes, scythes and broadswords, and covering the broken ground at a pace no southron soldiers could equal. At the sight of them the pack chose to face the unchancy waters of the Spean. The Highlanders saw them when they were shaking out water on the far bank and assumed they were dogs.

For the rest of the daylight the pack lay up in a great tract of forest bearing old signs of the firestick and the woodsman's axe: the high round was pine, with oak and hazel, rowan and holly, on the lower slopes, and alder and willow along the burn on its eastern boundary. Here red squirrels, voles and mice harvested

156

acorns, nuts and berries, and pine martens hunted the squirrels, voles and mice. Jays were gathering acorns from green-mossed uphill trees planted as acorns by earlier generations of their species, and burying part of their harvest to grow into new oaks that would produce acorns for jays and squirrels in the far away future.

At sunset a sickle of moon rose in a clear starlit sky and the pack left the forest, following the River Treig and then the east shore of the loch, and soon they were in the country of the deer, with the scent of them everywhere from Ardverikie to Mamore, big stags roaring, and Orion the Hunter, frosty-brilliant, astride the southern sky. That night they killed nothing, but at daybreak they drove a goat and kid from the rocks and threw them both on a downhill run, killing them as they rolled on the frosted ground. After eating they lay up to digest their gorge in a forest remnant on the loch shore, their noses on the alert for man-scent, and their ears pricking now and again in their half-sleep to the clear, haunting whistle of otters. In the afternoon they hunted twenty miles out into Ardverikie, where they killed a sickly hind: two days later they returned to Loch Treig and rounded its south shore to run on into Mamore, where they killed only hares. They were in Lairig Leachach, on the way back to Loch Treig, when they saw the white hind with her white calf.

White deer were not unique in that arrowhead of Lochaber between Loch Treig and the Spey, and were the stuff of folklore. In a land where the deer was often a legendary animal in poem, song, and story, white ones had a special place, and were noted for wondrous longevity. In the poetry of Gaeldom life-spans were poetically tabulated:

Thrice the age of a dog the age of a horse;
Thrice the age of a horse the age of a man;
Thrice the age of a man the age of a stag;
Thrice the age of a stag the age of an eagle;
Thrice the age of an eagle the age of an oak tree.

So in Badenoch there had been Damnh Mor, the Great Stag, whose life spanned two centuries; and there was that white hind of Loch Treig who lived for a hundred and sixty years in the wilds of Lochaber: she outlived the chiefs and their sons and was still young when boys had grown to manhood. That was the way the sennachies were saying it, and although modern man may scoff, knowing that the life of a deer is shorter than that of a horse, and that the noblest stag is decrepit before a man-child becomes a man, there is neither poetry nor music in his wisdom.

The white hind the wolves were seeing was full of the wisdom of her eight years and her stag calf was strong. There were two hinds with calves in her group, tailed by a wearied stag at the end of his days of roaring. As soon as the wolves lined out below to test them, the white hind turned uphill, flanked by her calf and followed closely by her group and a reluctant stag. When the pack pressed him, he broke away on his own along a hogback ridge, in full flight, and they let him run. The white hind continued uphill at a faster pace than the wolves, set on going right to the top and maybe she was knowing that tops at over 3000 feet are places where wolves would rather not be. Saighdear, as though reading her thoughts, ran wide to flank her followers on one side while Alba and Luath flanked them on the other. They turned in between them and their white leader, and forced them along a ridge of boulders and leggy heather. After a pursuit of half a mile they cut out a calf, Saighdear and Alba kepping while Luath harried the hind in a curving run away from it. Saighdear and Alba drove the calf to the top of a crag, and over it, and the fall broke its back. The pack was on to it within seconds in a three-pronged attack, and in a few seconds more it was dead. The carcass fed them to gorging and they did not kill again for three days.

Towards the end of October, on a day of August heat, blue sky and whiddering wind, with the birchwoods like a golden tapestry on the slopes, the pack halted on a high flat to view a hummel rolling in a wallow. A hummel is a stag without antlers, but not humble, and at the height of his powers is often a master during the rut. This was a young beast, not yet at the peak of his strength, although he was well muscled and rumped like a stirk. The wind was carrying the pack scent high over his head, so he could not smell them where they stood, but to get down to him they had to make a wide detour to keep themselves out of his nose until they could approach him upwind. This time they did not show themselves to test him. In the wallow, with his hooves

158

in the air, he would never be at a greater disadvantage. Saighdear touched noses with Alba and Luath, as though communicating, and when he moved they moved with him – in a bounding rush. The hummel, in the moment of awareness, struggled to rise, but he was on his back still when Saighdear leaped at his throat and Alba sank her tusks in his nose. Then Luath, with all the recklessness of Sgian, leaped on to his exposed belly and snapped between his hindlegs, gripping his testicles and shearing them off.

The hummel bawled and kicked his hindfeet in the air, at the same time trying to shake Saighdear and Alba from his throat and nose, but the pair were not to be shaken and Luath miraculously avoided the stabbing hooves. Soon the hummel was choking in his own blood, and when his kicking ceased, Alba left his nose to tear into his groin. And then he was dead. They had to feed on him where he lay, in the watery slush of dark, bloodstained peat, because they could never have dragged him clear; he was heavier than any prime royal at peak of condition. He was a lot of meat for three wolves, and the pack fed on him, and stayed with him, until there was nothing left but hide and a few bones.

On that last day, when the wolves left the debris to the ravens and crows, Prince Charles Edward Stuart and Lord George Murray were leading a Highland column south-east to the English frontier, while another under Tullibardine and the Duke of Perth was feinting towards Newcastle to hold Marshal Wade and his army there. The ageing Marshal at last had his army, and he was marching north to tame the Highlandmen; instead he passed out of history, although ecstatic audiences at Drury Lane were nightly singing his praises in a new verse that had been added to their national anthem:

God grant that Marshal Wade
May with thy mighty aid
Victory bring.
May he sedition hush
And like a torrent rush
Rebellious Scots to crush,
God save the king!

The man whose engineering feats had exposed the underbelly of the clan lands north of the Great Glen was now démodé. The rising star was the king's son William Augustus, Duke of Cumberland.

13

The November gales stripped the birches of their buskins and the hill burns bickered down carrying flotsam of gold; the first snow trimmed their banks with ermine and brought the deer from the high ground to the glens. The mountain hares, all in winter white, were invisible above the snowline, which the eagle patrolled, seeking those that moved on to the dark ground below, where they became conspicuous. In the river the first salmon kelts were drifting tail-first downstream, cock fish and hen fish who had spent their strength in the fast, cold, clear water of the spawning redds and were now on their way to the sea, which some would reach if they mended well and others unmended would not.

A lone dog otter was stirring up courting salmon in a holding pool when the wolf pack appeared and stopped on the bank to look for him. They knew where he was because they had been following his trail along the bank and it ended at the pool: but the only sign of him, which was no sign at all to a wolf, was his bubble chain on the surface. Their interest in him was more than casual; they were in their third day of empty bellies and he was food if they could catch him. When his face surfaced beside his last bubbles, he had in his jaws a spent fish which he carried to the opposite bank to eat, and they knew he was beyond their reach, too close to his own element even to be robbed of his fish.

But the gods who look after the destinies of wolves awoke from their slumbers, and suddenly there was a fish wriggling across the current over shallows with his back out of the water – a big redskin of a cock salmon kelt with a kype like the pincer of a lobster, too drained by milting after long fasting to know which way he was pointing. Alba was first into the water and headed the hunt. She caught the kelt in midstream, broke his back with one closing of her jaws, then splashed and waded to the opposite bank with her teeth firmly locked in him, all set to greet Saighdear and Luath with thunderous growls when they came ashore. The sight of three wolves at such close quarters sent the otter back to the pool, leaving his partly-eaten fish behind. Saighdear padded stiff-legged towards Alba with his tail up and his hackles on end, but she would not yield, and he had to growl at her with his lips drawn back from his teeth before she would part with the fish. Once he had it, he ate little of it and left her in peace while she bolted what was left. In the meantime Luath had snatched the partly-eaten fish left by the otter and eaten it.

Daily the snowline crept down to meet the lower squalls of sleet and rain. The wolves killed three more dying kelts in eddies before the first big snow, Saighdear and Alba scooping with a paw, bear-like, and Luath ducking for his like a hunting retriever. They also caught white hares, and killed an old thin-antlered stag with mocassin hooves that clickety-clicked when he was running; but such kills were lean living. The night frosts sharpened their claws, and the birches and heather remained silver in the short days of heatless sun. Then came skirling wind with whirling snow that blanketed the tops and covered the low ground to the foot-depth of a wolf. More snow, fine as sand, swept in brief fury along the glens like a white hurricane, and soon the wolves were walking hock-deep in drifts, for a big wind can do much with little. The sharp snow stung their eyes like an onset of wasps in anger, so they bellied down with their backs to it until they were mantled in white like the rocks among which they were lying. After the white storm had died, the wind scourged the drifts to a fierce creeping barrage of pinhead snow. The barrage lifted when the rant was over; the wolves rose and shook off their ermine wraps; and Alba knew that once more it was time for her to go.

That afternoon, when a gilded cat's claw of rising moon was facing a fireball of setting sun across a freezing sky, Alba left the rocks and led the way south into the white, empty vast; while a Highland army was facing north across the Scottish border after the long march from Derby, during which their rearguard had mauled Cumberland's dragoons at Clifton. They had marched from Lochaber into England to shield an English rising, but the English, except for the men of the Manchester Regiment, had not risen. And now they were homeward bound.

Alba broke trail for six miles, with the others in line treading in her tracks; then Saighdear moved to the front and she fell in behind Luath. Twelve miles out Luath changed places with Saighdear, and veered east; the adults followed in his tracks without questioning the change of direction. Either all of them knew where they were going or they were going anywhere. They padded on through the white starlit night until they reached a place of scattered lochans, dark as the sky, where the water was open and white snow was lying on the thin ice creeping out from the shores. Here Alba moved to the head of the line again. After another hour of slow-time in the dragging snow, they entered a tract of old pine forest above Loch Ossian, where the snow had been slotted by deer not long before. The wolves became excited at the scent of them on wandering flaffs of wind, but with twenty-five miles of hard travelling behind them they needed rest; the deer could wait until daylight. More snow fell in the night – great soft flakes pat-patting densely down or eddying on the almost windless air. In the last hour of darkness, when the sky cleared, it was lying deep in the forest.

The pack moved into the forest at daylight with Alba breaking the trail. In the muffled silence they could hear the soft fall of snow from the laden trees. Under a century-old pine, with wide-spreading muscular arms, they found the presses in the snow where three deer had been lying: the presses were stained dark with their droppings and urine. Their gashed going-away trails led to browse of juniper, rowan, hazel and blaeberry, and after half a mile the pack found them – two hinds and a calf, all facing their back trail with ears up and nostrils flared. The wolves wasted no time in testing self-display; they were hungry, keyed up and ready to run. Three wolves ploughed in slow-motion gallop down on three deer, and three deer broke away downhill in a storm of white to escape them. Gaining ground, the pack fanned out to converge, and drove the three into deep drifts where the calf was soon floundering. It cried out in despair for its mother, and the hind bucked through the drift towards it as Alba clambered on to its back. She killed it, but not before the hind had knocked her into the snow and pounded her twice on

163

the ribs with her forepaws. Saighdear, threatening her flank, drove her off and let her sprackle away. Then he helped Alba to drag the body of the calf from the blood-spattered drift, leaving Luath to go plowtering in vain pursuit of the hinds who were now on ground they knew and soon left him far behind.

Alba escaped with nothing worse than bruised ribs because the soft, yielding snow beneath her had lessened the impact of the hind's pounding hooves; but the bruises were painful and would slow her down and make her unfit to hunt for a week or more. When Luath, boring eagerly into the rib cage of the calf, knocked against her, she yelped and showed him her teeth. The calf had been strong, six months old, and still a suckler, so there was a lot of meat on him. The pack stayed in the forest for two days until they had eaten every morsel of meat and every eatable bone, with Saighdear guarding it from plundering ravens and crows. When they left the forest Saighdear was leading the line, with Alba following and Luath at the tail.

Frost had hardened the snow to a crust coruscating with stars of ice, but the wolves with their grip-fast pads were not slowed down. Alba set the pace, padding stiffly behind Saighdear and now and again carrying her right foreleg to ease the pain in her side. That day they travelled only sixteen miles, and after dark Alba rested in a thicket of burnside hazels and blackthorns while Saighdear and Luath hunted eastwards, following the bank to the dangerous neighbourhood of houses of thatch. Long after the people were abed they killed a four-horned sheep by the river where it was browsing on the shoots and bark of much-bitten alders. They were disturbed halfway through their eating by a roving cattle dog, who chased after them barking loudly and fiercely. When they were well clear of the houses they ambushed the dog, which they killed and ate; but they had to leave the partly-eaten body of the sheep for the women to dress into cuts of mutton and share out among them. Highlanders, like wolves, wasted not food.

In the blue and white morning of sun-glare and ice stars like diamonds glittering, Saighdear pointed the pack south, padding at a dog-walk or wolf-trotting in slow-time through white miles of empty glen, following the river bank to Loch Eigheach, now a frozen snow-field, where seven whooper swans were parading with heads high and necks straight, searching in vain for open water. The wolves crossed the frozen loch, sending the whoopers footing away into creaking flight. On the far shore Alba stopped in a hollow to rest, lying on her side with her bruised ribs to the sun. Within half an hour she was on foot again, trotting behind Saighdear, who kept heading east, holding to the low ground, until they reached a pine forest which was another remnant of the ancient Wood of Caledon. There he signalled journey's end by sitting down and howling. Alba and Luath joined in, and the three sang solo in wolf harmony before throwing down to pant and lick their fur. Behind them stretched a line of shallow foot-slots in the snow, marking their route for twenty-four miles.

They were now in Rannoch of awesome folklore and fearful repute, the dark, menacing vast of wilderness from Schiehallion to Black Mount that once was the ancient Wood: an unchancy place, shunned by travellers at night like the mouth of Hell for fear of the wolves lying in wait to devour them. Men feared them more than they feared the spectres or the fierce water-bulls of legend, and they fired the forest until the dreaded quavering cries were heard no more. Now all that remained of the once great Wood that the Romans knew were remnants in the glens and on the moraines sculpted by glaciation; but in the graveyard of the peat were preserved the stumps and roots of trees that were old before the proud Legions set foot in the Caledonia they failed to conquer, and where the peat shroud had eroded, relics were exposed to bear witness to dead centuries and millennia.

Saighdear, the first wolf to howl there for the lifetime of a man, knew the moor and its remaining forests; where the men-animals lived; where the shielings were; and where cattle, sheep and goats grazed in summer. But this was winter, and he knew that the shielings would be deserted and the cattle inbye. He knew he had to explore, and he knew where he would be going; but first he needed to rest. Leaving Alba and Luath asleep on the edge of the wood, he padded deeper into the snow-bright, testing the wind and listening, and when he found a press under a tree where a stag had been lying he lay down on it and fell asleep, with his nose against his flank and his tail screening his face. He slept his waking sleep until far into the morning, and when he rose to stretch and yawn his breath vapoured in the light of a silvery half-moon shining through the trees and casting their shadows on the snow. Saighdear howled – and not to the moon. He was signalling to his pack mates, and they replied. But only Luath came to him.

The forest was silent, like a cathedral, until a wolf pair trotted into the depths, lost in the tree shadows, spotlit between them. The silence was first broken by red deer crashing away, downwind. Next a roebuck *boughed* twice, running. Then a dog fox yapped thrice and was answered by the *wauling* cry of a vixen. The wolves held to the east, into the open and across the moonlit snow towards the towering pyramid of Schiehallion. Saighdear knew there were houses of the men-animals along the loch shore and round behind the mountain, and shielings in the glen to the south: a horseshoe of danger, open only to the west, and into this he was leading. He knew there were hares there, now in winter white; and he knew they would be wherever there was ground blown clear of snow.

The pair probed into the open end of the horseshoe but there was no black ground; even the most exposed ridges still had a scowder of white. Against such a background a white hare could not be seen, and there was no scent of any kind on the wind; but Luath ran on top of one sitting at the entrance to its snow cave, and was as surprised to find a hare under his feet as the hare was to find a wolf on top of it. It kicked out and tried to scramble clear, but he broke its back and ate it on the spot, defying the growling Saighdear who wanted possession, which is about the same number of tenths of the law among wolves as it is among men. Saighdear sniffed where Luath had eaten and ate a mouthful of the bloodied snow. Then the pair padded round the southern face of Schiehallion, well above the empty shielings, testing the wind, seeking trace-scent of hare. Then, just as they were about to turn back, they saw a sight wondrous for any pair of wolves to behold.

The snow ahead of them, and above, began to erupt. No trick of moonlight this, or glamrie. The eruptions became wraiths in the shape of hares – dawdling, hopping, leaping down, always down, on a broad front, like a retreating army, as indeed they were, until the whole hillside seemed to be moving. The ptarmigan were already down below seven hundred feet, burrowing in the snow to reach heather leafage. Now the hares

166

were deserting the high ground after hiding for days in snow burrows to save their fat. The sight of them – phantom shapes of flesh and blood hares and their dark shadows – stimulated the wolves to instant action, and they rushed into their midst with teeth flashing and mouths spouting vapour. They slashed, chopped and released; they bowled hares over and ripped them; they leaped, and fell, and rolled. But always their jaws were tearing, disabling and killing.

When the rampage was over, and the escaped hares had scattered in all directions on the snowy slope of Schiehallion, the wolves sought out the wounded and the dying and made them dead. In their brief, hectic, bloody action they had killed twelve hares, so they had enough meat to feed four wolves to repletion and they were only two. They ate five hares between them, cached five in a rocky hollow out of sight of ravens and crows, and carried away two. The sun was rising amidst waves of gold and yellow and saffron when they started off across the white emptiness, following their own out-trail, on the ten-mile run back to the forest where they had left Alba.

Inside the first tree cover they scraped holes in the brushwood, cached the hares and nosed snow over them. Then they howled in duet, and were answered by Alba, who presently came to them at the fluid lope of the long-distance runner, showing that her aches had gone and she was fit to run again. The pair greeted her with tails wagging, and she nuzzled the side of Saighdear's mouth like a pup begging for bocks. He held his chin high for her, and when he turned his head away and walked towards the caches she followed him, mouthing his neck and biting his forepaws, a form of rough play which he accepted without growl or grimace: he was the ranking wolf letting his mate take liberties. As soon as she found the cached hares the others bellied down, chins on forepaws, to watch her tearing and swallowing, half-choking in the urgency of hunger, ignoring her bristling and snarling and show of teeth when she thought they were showing too much interest in her. But it was not in their minds to question her right to the prey.

That night Saighdear fronted the line back to Schiehallion by star-shine and snow-light, although Alba, running tail, could likely have found her way to the hare ground by the places her pack mates had marked with their scats and urine the night before. Before they reached the cache their nostrils were owning the rank taint of fox on the air. A dog fox and vixen had been there at nightfall and eaten the fore-end of two hares, leaving two haunches and one intact carcass; the other two they had carried away. Hackles up and growling like thunder, Saighdear snatched the intact carcass and walked away with it, leaving the haunches for Alba and Luath. After eating, the three picked up clots of bloody snow and gulped them down, making water of the melt. They followed the fox trail for a few hundred paces, whether by accident or intent only they knew, then moved down towards the shielings where ptarmigan and red grouse were in packs, not mixing, burrowing in the snow to reach the heather. Of hares there was not even a scent-trace, for they had deserted the hill and were across the frozen river on the other side of the glen. The wolves soon found them there and each killed one in snow burrows after losing many more in hard coursing, for the hares were warier now and widely dispersed across the hill.

The pack hunted by night and lay up by day, untroubled by man-presence or threat, living hard, eating enough but never feasting, until one morning, after forty-eight hours of empty bellies, Saighdear led them into the danger zone. A crescent moon was rising. The houses were in darkness, and on the snow nothing was moving; but the tantalizing odour of cattle and sheep lay thick as a mist along the glen below the forest edge. Three kyloes had broken out of a ramshackle paddock beside a shelter roofed with thatch and sod, and were foraging slowly towards the forest, nipping windlestraes as they walked and stopping every now and again to scrape through the snow to the heather. When they saw the wolves in the moonlight, with their ruffs hooded and their eyes glowing green, they stood at gaze, curious but not afraid – until the rush. At sight of the pack galloping towards them they turned about and bolted for the cover of the forest, which was familiar ground to them, for they had browsed there on juniper, blaeberry and cowberry before the big snow. Two of them reached the trees, but Saighdear and Alba leaped on the laggard and pulled him down, slashing at his rump as he fell. When he was slumped on his chest, with legs splayed, bawling, Luath took his favourite nose-hold and remained locked there until the others killed him.

The kyloe was lean, and they had to work hard to scrape the

168

thin layers of muscle from his bones. They left paunch and entrails, hip bones and shoulders, but carried away spine and ribs, leaving a blood-trail far into the forest. They knew they would not be returning to the kill.

Alba now fronted the pack and led them west, but not along their outcoming trail; she held farther to the south, following the glen bottoms where all the burns were frozen under snow, crossing the slash trails of deer and the neat in-line-ahead tracks of fox and wildcat, and reading as though waywise the treacherous ground ahead. She had no idea where she was going except into the clear – free to wander where she listed, to kill then disappear into space, perchance to settle for a little while where men were not, having no pups to tie her down to trysting places now Luath was a strong wolf running. Like the wolves of the tundra they were now wanderers, but they would wander where they willed instead of following where a migrating prey species might lead them; and if they killed a sacred cow they could be forty miles away before the men-animals found it to ponder over.

Twelve miles from the place where they had killed the kyloe they halted and lay down to crack, crunch and eat the bones they had been carrying. Behind them a pallor was spreading across the sky like a slow tide; ahead, the crescent moon was paling towards its setting. Before Alba had them on foot again, dark clouds like cobwebs sagging were smothering the tops and ridges to the south-west, and soon they were running into rain-mist that webbed their eyebrows and ruffs like gossamer. Their pads sank deeper into the snow crust. After another fourteen miles they were again in forest, on the edge of the desolation of blanket bog, dens, hags, waterways and lochans that was the Moor. They slept in the forest during the rain and thaw of the day, while the snow-melt trickled down the slopes to the burns and made pools on the ice of the lochans. In the white-dark after nightfall they padded into the open, but quickly turned back into the cover of the forest when they were faced with heavier rain and sleet on a gusting wind.

At daylight the wind backed and the rain dripped to a stop. Under the grey sky the frozen burns were leaden veins in the glens. The pack left the tree cover, led by Alba, who continued to run west. Within an hour they were in broken, hillocky

169

terrain with a network of lochans, some still patchy with snow, others rain-washed through to ice gleaming dully like pewter. Alba veered south through the network until they were running with a forested ridge on their left flank. Suddenly they halted, with their noses to the wind and their tails excitedly wagging; the wind was saying deer-scent, and the source was among the trees, upwind and not far ahead. After a session of seeming communication the pack moved across the wind and round to test the deer by filling their nostrils with wolf-smell. Five stags trotted from the tree cover and stopped to look back, then fled when they saw the wolves coming on. That roused the pursuit response and the pack followed at the gallop, splashing through dubs, slithering in the slush, and wading the floodings. Four stags drew slowly away from the pursuit, but the fifth was barely holding his distance ahead, and after a mile he was falling back. At two miles, with the pack closing up, he swerved away from the soft snow to a frozen lochan, where the grip-fast pads of his pursuers gave better footing than his hooves. Before he could reach the far shore they were at his heels, ready to leap, and at that point the gods who look after the destiny of wolves must have fallen asleep.

The stag was old, going back as they say – losing with age the head-gear he had grown before ageing – and there was slow death already working in him. He had brow forks and bay tines only, with naked dirks aloft. He was almost dead on his feet before he fell, with Saighdear and Alba on his rump and Luath reaching for his nose. So he should have died out there on the ice; instead, with the crash of him, and the weight of wolves on top of him, he went through it. In the belly-depth of water he found his feet again. He ducked Luath, forcing him to release his nose-hold, and threw him on to the creaking ice. By then Saighdear and Alba were in the water, trying to climb clear. With new-found strength the stag thrust at Saighdear, forked him over, and ripped open his abdomen clear through to the rib cage. Alba clambered on to his back while he was still brandishing his antlers and leaped clear to join Luath. They had to stand helplessly by while the stag gored the dying Saighdear again, and pushed the body under the ice; but when he tried to beat a channel to the shore they pulled him down and killed him in two feet of water. They squatted on the ice and fed on him

170

where he lay in the clearway he had broken open with his hooves. They did not seek Saighdear where he had died, perhaps because his death was beyond their understanding. But at darkening they howled a duet, and no man can know whether their eve-song was summons or mourning.

What many men did know at that darkening was that a Highland army, reinforced by Frasers, Mackenzies, Farquharsons and four hundred Mackintoshes, had routed the brutal General Hawley at Falkirk – the general who later hanged many of his own soldiers on gallows meant for the Jacobite prisoners he had hoped to take but did not.

14

Dead now was the master wolf Saighdear, and no sennachie to tell of him, nor piper the pibroch sounding; but Alba and Luath howled evening and morning song for the ears no longer waking, and hearkened with their own for the reply they would never hear again.

They stayed with the kill to the last bone, guarding it from ravens by day, stripping the meat on the exposed flank from neck to haunch until the ice melted under them and they had to eat standing belly deep in water. When their strength was equal to the task they hauled the carcass by neck and antler into the shallows, where they turned it over to reach the meat on the other side. While they were shearing flesh from haunch and spine a black water-shrew swam into the rib cage, probing for morsels with its whiskered trunk-snout. Luath dabbed it underwater with a massive paw, and when it surfaced again it was dead. The pair stripped the bones clean of flesh, ate out the body cavity except for the paunch, and tore off the lower jaws to reach the tongue. Then they let the ravens come down to peck out the eyes, seek in vain for the tongue, and pluck the hair from the hide in frustration.

That was on the fourth morning after the death of Saighdear. All the low ground was clear of snow, except in hollows and gullies lying away from the sun. A skirling wind, threatening snow and like a banshee wailing, combed the thick fur of the wolves and stirred a tide-race of wavelets on the lochans. Westward the dark emptiness of the moor stretched endlessly away, wide as the sky, an immensity of desolate grandeur, tormented by wind, with a wan sun glinting fitfully on fretting waters. In olden times of the forest men feared the grey wolves hiding in it; now they were in awe of the tameless wilderness of sullen moods and dangerous tantrums where a man, not waywise, might vanish and never be seen again.

Alba and Luath trotted back to the forest where the pack had roused the stags, but there were no deer to be seen there, nor smell of them. They stopped suddenly when a heron, weak with hunger, flapped heavily away from the roof of a pine on eagle-spread of wings. On the ground nearby another lay folded in death, uninjured, shrunken, a meatless cadaver of feathers, skin and bones. The wolves sniffed at it and padded away. On a snow-field covering a gully they found a deep hole smelling of fox, and the fox was still there, but they knew it would take them the rest of the day to dig down to him, and they were not yet hungry enough to want to eat him. Far off, in the open, dark deer were moving on dark ground, but the wolves could not see them and they were on the wrong side of the wind to be smelled. Alba turned west again to face the wilderness of bogs, lochs, lochans and waterways between the forest and the snow-capped peaks of Black Mount and Glen Coe.

The wind was on their right flanks, with blasts of powdery snow, and they had to lean into the sudden gusts to hold course. Within an hour they were on the shore of Loch Laidon, running north-east into the Arctic fury of the wind, with the first granite grains of a snowstorm stinging their eyes. They padded on at tireless slow-time pace, and before they reached the first tree cover they were facing a shrieking barrage and whirlwinds of spindrift. The wood was a swirling chaos of white. Under a buirdly pine tree, in the lee of a drift, three hinds and two calves were lying, upwind of the wolves, without scent-warning of their coming, hearing nothing above the wind's skelloch and seeing nothing in the blinding storm of white. The deer's scent was wayward but Alba and Luath placed them. They stalked in on noiseless pads, like Arctic wolves in their white snow-spun, and were within rushing distance before the leading hind jumped to her feet with a gruff bark of warning. Storm-bound, half-asleep and off-guard the group had been, but their reflexes were like a light flash in face of visual peril. All were on their feet as the wolves leaped, but in the breakaway from the bourach a stag calf was bumped, and before he could recover from his stumble Alba was on his back. He went down face forward into the snow, bawling for his mother. Then Luath had him by the nose and soon he was dead. The hind lingered in the wood until she knew he was not coming to her, then trotted away to find her group.

The calf was big and strong, and fat with forest living, and after the wolves had fed on him to repletion there was meat enough left on him for two more eatings. So they stayed with him, under the trees, seeking no cover, but rising every now and again to shake off their mantle of snow. Halfway through the long night they fed from him again, gorging truly like beasts who know not when they will eat again. By morning the storm of snow had passed over, the sky was luminous blue and the white-caped peaks glowed pink in the sunrise. But the wind was still in rumbustious mood, ripping branchlets from the pines, felling the falling, loosening the rootholds of the shaken, and scouring the drifts to spindrift. At mid-morning it died away to a breeze, and suddenly there were goldcrests making mouse-squeak in the trees and a red squirrel running on a branch shaking loose the snow. The wolves wandered through the wood to the loch shore, leaving scats and urine stains beside the carcass. Two herons were standing in snow spume on the loch margin, and out in the open water five whooper swans were sailing with heads held high. A dark, rounded bosset in the shallows was the pate of an otter snorting surface bubbles. The wolves lapped water from a dub then padded back into the wood where two greyback crows were perched on a branch looking down at the carcass. They were hungry, and eager to fly down, but the return of the wolf pair was off-putting, so they waited on to see if they would go away.

Alba and Luath settled down beside the carcass and scraped it almost to the bare bones, leaving the internal organs and the tongue for the next eating. Then they backed off and lay down with hindlegs drawn up and their cheeks resting on turned-in forepaws. Alba, showing no interest in the crows, fell into a half-sleep; but Luath was interested in them and remained awake, with his eyes slitted. By the time they had the courage to fly down he had almost lost patience, so instead of letting them settle to over-confidence he rushed at them too soon and they left him snapping air. If he had a mind to become a crow-catcher

174

he would have to live to be a lot older before he could hope to match the deadly skill of Saighdear.

Before dark the pair dismembered the calf, eating the tongue and internal organs and most of the bones; after midnight they cleared everything a pair of wolves could clear, and were ready to go. Alba led the way into the white starlit night. They trotted west through Black Corries, then across the Blackwater, where they rested for an hour. From there Alba pointed north. She knew where she was going. In her head-place was a picture of Lochaber, where she had spent the previous winter, and she was going there by Loch Treig of the white deer, and Lairig Leacach, then across the Spean to Glen Roy. By morning light, with the sun showing behind an eruption of sepia clouds limned in gold and amber, she was in a wide glen ringed by white-crowned mountains bathed in rose and amethyst. A soft, thawing wind was blowing up the glen when the wolves crossed the burn by an arched snow-bridge formed by the current in spate undercutting a drift. The snow was already printed by the webbed feet of an otter and the soft-edged slots of a wildcat. Dippers were arrowing upstream and down, flying under the snow-bridge.

Alba followed the west bank of the burn north, and soon she was owning hare-smell on the wind. But only a mile ahead were woods, then greater forest, and she wanted cover before thinking about hunting. They trotted through the small woods, sending black grouse whirring from the birches, and on the edge of the big forest they found a nanny goat down on her side, struggling, with the legs of twin kids born and the remainder of them locked and not following. She struggled to her feet, but fell on her side again, with the protruding feet feebly kicking, and she would have died there, slowly, trying to give life. Instead she died quickly, almost before she could bleat.

The low ground cleared in a day, and in continuing thaw the white hares moved up with the retreating snowline. This was their mating season, with bucks hopping uphill and down in slow pursuit of does. The wolves hunted them over twenty square miles of hill, on both sides of the glen, crossing the burn by the snow-bridge until it collapsed in the thaw and like ice floes was carried away. On nights when they killed more hares than they could eat, they cached the surplus in the forest out of

175

sight of the ravens and crows. One day, deep in the forest, they killed a deer calf after separating him from his mother and running him into a lochan, where they held him throughout the night and far into the next morning, kepping like two collies holding a sheep, until he staggered ashore and collapsed, with the power gone from his legs and death in his eyes. They stayed by the lochan for two days until they had cleaned the carcass, then returned to the glen. And there they were met by the scent of men-animals in the wind.

There were ten Highlanders in the party, displaying the white cockade, travelling light in wolf-time up the glen. They were Glenmoriston men who knew every mountain pass and hill track from Lochaber to Glen Garry, scouting ahead for the Prince's column, then at Blair Castle, which was preparing to march by Wade's road to Inverness while a second column under Lord George Murray approached by the low road on the coast. The men were on their way to Fort Augustus to check on redcoat strength and troop movements between there and Inverness, where they would rejoin the Prince. They passed within hailing distance of the wolves watching them from hiding among the rocks and rowans on the knoll.

Alba and Luath remained on the knoll for the rest of the day and far into the cloudy dark. Luath was restless, eager to go hare hunting again; but Alba was under stress, knowing the men had gone where she wanted to be going. She made no move to follow Luath when he left her at midnight to hunt alone. An hour later she howled her high-pitched, quavering solo and padded down to the burn where she turned north, just as Luath answered her summons from four miles to the south. He caught up with her on the south bank of the Spean and they swam the river together below the first of the ancient beaches. They turned west to the River Roy and followed it north. Near the green flats where they had killed the kyloe they left the river and crossed the beach into the wood where they had hidden before. Alba was remembering the strath below with its black cattle, and likely it was in her mind to visit the place again; but she wanted first to reconnoitre, so she lay up in the wood all night to wait for viewing light, and Luath stayed with her. The morning was dark, with rain turning to sleet, and it was late in the day before the sky cleared and the pair moved down to the strath, where three kyloe cows were snatching lean bites along the river bank and reaching up to browse twigs of willow and alder.

Voices were coming from the nearest houses of thatch, and the wolves had to wait five hours for silence. Then they stalked to the river, between the beasts and the houses, and rushed abreast towards the nearest kyloe. Like the others she was big-bellied with calf, lean on back and haunch, but fit. At first she did no more than stand there, unalarmed, watching the wolves coming on; then she lowered her head and shook it at them; and they were swerving to get round behind her before she turned about and galloped away, bellowing, with her tail in the air. While the others scattered she ran to the river, and was plunging in a pool when Alba snapped at her flank and forced her back up the bank. In her blind, mad panic she tried to run between the twin trunks of a forked alder, where she wedged herself, and before she could pull out again the wolves were on her back, shearing at her rump and loins. They pulled her clear as she died and the body rolled to the water's edge where they ripped it open, spilling out the calf and eating it between them. There was no sign of men-animals, so they stayed with the kill for most of the night and gorged on it again before leaving in the sleety morning dark.

They ran north after making a detour to avoid the house, and at daylight were back on Corrieyairack, passing close to the place where lay the hide and few bones of the shaltie pony. At mid-day, when they were lying high above the Pass, two redcoat horsemen rode through on their way to Fort Augustus. Suddenly the wind rose, bringing a short, savage blizzard, and long before the redcoats reached the fort their horses were over the fetlocks in powdery snow and beating through drifts up to their hocks. The wolves crouched on a knoll, exposed to the blizzard, and when it was over they were mantled in white. After nightfall, by the light of a half-moon, they followed the high ridges eastward, keeping to ground scourged to the bone by the wind, and had reached Wade's link road to Ruthven when they were confronted by the spectacle of a sunrise at night – a red sunrise that was the glare from Ruthven Barracks burning. The garrison had surrendered to the Prince's Highlanders, and he had ordered the barracks to be burned down, an order that delighted the clansmen, who loathed the forts of George,

Augustus and William and all other symbols of Hanoverian military occupation of their country. Before they burned the hated place down, they stripped it of all stores and equipment and presented the booty to Cluny Macpherson, because the barracks were on the territory of his clan. The men of the garrison were treated as prisoners of war.

To the wolves the flames painting the night clouds, like the northern lights flickering, were no more than another brightness in the sky, without meaning and beyond their understanding; so when Alba led the way towards the glare she was going where she wanted to go and in no way a wolf-moth attracted by light. The meaning of the brightness began to make pictures in her head-place when she found the man-smell at the head of every glen between Baltach and Gynack, and the fire-smoke came to her nostrils when she was high on Creag Bhalg within nose-distance of the flaming barracks. The men in the glens were Macpherson scouts, and there were others south of the Spey – all watching their backtrail for the approach of the Duke of Cumberland and his army. The wolves saw nothing of the clansmen whose scent they were owning, for they were men of the place, Macphersons, waywise, and not likely to make silhouettes of themselves against the snow. But in the strath, in the light of the burning barracks, men were everywhere to be seen, dark specks against the white, eating, talking, shouting slogans and cheering on the flames. Black cattle, lifted or requisitioned to feed the army on the march, were strung out along the strath in straggles and bourachs. They were downwind and down-river of the flaming barracks, in the white night beyond the snow flats flushed pink by the fire – all of them uneasy and all on foot, irritated by the smoke, and working up to the point of stampede. There were men on their flanks and down the strath, unseen and wrapped in plaids, but they were sentries not herders.

The spectacle of men in such mass and at such close quarters unnerved Alba more than the sight of Cope's army had done on Drumochter, and she wanted to be away – north into the unknown or back to the known Corrieyairack and the mountain wilderness of the west. But Luath wanted to be among the cattle. The sight and smell of them was drawing him on more than the proximity of men was putting him off. There was in

178

him some of the wilfulness and rashness of Sgian, and the bond with his mother was being strained by the tempting of the kyloes. He was going on, and just as surely Alba was not. She followed him reluctantly down into tree cover closer to the river; but that was her limit, and Luath read the signs. After dutifully nuzzling her muzzle he moved out and down, looking back twice, but not turning about, even when she left the tree cover and padded uphill, pointing north. Hunting the kyloes he would be, and he would join up with her later, as he had done in the glen of the hares.

He did not have to cross the rushing waters of the Spey. On the north bank he winded and stalked into a parcel of five kyloes – three heifers and two cows, all in calf and lean after wintering – browsing and scraping for a bite, not unsettled like the beasts on the strath because they were on their own ground. They stood at gaze when they saw him approaching. Dogs they knew, and they would be thinking he was some kind of hound; so he was into his wolf-rush and almost among them before they broke away with their tails in the air. Within seconds he had picked out the laggard heifer and turned her away, and this time he was not fronting for a nose-hold; he flanked her, leaped on her back, and bore her down, bellowing as she slumped forward with her chin furrowing the snow. He tore at her rump and groin, while she kicked out with a hindfoot and tried to hook him with a horn. Lean though she was, and pregnant, there was fight in her, and she fought him, and threw him, and staggered to her feet, snorting and bellowing, and faced him, swaying, with her head low, threatening with her horns. But the wound in her groin was mortal, and Luath held back until she buckled at the knees and collapsed in a pool of blood. Then he killed her.

After spilling out the calf he gorged on the heifer, devouring sixteen pounds of meat before cleaning his bloody face in the snow and sitting down to lick his feet. When he left he followed his back trail to track Alba from the place where he had left her. He knew he would not be returning to the kill; that much wolf-wisdom he had learned. A quarter of a mile from the kill he stopped on a knoll to howl – a solo lasting almost a minute: a call for contact, not a summons, which was faintly heard by Alba on Creag Bhalg. She replied, and her reply was faintly heard by him. And it was at that moment that the wind brought to his

179

nose the scent most dreaded by wolves the world over – the scent of the man-animal. He could see nothing, but the wind was saying; and in that space of a heartbeat between recognition and wolf-reflex the shot was fired from close ambush – a musket ball that smashed into his thigh, shattering the femur below the neck and almost tearing the leg off. As he lurched away towards the river, with the useless leg trailing grotesquely and leaving a blood trail in his slots, a plaided figure rose from hiding, laying down his musket and shedding his extra plaid – a broad Glenmoriston giant of a man who had been at Prestonpans, Clifton and Falkirk. He had been on sentry duty when he heard the bellowing of the heifer, and had stalked into his ambush when he saw the line Luath was taking after the kill. He was thinking he was dealing with a rogue hound, although he had never known a hound kill a kyloe before. After wrapping his musket and broadsword in his spare plaid he left his ambush at a jog-trot to follow the blood-trail, armed only with his dirk.

Luath reached the river bank with the blood draining from him and fell six feet on to a shingle spit, where he backed under the exposed roots of an alder and collapsed. His tracks in the snow, dark with blood, were easy to follow in the half-moon's light. Soon the Highlander reached the bank and leaped lithely down to the shingle to confront the broken wolf, which he still thought was a dog of a kind he had never seen before. Luath raised his head weakly to stare at the man with pale say-nothing eyes. He could have moved; but he stayed. He could have defended himself with his great rending teeth; but he did not. The thought of attacking the man never entered his head-place. In him was the deadly fear of the human animal, and meekly he crouched there, staring without savagery, with death beginning to say in the eyes of him, awaiting execution.

'You bloody turncoat,' the Highlander accused him, still thinking him a renegade hound. 'You'll kill no more kyloes!'

Luath, with eyelids beginning to shutter, nodded his head feebly, as though in agreement. The big Highlander stepped forward, buckled with him, grabbed him by the throat with his left hand, hoisted him almost clear of the ground, and with his right hand stabbed him to the heart with his dirk.

15

Alba was ten miles north of the Spey, holding to the high ground above the tree-line, when Luath was killed, and twice more, before moonset, she stopped to howl contact and summons. But there was no reply. Understanding nothing of death in the abstract, or the reality even when she had a warm prey at her feet, no thoughts formed in her head-place that Luath might be dead: all she knew was that he was not answering her, which signified nothing. Sooner or later he would howl for contact and soon appear to run with her again.

That night it seemed there was not a lonely, deserted glen in all the Monadhliaths. Almost everywhere the man-taint was on the wind – Highlanders scouting northwards towards Inverness, which was being held for King George by Lord Loudon and 1700 men, and westwards to check on troop movements between there and Fort Augustus. There were even clansmen homing in quick-time on a brief visit before rejoining the Prince. Alba padded in slow-time along the ridges, not waywise but skilled in reading ground, so she avoided drifted hollows and snowbanks and broke trail where the cover was no deeper than her hocks. The rocks were already dripping melt-water in a sudden thaw. Behind her the fire-glow in the sky over Strathspey was fading. At daylight she was above the headwaters of the Findhorn. She swam two burns running milky with clotted snow, then trotted downhill, splashing belly and brisket with melt-water, into a tract of pinewood where she found a lying-up place among the rocks below the tree-line. Here was no taint of the men-animals, although far down the river, out of her sight, men were moving in small groups at

Highland pace on the way to Inverness, where they expected to meet up with the Prince's army.

The thaw quickened and melt-water dripped from the rocks, pocking the snow where Alba was lying. Rain, fine as mist, webbed her ruff like gossamer. Below her the ground fell away so steeply that she had an almost eye-level view of the nearest pine tops, in one of which a hen capercaillie was feeding, shaking down a light snowfall each time she pulled on a shoot. Alba had lost interest in the bird and was dozing, when the wind brought to her the scent of cat, and presently he appeared high-stepping through the soft snow – a big wildcat, thick-furred, with ears up and out-pointing, heading for home with a red squirrel in his jaws. Whether she had a mind to hunt the cat or pirate his prey, only she knew, but when he was passing below she uncoiled from her seat and bounded down on him. The cat was taken by surprise, but he was on his home ground, waywise, not having to look before he leaped, and knowing where he was going when he did. Alba was within a few bounds of him before he moved – into the capercaillie's tree; and he was on the first branch, wailing his war-song, when she slithered to a stop, ploughing the snow at the base. The capercaillie crashed from the tree, showering Alba's head and ruff with snow, and with the snow fell the squirrel, dropped by the cat when he looked up to bare his teeth at the seeming new peril from above. And Alba bolted the squirrel where she stood, while he glared down at her, hottring with venom.

At nightfall, after howling for contact without reply, she left the wood and padded north in slow-time, with the west wind gusting skytes of sleet and brief squalls of rain, a lone dark speck in the vast snow white – the lone wolf not yet knowing it, and who would never know she was the last. In Glen Mazeran she howled again – and a mere man might have imagined a coronach in the quavering of it – but again there was no reply. Five miles south of Wade's military road, in the Mackintosh country, she ran three hinds with followers but quickly broke off the chase because the hock-deep snow slowed her more than it slowed the long-limbed deer. Later in the night she surprised a white hare squatting at the mouth of its snow burrow and the kill took the edge off her hunger. She was two miles south of Wade's road, on the low ground north of Carn na h-Easgainn, when she halted suddenly on a knoll, and bellied down, with the scent of deer coming to her on the updraught. They were bedded down in the shelter of the hollow, relaxed and cudding, and this time the gods who look after the destiny of wolves were on Alba's side: she was close in, above them, on the right side of the wind, with the advantage of surprise. Her downhill rush was irresistible, and she crashed into the nearest beast before it was rightly on its feet, knocking it over on its back with its legs stabbing the air. She was at its throat, straddling its middle, before the others were clear of the hollow with the snow flying from their hooves.

Three times before daylight the dead hind's calf came upwind to the knoll and finding the wolf still there went away again. Alba could see the head and ears of him on the knoll, but she had no urge to hunt him. It is unlikely that she had any idea that her prey was his mother. After daylight, when she had withdrawn uphill to lie on a boulder with a view, he came to the hollow and nervously approached the mutilated body of his mother. After tapping her face with a forehoof he *baáed* once, then trotted spring-footed from the hollow. Alba did not follow, and that was the last she saw of him.

The kill was a big one – a strong hind well fleshed and fat with forest living – and this time, finding no sign or taint of the men-animals in all the white, Alba stayed by it, eating at night and lying on the boulder by day, which was close enough to discourage visiting ravens and crows, and a pair of eagles, from flying down to the carcass. By the fourth day she had eaten the carcass down to the hide and a few bones, and she left at darkening to continue north; but within an hour she encountered the man-smell again when she was on Wade's military road, travelling west. All movement of the men-animals was from west to east or north, where history was in the making. Alba continued travelling west for several miles, high above the road, then south-west towards Strathnairn, and at daylight she was in a forest above the river, looking down on a wooded strath and scattered settlements. Black cattle were moving among the trees, scraping for a bite where the ground was clear of snow; but people were moving there too, and Alba knew she would be travelling again at nightfall. At owl-light she left the forest, running south-west for Stratherrick.

That night the Prince was at Moy, being entertained by the

Lady of Mackintosh, whose husband, the Chief of the Clan, was serving at Inverness with Lord Loudon in the Hanoverian army. The Lady had called out the clan for the Prince, and so became Colonel Anne, *la belle rebelle*. When Loudon learned that the Prince was at Moy, with only a handful of men, he had the idea of making a surprise night attack and capturing him, and maybe the Government's £30,000 reward, on offer for the person of Charles Edward Louis John Sylvester Maria Casimir Stuart, influenced his bold decision. But the Lady of Mackintosh, uneasy about the Prince's safety, had sent out her Fraser blacksmith and four servants to reconnoitre beyond the sentries, and the five became magnified into a regiment in the heated imagination of Loudon's soldiery, who fled back along the Inverness road in disarray.

About the time the comedy of the Rout of Moy was being enacted, Alba was on the high ground at the head of Loch Mhor, facing the bluster of a thawing westerly, howling for contact and not knowing in which direction to seek it. Twice in the next hour she howled again – for Luath, or any wolf within hearing – while the wind died away in a driffle of rain, and the clouds rifted, revealing a silver claw of moon and stars in the clearways; but the only reply was from a dog in one of the settlements in the glen below. Downhill she went, following the trail of a mountain fox whose pad marks had thawed to slots bigger than her own, until she realized she was approaching the habitations of the men-animals. That turned her about and she pointed eastwards, running in slow-time for fifteen miles before turning north, not halting until she was in the white mountain wilderness between the headwaters of the Nairn and the Findhorn, where there was neither human habitation nor sign of man. In the glens the snowline was retreating, and white hares were grazing on the dark ground below. Deer were also moving there or sheltering in patches of forest. Alba could not see them but she could smell them; she could also smell voles and the wayward scent of goat. She moved down from the snowline, disturbing the hares, but not hunting. First she had to find a day-place – a place with a view.

In the heart of the wilderness, in Mackintosh country, she found what she was looking for – a rock flat at the head of a glen, with threshy ground below and a hill burn spilling down. The flat was clear of snow, but wet, and she bellied down between two fissures brimming with melt. While the moon moved down the sky she stayed there, dozing with chin on forepaws, sniffing the air and listening; then in the last hour of darkness she moved out to hunt hares, killing one and chopping three voles in their grass creeps before returning to the flat in the first flush of dawn. There, standing tall, facing the east, with the light in her pale, half-slitted eyes, she howled, and many ears, not human, heard. Deer, grazing far down the burn, threw up their heads and swivelled ears to listen, unalarmed; hares across the glen sat up for a moment, then went on with their nibbling; crows in the wood below ruffled feathers and croaked comment; a homing mountain fox with twelve voles inside him changed direction to avoid the rock flat, knowing the sound was coming from there and thinking the voice was a hound's. Alba remained on the flat throughout the day, sleeping her waukrife wolf-sleep, howling at intervals, unsheltered, in full view of raven, buzzard and crow flying over: the lone wolf relaxed in good game country, not knowing that men were absent because it was winter, because many were out with the Prince, or because of events shaping in the north.

So she stayed between the two rivers, hunting sixty square miles of hill, glen and forest, killing hares and voles and a weakly orphaned deer calf, until the wild geese were flying north and the curlews were sounding their pibroch again on the low ground. By then the snowline was high and the high burns running full. All her calling for contact with her kind having been in vain, she was now ready to go, driven by a commanding restlessness. Luath she was not remembering, although in her head-place he would never be forgotten: the wolf, like the dog, has instant recall after the not remembering of years, and she would have recognized even the pups killed long ago in Kintail if they had suddenly appeared.

She left the country of the two rivers on a starlit night of east wind and frost, keeping to the middle heights away from the Findhorn, across the head of Glen Mazeran, then followed the snowline into the silent heartland of the Monadhliaths. When the moon rose, frosty brilliant, mirroring the white tops on shining waters, she was back on the heights of Sherramore, heading once again for Wade's road and the Corrieyairack; and

185

at sunrise, when the frost smoke was rising from the river pools, she was on the spur above the meeting place of waters from which she and her band had watched the Highland army on its march to Garvamore. On the spur she howled, then harkened for a reply; but there was none. At darkening, after howling again, she moved down to the river and followed the bank to the bosky place where Dileas had died, and perhaps she knew in her head-place that the skull with its eyeless sockets was her sister's, although she did no more than notice it with her nose and pass on. For a few nights she hunted over Sherramore, into the Pass, and on to the ground where the pack had killed the shaltie; then the restlessness stirred in her again, to drive her out on the quest for her kind.

The night was moonless when she left the Pass, after killing a hare patchy in the moult, and at daylight she was on the snowline above little Loch Tarf of the wooded islets north-west of Fort Augustus. Patrolling there, on Wade's road, were Highlanders of the Prince's army, which was then at Inverness where they had blown up Fort George after removing sixteen cannon and a hundred barrels of beef. The men patrolling by Loch Tarf were one of the outposts protecting the Irish picquets and the regiments of Lochiel, Keppoch and Drummond, who had taken Fort Augustus and were systematically destroying it. Alba spent the daylight in forest cover below the snowline, while deer rested and cudded on high ridges in the misted sun-glare, and curlews and oyster-catchers flighted and whistled along the river. After dark, she walk-trotted south to the River Tarf, which she splashed and waded across half a mile from the Fort, where the dying fires were sending up flickers of light like elf-caunles. She knew the men-animals were there in force, and Highlanders were as much to be feared as the Red Army of King George. She skirted the village, once called Killichuimen and now Fort Augustus after the king's son William, Duke of Cumberland, a brutal soldier still smarting from the humiliations of Prestonpans, Clifton and Falkirk, within months of his defeat in France by the Irish brigade of Marshal Saxe's army. Once round the village Alba pointed north, holding well away from the Fort and the exulting clansmen, and padded under cover of the forest until she reached Invermoriston, where she turned west.

Her days south of the Great Glen were over. Now the west was beckoning, and perhaps in her head-place she was seeing pictures of Kintail of unhappy memory, or maybe Lochaber. Whatever the pictures, she kept pointing west, and towards morning she was in the forest of Glenmoriston, running below the snowline, with thirty miles behind her by the way she had come.

The low ground was grizzled with frost, and mist like smoke was drifting on the river. At sunrise black grouse flew down to feed in the trees along the banks, where siskins, fieldfares and redwings were moving. Late in the day a gelid east wind began to shake the trees, and when Alba left the forest at darkening to hunt the glen bottom, its rant had silenced the night cries of the curlews and oyster-catchers. The river, running full and open, was carrying wreckage of oak and alder twigs. The side pools had a film of ice and every rush clump was a porcupine rattling quills. Alba surprised a polecat hunting early frogs among the kingcups on the edge of a flood pool, and rushed at him as he pounced on a fat female three days out of hibernation. The frog escaped the polecat by leaping into the pool and through the ice film, while the polecat escaped the wolf by finding refuge below an undercut alder, from which safety he assaulted her nostrils with his stink-smell. Having no real interest in polecat, and not being hungry enough to want to eat him, she left him hissing and stinking in his refuge, trotted a few paces, and killed a water vole in a rush clump.

Although not irked by hunger, she hunted on and off through the night from the river to the snowline. She ran a parcel of three hinds and two calves down-wind for a mile then broke off, realizing there were no laggards or weaklings among them; but towards dawn, when the wind's fury was spent, she roused a pining yearling from a hollow and killed him after a straight run of five hundred yards. He went down without a struggle and grunted only once before he died. Unhungry though she was, she had ten pounds of him inside her when she rose to her feet and howled. After listening for the reply that would not be coming, she dragged the carcass into the cover of scrub willow to conceal it from scavenging ravens, buzzards and crows, then trotted uphill to hide in the forest for the day. At night two foxes took possession of the kill, but they stopped eating when their noses found her on the wind and were in full flight when she appeared in view. Being no fox hunter she let them go and bellied down to eat. With her stomach again gorged she prowled into the black and white night, howling and listening, testing the wind, sometimes whimpering, and made a twenty-mile circuit before returning to the kill, which she ate down to the hide and bones.

For four more days she roamed high above the glen, east and west, coming down on the last night to kill a sheep near one of the settlements. She gorged on the kill and carried away a leg, knowing she would not be returning to it. The restlessness was commanding her again, but now it was more than the urge to travel in search of her kind or to avoid the men-animals. She had just felt the first flicker of life inside her, which was the stirring of Saighdear's puppies, and the new compulsion was to find a denning place where she could give birth to them. When she left the glen, from which many men had gone to join the Prince, she ran true through the mountainous wilderness towards Kintail, guided by the compass in her head-place, as swallows are guided by astral bodies from the remotest glen to Africa, or salmon homing from the sea find their native river by smell. She came in by the headwaters of the Affric, east of Ben Attow, and when the crescent moon was setting she was on a crag above Glen Shiel, looking down on the military road, scene of the abortive Rising of 1719, when a small Spanish force under Tullibardine, supported by a few Highlanders, was broken by the mortar barrage of General Wightman's Hanoverian redcoats.

Alba was on familiar ground, remembered in her head-place, between the sierra of the Five Sisters and the necklace of lochans to the north. Here was a great solitude of frowning glories and peaks wild and majestic – a silence of wind's rue and water-song broken only by the croak of a raven, the mewing of buzzards, the yarring of crows or the *tut-tut, hurry-hurry, go-back, go-back* crowing of grouse. But it was not a remote solitude. Down in the glen, to south and west, were habitations of the men-animals, some of them without men because many were away being soldiers. Near the habitations, on the river flats along the glen, black cattle and sheep were grazing, finding a bite on unfrozen ground clear of snow. In Glen Lichd Alba visited the place where her first puppies had been born, but she did not linger, and likely she would be remembering what had happened to them there. Night after night she roamed the vast, high-flung wilderness north and east of the Five Sisters, from Kintail Forest to the headwaters of the Affric, and from Inverinate to Benula, prospecting at old fox dens, searching in rock outcrops, screes and forest, and on some mornings she entered likely places and slept there for the rest of the day. She was in one of them on the day the Duke of Perth routed Lord Loudon at Embo, taking many prisoners, among them the Chief of Mackintosh whom the Prince sent home on parole into the care of his wife, Colonel Anne.

But none of the places she looked at pleased her. Soon she was fidging to be moving again, and one night, when the moon was in its last quarter, a gleaming talon in the high cloud-race, she hunted down to the glen and killed a kyloe, and after she had filled herself with meat she withdrew to the high ground to watch during the day. In the morning two women found the kyloe and ran to one of the houses of thatch, and when they returned with an old man and a dog she knew that once again it was time for her to go. Before moonrise she swam the river to the military road, then walk-trotted up through the forest and over the heights of Rattachan, exploring for a den, not hunting, as she travelled. Soon she was looking across the sea to Skye, but down there boats were crossing and men-animals bustling, including fugitives from the Battle of Embo, so she turned back along the military road into Glen More, and from there ran the forested low ground south to the massif of the Saddle. Her quest for wolf-contact and a denning place was now more important to her than hunting, but when she found a goat and kid in a corrie she killed them, and next day she stayed with the remains while the cock eagle from an eyrie four miles away quartered the middle heights and the lower slopes, hunting for his mate who was sitting on two eggs. That night she reduced the goat and kid to skin and bones, and when the grey crows flew down in the morning, looking for leavings, all they could take away was goat hair for nest lining.

From the Saddle she pointed south-east, and by midnight, in a fine drizzle of rain, she was running west from Loch Quoich to the River Carnach, which she crossed beside an old shieling near its source. Within the hour she was between the horns of

Knoydart – Loch Nevis, the place of Heaven, and Loch Hourn, the place of Hell, where once, according to Gaelic legend, dwelt *Domhnull Dubh*, the Devil himself. But Alba could see neither Heaven nor Hell, for the mists were crawling on the waters and in the glens, and the mountains were in shrouds and the rain teeming, and not a glimmer of moon in all the dark, wet, brooding night, and maybe the Devil himself was down there at Hourn, which is a corruption of *Iutharn*, which is Gaelic for Hell. Even when she was high on Meall Buidhe, long after the sunless sunrise, she could see nothing in the sagging cloud gloom and crawling mists as she crossed slippery slopes of glissading water and under rocks where every drip of rain had become a cascade. When at last she lay down to rest under an outcrop, her wet mane was bristling like a porcupine's quills.

The rain ceased at mid-morning and a prowling westerly stirred the mists, setting them drifting, billowing, swirling, and spiralling up from the depths. Alba rose, facing the Nevis horn, and was shaking herself when the wind, in sudden gust, rent the mist asunder, revealing a mirror of intense brilliance, which was the sun's light on the Loch of Heaven, and maybe God was showing the one on Hourn how to make the darkness light. Down there, along the green of Heaven's shore, were human habitations – the only settlement in the trackless, sea-girt grandeur of Knoydart. There would be kyloes and sheep down there, and maybe goats as well, but Alba was not drawn, although she made a picture in her head-place.

She began to explore the gloomy, silent wilderness for a denning place, from the heartland to the Sound of Sleat and the shore of Loch Hourn, finding no taint of men-animals but seeing deer, goats and a few hares now back in summer fur. In the end she chose a rock fortress on Ladhar Bheinn, with her nursery-to-be at the end of a nine-feet tunnel where no man could reach her. Although so close to whelping, she was still strong and active, and two days from her time killed a yearling deer after running him uphill on a steep gliddery slope where he slipped and fell back on top of her. She killed him when they were rolling downhill together in a fankle of legs. When she had eaten her fill, she carried home meat and cached it near her den, then laboriously dragged the remainder of the carcass to within a mile of it – the lone wolf, with none to help her, storing surplus near at hand to see her through the critical days when she could not leave her puppies. Beyond that she was incapable of thinking.

On the third day of April she gave birth to five puppies on the bare ground at the end of the rock tunnel, and for the next four she lay up with them, leaving them only for short periods when she went outside to eat. In a week she did no hunting, but the drain of five suckling puppies did not show on her so long as she had a deer carcass to feed on. By the end of that week she had devoured every morsel of meat from it, including tongue and brain, and eaten every eatable bone. Since the birth of her puppies she had called only twice, in the early morning, but the men-ears at the Loch of Heaven were too far away to hear her. On the eighth day she left the puppies for three hours, during which she killed a hare and two leverets; these took the edge off her hunger and kept her milk flowing. From then until the twelfth day she had only two leverets and a mouthful of voles. By then she was already ravenous and becoming lean, and the picture of the green shore of the Loch of Heaven became clear in her head-place, beckoning; but she did not run there directly after leaving her protesting puppies. Hunger had not yet made her bold enough to enter a settlement of the men-animals alone, so first she hunted north and south, facing squalls of sleet in the black night of cloud-smother, rousing and running deer, then breaking off, and by midnight she had run off more weight than she gained from the one vole she caught and swallowed. Wet and griped by hunger she returned to the den to suckle her puppies before pointing south-east towards the Heaven in her head-place.

The moon had risen while she was with her puppies, and by the time she was nearing the green and the hard-won arable on the shore of Heaven it was a glow in the cloud-race and gleaming in the clearways. There were no lights in the houses of thatch; the people were abed, and there was no sign of men or dogs. Alba prowled round the houses on a wide circuit and her nose quickly told her that here were cattle and goats, but they were all close to the dwellings and the fear in her kept her away. On her second foray she followed the river for half a mile, and presently winded a small flock of sheep just as the moon appeared in a rent in the cloud ceiling. Without preliminary stalk or self-display

191

she rushed in among them and cut out an in-lamb ewe which broke towards the settlement. It ran mute until she closed on it, when it began to bleat, and its bleating started a dog barking in one of the houses of thatch; but no one paid any attention to him because the night cries of sheep made no special pictures in the head-places of men and only he recognized the distress in the far-off bleating of the ewe. Alba tore out her throat, licked the warm blood and gorged on the haunch, then left half-dragging and half-carrying the carcass, which she cached in a corrie three-quarters of a mile from the killing place. There she left it while she returned to the den to suckle her pups, but within two hours she was back, to feed from it again and drag the remains still farther from the killing place and nearer home. The loss of the ewe was a serious one in such a small community. She was missed in the morning, and a few tufts of bloody wool found, but her disappearance remained a mystery.

That morning Alba's puppies opened their eyes in the darkness of the tunnel, unaware even of the light at the end of it. It was the thirteenth day of their lives and the sixteenth of April, and Alba went hunting in the mist and rain of the morning, while on the other side of the country, on Culloden Moor, the armies of Prince Charles Edward Stuart and the Duke of Cumberland were facing each other, arrayed for battle.

A battle there had to be, but not on that day or that field. The clan muster was not complete. Detachments were fighting elsewhere; many others were on the way. The Macphersons were at Moy, marching to join the main army. So the Jacobites were under strength – barely 5000, tired, wet and hungry after an abortive night march, with hardly a horse and only a few cannon, facing Cumberland's 9000 regulars and mercenaries, horse, foot, and artillery. 'There could never be a more improper ground for Highlanders,' wrote Lord George Murray, the Jacobites' ablest general, of the field chosen by the Prince's flattering sycophant O'Sullivan. So the result was never in doubt. After the battle Cumberland earned his title of the Butcher, murdering the wounded on the battlefield and off it, cutting down innocent bystanders in the pursuit and the throats of exhausted clansmen asleep in the grounds of Culloden house. He had his Final Solution to the Highland problem, which was to carry fire, sword and rapine into the glens, giving roofs to the flames and flesh to the eagles, and this he proceeded to do, using reinforcements daily arriving. His men swept through the glens like a pestilence, looting, burning, killing; lifting sheep, cattle and goats. Starving the people was part of his solution. All over the west his men pillaged and killed – in Lochaber and Strathglass, Keppoch, Appin and Moidart, then soon to Knoydart and the islands. They were hunting rebels, but they were also hunting a fugitive Prince with £30,000 on his head.

One day on Knoydart a detachment of redcoats stopped to rest at the rock fortress on Ladhar Bheinn. Alba, newly home from an unsuccessful hunting trip, had seen them coming across the heights in open order and was in hiding nearby, the bond with her puppies being stronger than her fear of men. While the men laughed, talked and munched biscuit from knapsacks, she remained out of sight, watching; but when two of them squatted down at the mouth of the den she became so distressed that she showed herself, and circled them, whimpering. The squatters jumped to their feet and every man in the patrol watched her, thinking she was a big dog. One of them raised his musket and took aim.

'It's only a bloody dog,' a sergeant said. 'We're supposed to be hunting rebels.'

'Anything on four legs we take, sergeant, alive or dead,' the soldier said, and fired.

The ball broke Alba's back, making a gaping wound, and she went down on a hip with her spine at a grotesque angle. She watched the approaching soldier with her pale, say-nothing eyes, all fear gone from her, knowing only a numbness without pain.

'I'll give it another one,' said the soldier who had shot her.

'Save it!' the sergeant said. 'The bayonet'll do!'

Alba, looking death in the face without knowing it, watched calmly as the sergeant lunged at her with the bayonet and drove it through her chest.

'Funny kind of brute that,' he said. 'Quiet as a mouse.'

Clouds came over, bringing fine rain, and the lights went out on the Loch of Heaven. Later in the day the crows found the

193

body of Alba and took her eyes, and the day after, in warm sunshine, the flies held revelry on her. By then her puppies were cold and mewing their plaint, and in the night they slept to death.

Epilogue

Lord President Duncan Forbes of Culloden – king's man, agent of the Hanoverian parliament, and a much respected figure in Scotland – tried in vain to curb the excesses of Cumberland and his henchman General 'Hangman' Hawley, drawing their attention to the laws of the country. 'By God, I'll make a brigade give the laws!' Cumberland told him. And later, writing to London, he referred to Forbes as 'that old woman who talked to me of humanity'. One of his own officers wrote that the troops slaughtering on the moor 'looked like so many butchers rather than Christian soldiers'. Dr Samuel Johnson, the great lexicographer, had his say when he toured the Highlands: 'They have made a desert and called it Peace.' And the murder and mutilation on the moor were later to be described by an English historian as 'such as never perhaps before or since disgraced a British army'.

Cumberland did what old Marshal Wade had failed to do, or ever attempted: he tamed the Highlands. His hatred of Jacobites was natural; they were a threat to his father's throne. And in the clans he saw the only instrument that could make the threat a reality. To the prime minister he wrote: 'Jacobite rebellious spirit is so rooted in the nation's mind that this generation must be pretty well wore out before this country will be quiet.' He set about wearing it out by the harrying of the glens. People, driven to the hills, died of hunger and cold. None dared beg near the forts. In May sixty-eight Glenmoriston men marched to Inverness to hand over their arms, under guarantee of a 'written protection'. Cumberland had them arrested, taken to London and thence to the Barbadoes. This gave rise to the saying: *As safe as a Protection.* Prisoners were taken to London to be hanged without trial, in direct contravention of the Treaty of Union. The Butcher's idea of a final solution was the transportation of whole clans, especially Camerons and Macdonalds, and there were those who would have planted civilized Southrons in their place. In the meantime the killing, looting and burning went on.

This was the man who returned to London with his pay increased from £15,000 to £40,000 a year, and to a hero's welcome akin to a Roman triumph. A grateful parliament approved his war crimes and crimes against humanity and indemnified him; two centuries later he would have been arraigned before the Nuremburg Court with kindred racists like Eichmann, Heydrich and Himmler. The celebration bonfires burned, the bells rang out, and the populace sang 'See The Conquering Hero Comes', which had been specially commissioned for the occasion – a sad and revealing comparison with the compassion and humanity shown by the Prince and his Highlanders after Prestonpans. Tyburn was aptly renamed Cumberland Square, and the Butcher became Baron Culloden. The City breathed again. The General Assembly of the Church of Scotland, predictably, congratulated the Butcher for his 'generous resolution in coming to be the deliverer of this Church and Nation.' The Episcopal and Roman Catholic Churches would not have agreed. All clergy were obliged to pray for the king and all members of his family by name, in case there was any nonsense about the one over the water.

Parliament quickly found time to update the old Disarming Act. Highlanders were forbidden to carry arms of any kind, and must surrender any they had on pain of imprisonment or transportation. Highland dress in any form, and the bagpipe, were forbidden to all except the forces of the Crown, and penalties for breach of this regulation were severe. So the Gael was stripped even of the clothes on his back. The clan system was abolished, and the chiefs became rent collectors without power. School teachers and university lecturers were vetted for reliability and told what they could teach, and the results of this can be seen to this day. Most Scots know about Magna Carta, but few have heard of the Declaration of Arbroath. Cumberland and Parliament set out to destroy Gaeldom and its culture, and they succeeded.

196

After Culloden the Butcher never won a battle. He was defeated, for the second time, by Marshal Saxe at Lauffeld in 1747. He was defeated by Marshal d'Estrées at Hastenbeck in 1757. And in September of that year he had to surrender, with a promise to evacuate Hanover. Culloden remains his memorial, his epitaph and his disgrace. Old Marshal Wade, whom God did not after all choose as His instrument for crushing rebellious Scots, is remembered for his roads and bridges and a memorial which a grateful government allowed him to pay for himself.

After Culloden the Gaelic way of life, its culture and economy were progressively destroyed, and the process continues. Before Cromwell's day the natives had burned tracts of the old forest to smoke out the wolves; by the time Cromwell arrived to smoke out the rebels and mossers the wolf was staring eternity in the face. After the failure of the 1715 Rising entrepreneurs from the south moved in to grab the forfeited lands of the attainted chiefs, and the axe took over from the firestick. The furnaces devoured the forest with the appetite of Moloch, and some of the lairds joined in the rape of their heritage to feed them. The clansmen, disarmed, could do no more than obstruct, and their obstruction saved many priceless remnants of the forest. They won some battles, but the axe won the war.

After 1746 the rape of the Highlands went on. The ring of the axe was a paeon to Mammon in the highest and the forests were felled to his greater glory. The human population rose as the trees fell, and then there was pristine grassland and leafy heather. The sheepmen from the south looked upon the pastures and saw that they were good, and the sheep began to move in. Within fifteen years of Culloden the Blackfaces were crossing the Highland line. Thirty years later, by which time Glenmore forest had disappeared and Rothiemurchus had been torn apart, they were all over the Highlands and on some of the islands. At the turn of the century the Cheviot sheep were beginning their invasion of Caithness and Sutherland. And soon sheep became the new army of occupation in the Highlands and islands, sounding the death knell of the clan-folk in the glens with their subsistence farming of oats and barley, and then potatoes, and their rearing of black cattle for the trysts of the lowlands. The people had to go, and the time of their going became known as 'The days when sheep ate men'.

197

The lairds achieved what Cumberland had wanted to do and failed to do: they emptied the glens. Many of them were as ruthless as the Butcher, although they stopped short of burning down a house while the family was still in it. The clansmen, disarmed and disillusioned, accepted their fate with little show of fight. There was no leader to sound the battle cry: *Claymore!* And there were some clergymen around to tell them that it was God's will. Some of them moved to the coast, there to begin a precarious new life; others opted for the migrant ships and Scotland's loss was the New World's gain. The Butcher won in the end, and there was Harriet Beecher Stowe with her Uncle Tom-ism to put a face on it. And soon the great Highland war-pipes were sounding again – not in a new Rising, but on distant battlefields where kilted men fought and died in England's wars to build a British Empire.

In 1751 Lord Morton believed that the wolf still existed in some parts of the Highlands, and there is a persistent tradition that the last one died in 1760 while the Butcher was living in disgrace at Windsor. It makes little difference now. The only wolves in Scotland today are in zoos or private collections, two of them being the pair to which this book has been partly dedicated.